72 HOURS

Karen -
Enjoy!
Thank you for
always bringing
a smile! You shine!
megan Barr

72 HOURS

MEGAN BARR

TATE PUBLISHING & Enterprises

Published by Tate Publishing & Enterprises, LLC
127 E. Trade Center Terrace | Mustang, Oklahoma 73064 USA
1.888.361.9473 | www.tatepublishing.com

Tate Publishing is committed to excellence in the publishing industry. The company reflects the philosophy established by the founders, based on Psalm 68:11,
"The Lord gave the word and great was the company of those who published it."

Book design copyright © 2011 by Tate Publishing, LLC. All rights reserved.
Cover design by Amber Gulilat
Interior design by Stephanie Woloszyn

Published in the United States of America
ISBN: 978-1-61739-595-6
1. Fiction / Thrillers   2. Fiction / Suspense
11.01.24

ACKNOWLEDGEMENTS

This book is a product of love, and would not be here without the incredible love and support of my family, and my writing coach, mentor and friend, Linda K. Wendling, without whose support this creation would have remained in a desk drawer. I also want to thank my good friends Kat Hinkle, for making me beautiful for my photo shoot, and Julie Potter for taking those amazing pictures. Enjoy!

PROLOGUE

The smallish room gleamed under the swinging bulb, striking a startling contrast with the remainder of the basement. The one dignity he would grant her, even though she deserved none, was that of dying alone. Turning off the lights and shutting the door, he heard the first one drop to the floor. Soon they would all descend. Without even so much as a last cursory glance in her direction, he turned and left the forsaken place, the beginnings of a malevolent grin tickling the corners of his mouth.

Outside, the sky had turned a brilliant shade of red, casting the morning with a fiery glow. "Red sky at morn, sailors take warn," he repeated the old mariner's rhyme predicting stormy weather as he climbed into the driver's seat and started the van.

As he backed out of the drive and pulled onto the quiet boulevard headed into the blazing sunrise, he said, "Here comes the storm."

CHAPTER 1

November 1, 7:28 a.m.

Sadie woke to the shrill sound of the telephone; the clock read 7:28 a.m. "I am so dead! He's gonna kill me." Grabbing for her cell phone on the nightstand next to her bed, her hand found nothing attached to the charger. "Of course," she moaned. Half in, half out of bed, she searched the floor frantically for the phone. She found it halfway under the bed. As soon as she had hold of it, she flipped it open uttering a breathless, "I'm on my way."

Silence.

Then she heard a muffled ringing coming from another part of her apartment. The house phone—no one called the house phone anymore but telemarketers. She wasn't even sure why she still had it except that she'd been too lazy to have it disconnected. Still it had to be Andre, her boss, wondering where the heck she was.

Whipping the covers off, she sprang out of bed, disrupting her cat, George, who gave her an annoyed glare before jumping onto the window seat and away from the commotion. Sadie ran for the phone, smashing her right shoulder into the doorjamb as she rounded the doorway too fast.

"That's gonna bruise," she said without slowing down. Sliding in her stocking feet like a professional skater for the phone stand, she realized that phone wasn't in its cradle either. Standing still, she listened for a second; the ringing was coming from the kitchen. Executing a leap that would have made any Olympian jealous, she cleared a basket of laundry blocking the doorway between the living room and kitchen; still no phone. The ringing, though still muffled, was louder in here; she was close. Then she remembered the last time she'd been on it, she was also making a bag of microwave popcorn. Turning to the counter, she opened the microwave and retrieved the phone, shaking her head and rolling her eyes. Sometimes she amazed herself.

Upon rescuing the phone, she looked at the caller ID. The number displayed was Rapture's, the shop where she worked as manger and where she was supposed to be already.

"Damn." Pressing the talk button, she started in before the caller could speak. "Andre, I am so sorry. I have no idea why my alarm didn't work. I checked it twice last night. I'll be there in five … Andre? … Hello? … Are you there?" She could hear quick, shallow breathing on the other end of the line.

"Ugh." Sadie felt sick. Andre had never given her the silent treatment before. She looked at George, who had come out of the bedroom for a snack. "Think you could find a job?" Of all days to be late, today was the worst. Today was to be Sadie's first official art showing, which Andre was generously hosting at Rapture, a work of art in and of itself. Sadie, via the grace of God, Andre's keen persistence, and his vast Rolodex, had been selected by *Style Magazine* as this year's up-and-coming hot new artist—the one to watch out for. This would put her on the map. It would mean the difference between popcorn for dinner every night and real food.

Critics and journalists from across the country were already beginning to gather for the show, and she was nowhere near ready. There was still a ton of work that needed to be done in the shop to prepare for the event. Andre had gone out on a limb for her, shutting down his shop for the day to help her prepare. He'd even gone as far as to throw her a huge celebratory party the night before.

Sadie made quick work of jerking her long, blond hair into a ponytail and was in the middle of pulling jeans over her hips when the phone rang again; this time it was her cell. Lunging across the bed for the phone, she answered before the end of the first ring, but before she could say anything, the caller said something that made chills dance up her spine.

"Don't come." Though strained and hushed, she recognized Andre's lilting British accent.

"What? Andre? Look, I know I'm late, but it's my showing." This was bordering on ridiculous. He couldn't seriously be mad at her for oversleeping.

No response.

The line went dead.

Panicked now more than anything, she ran out of her apartment, rushing right back in when she realized she didn't have her purse, her keys, or her shoes. It took her less than a minute to grab what she needed and head back outside. Locking the door with one hand, she balanced on one foot, slipping a shoe onto the other with her free hand and then wriggling into the other. Shoes on, purse in hand, and door locked, she flew down the outdoor stairs that attached her attic apartment to the street below. Lucky for her, her apartment was just across the street from Rapture, so she didn't have far to go.

CHAPTER 2

7:45 a.m.

The innocuous brown paper that covered the shop's large picture window gave it an ominous aura. The paper served as a shield, preventing prying, curious eyes from seeing Andre's current masterpiece before it was finished. Today it shielded *her* masterpieces as well. What sat inside the store now represented a decade's worth of Sadie's soul.

Nearing the door, she considered crossing the threshold on her knees, in an act of supplication, an act that had earned her a chuckle and forgiveness in the past. She disregarded the notion as soon as it came to her. She had a feeling it would take more than casual playfulness to correct this mistake.

Taking a deep breath, she grasped the handle and gave it a good tug. It remained tightly in place. Frowning, she tried again; the door was locked. "Huh?" Her brow wrinkled as her heart sped up. Andre always left the door open for her, relying on the "Closed" sign to keep customers at bay until the shop officially opened. "This day just keeps getting better." Sadie frantically tore through her purse, looking for shop keys, snatching them up after what seemed an eternity. She slipped the key into the lock and raced in as the door swung open. From her vantage point, she could see only a portion of the store and the little hallway that led to the backroom, which connected the shop to the alley. The main portion of the store was off to her left and remained out of sight.

"Andre?"

No response.

"You scared me."

Again, no response. An ominous quiet filled the air. Sadie felt conspicuously alone. Just then the curtain to the back room fluttered as someone walked behind it. Taking a deep breath, she made her way through the store to the back room. Andre preferred the look of a curtain to a door, insisting that he never wanted his patrons to feel cut off from him.

"Andre?" Sadie tried to sound light against the oppressive feeling in the normally cheerful place.

No response.

Except for the subtle sounds of her footfall on the hardwood floor, the shop remained quiet around her. The silent alarm in Sadie's head began sounding louder and more insistently. Pushing her fear aside, she continued toward the now still curtain and the back of the store.

"Can you believe I even bought a new alarm clock? A lot of good..." Sadie's words fell heavy in the silence. She pushed aside the velvet curtain and stepped into the back room. It was empty. The back door was standing wide open, a fresh smudge of what looked like red paint on the handle. Cocking her head to the side and frowning, she looked at the smudge. Andre never left smudges. He hated smudges.

Stepping outside and looking all around, she could see that the alley was empty and hurried back inside, pulling the door shut tight behind her against a sudden icy draft. The bad feeling in her stomach now coursed through her limbs, and her hand shook as she thumbed the lock into place. It felt sticky, along with the door-knob—she'd forgotten about the paint. Grabbing a paper towel, she was about to wipe it off when it occurred to her that this neither looked nor felt like any paint she'd ever seen. Swallowing thickly, she raised her hand to her nose and inhaled the coppery aroma—blood. A cold sweat broke out on her neck, palms, and forehead.

"Okay, so he cut himself and went out into the alley to get help instead of dialing 911 or telling me he needed help when he had me on phone, because…That makes no sense." Sadie wiped her hand furiously on a paper towel as she looked around the office for any clue as to what was happening. Everything was in its place, perfectly stacked and neatly organized, just like Andre, except for the blood. A wave of queasiness washed over her, and her heart began to race; all of her nerve endings seemed to stand at attention. Her intuition told her that there was something very wrong here. Extracting her cell from her pocket, she flipped it open and began to dial 911 just as the phone's battery died. "Perfect."

The shop had two phones, one in the back room where she was and the other near the register. She could see that the phone here was not resting in its charger where it should be. In fact it was nowhere to be seen. It took all of her remaining will to part the curtain and step out into the store.

All was quiet.

The shop appeared empty. At the front of the store, another set of red velvet curtains hung from the front of the display case, guarding it from prying eyes on the inside, as the brown paper did on the outside. When the display was finished, the heavy crimson curtain would be secured on either side with heavy gold tassels, framing the newest panorama, which would now feature Sadie's own glass-blown creations.

For the first time she could remember, that curtain looked sinister, and she was afraid of what she would find behind it. Crossing the distance to the front of the store seemed to take an eternity. As she passed the register, she noticed this charger was also missing its phone. Inside, her common sense screamed at her to get out, to get the police, that things were not right. But she couldn't make her feet stop moving toward the front of the store. Feeling her mouth go dry, her hands trembled as she reached out to part the curtain.

She screamed.

Stumbling backward, she crashed into a good-sized display table loaded with her life's passion, sending it and herself crashing down. Sadie landed hard on her tailbone and hands as all around her dozens of delicate, hand-blown glass ornaments, vases, paperweights, and bowls cascaded down around her, each sounding like a small explosion as it shattered on the hard floor. She was unable to tear her eyes away from the gruesome sight before her.

Nothing more moved in the eerie quiet of the store. Finally, she managed to push to her feet. Ignoring the shooting pain in her lower back, hip, and hands, she ran out into the street and fainted.

CHAPTER 3

7:55 a.m.

"Honey, I think there's trouble at Rapture," Anna St. James said, slowly rising to her feet, a look of concern worrying her brow. Following his wife's gaze out the café window Rocco St. James turned just in time to see Sadie collapse. Without a second's hesitation, he rushed out of the café and across the street, Anna close on his heels, dialing 911 as she ran.

Rocco raced across the cobblestone street, dodging a car, a couple on a tandem bike, and a few early morning tourists on the sidewalk, all rendered immobile by the drama unfolding before them. They all stared at the unconscious woman on the cold sidewalk, but not one of them moved to help.

"Tourists!" Exasperated, Rocco wove through and around them to Sadie's side. "Sadie! Sadie! Are you all right?" Rocco dropped to his knees beside her on the sidewalk. Her hands were masked with gloves of blood, and Rocco could see a wicked-looking shard of colored glass sticking out of her right palm. Stripping off his jacket, he wadded it in a ball and lifting her head gently, placed it underneath. As he did, Sadie's eyes flickered open, and she found her voice. "He's ..."

"Sadie! Where is Andre?" Rocco looked toward the dark shop front, chilled by the haunted look on Sadie's girlish face.

"Dead." Overwhelmed by ghosts of whatever it was that she had seen inside the usually cheerful store, she fell silent.

"Where the hell are the police?" Rocco shouted to no one and everyone.

"Here," a familiar voice said, parting the crowd with easy authority. "Stand back. If you don't have business here, you don't belong. Mackey, get these people back. I want a fifty-foot perimeter. Seal it off now." Dan St. James, Anna and Rocco's only son, and Crystal Springs lead detective, took effortless control of the situation.

"What happened?"

Fighting back a wave of nausea, Sadie had just pushed herself up into a sitting position as she felt protective arms wrap around her and realized that Anna had joined them on the curb. Still in shock, Sadie sat quietly and allowed Anna to comfort her while Rocco stood to fill in Dan and his partner, Mike Johnson.

CHAPTER 4

8:21 a.m.

The street was alive with gawking people, insistent reporters and pushy photographers all held back by a few frenzied police officers. Sadie sat in the open back of an ambulance, her legs dangling over the edge, watching the scene outside unfold around her. Many of the people in the crowd, she knew, had come to town for her art showing. *This wasn't exactly the sort of show she'd had in mind.*

"How does your head feel?" Dr. John Conway asked as he bent over her, examining the part of her head that had connected with the pavement when she'd fainted.

"Everything hurts."

"Any dizziness or nausea?" he asked, placing a cold-pack in her left hand and placing it gently on the bump.

"I'm fine, Doc," Sadie lied.

"You know, this false bravado you've adopted isn't fooling anyone, most of all me." Doc Conway said, as he began extracting several small shards of glass from her right hand.

"I can't let go now, Doc. If I do—." Sadie found the rest of her sentence threatened by choking emotion and fell silent.

"You're too independent for your own good sometimes. What were you thinking going in there like that?" Though his tone was low, she could read frustration and anger behind it. Doc Conway had been very much a father to her after having lost both of her parents over the years.

"Don't be mad at me, Doc. Please, I can't take that right now." The words came out barely audibly.

"I'm not mad at you." He removed the last sliver of glass. "I love you and that gives me the right to worry about you."

Sadie fell silent.

"You're lucky you're alive." He tenderly swabbed her wounds with an antibiotic salve before applying a bandage and then wrapping her hand with soft cotton gauze.

"I know." Sadie caught his eye and held it. "I know."

For a few moments neither one said anything.

"It looks like a mummy's hand." She couldn't restrain herself. Sadie knew she was being flip, but it was her way of protecting herself from the tsunami-sized wave of emotion that threatened to overtake her.

"You always liked *Curse of the Mummy*." Now that he had made his point, he relented a little.

"It's cheesy but good." Just then the crowd parted, and she had a straight line of sight toward Rapture's front window. Although it was still covered with the brown paper, she could nevertheless see what lay inside. "Oh God, I think I'm gonna be sick."

"Put your head between your knees and breathe." Doc Conway pushed gently on the back of her head, urging her over as he continued to talk gently to her, soothing and reassuring her.

"Looks like oversleeping finally saved your life." Doc gave Sadie's shoulder an encouraging squeeze.

"Lucky me. My alarm clock didn't work." The onslaught of emotion was getting harder to control, and a tear escaped, coming to rest on her lip. Licking it away, she could taste the salt. Even though she knew she could let go around Doc, she still refused to give in to the tears. For that she would wait until she was alone.

"Well, I, for one, am glad that it didn't. I can't imagine Crystal Springs for one day without Sadie Elizabeth Mozart."

"Thanks, Doc. I love you too."

"Are you are going to be okay for a little while? I think I'm needed inside."

"It's okay. Go take care of Andre. And, Doc—thanks—." Her voice broke a little, and she cut herself off, letting the rest of her sentence fall away.

The older man locked her gaze with his own. "It will take time. Probably a lot, but you will get through this. You know I'll always be here for you." Still he didn't stand. He didn't make a move to leave; instead he stared hard at her, looking for any sign that she wouldn't be all right.

Finally she nodded. "I'm okay, Doc. Really, I'll be fine," she said, putting on a brave face.

"I know you will. I'll check in on you later." He winked, giving her shoulder one more squeeze, then got up and walked toward the yellow crime scene tape and the building beyond.

When he turned away from Sadie, he frowned and inhaled deeply, steeling himself for what was about to come. He would grieve later; Andre had been a dear friend, but right now he had a job to perform—a job that most of the time he loved but now hated. Doc Conway was the town's medical examiner. It had been years since he'd tended to a living person, but Sadie was special. For years, they had been each other's "family." Looking back once more he gave a nod of thanks to the paramedics who had gracefully stepped aside and allowed him to administer to their rightful patient. After convincing himself that Sadie was going to be okay for a few minutes, he made his way through the throng of people crowding the sidewalk and disappeared into Rapture.

CHAPTER 5

8:50 a.m.

Inside the store, it was as quiet and organized as it was loud and disorganized outside. Adam Gonzales, one half of the town's pair of crime scene investigators, was busily snapping photographs of the body and the shop from every angle while his partner, Evie Misae, gingerly lifted fingerprints from the register. Evie and Adam were two among the best-of-the-best. Doc couldn't figure out why neither of them had left Crystal Springs for more lucrative and auspicious pastures, yet he was nevertheless happy to have them both in town and working the case.

"We haven't touched the body yet, but we're about ready. Just waiting on your go." Adam rearranged himself for another shot with his digital Cannon Rebel.

"I'll be right with you, as soon as I check in with the chief." Even though he couldn't see the chief of police, he was nevertheless easy to find—all he had to do was follow the sound of the yelling.

In the back room, Doc Conway found a very agitated chief of police, Eddie Baxter, barking orders at two rookie cops while pacing and pulling hard on a Marlboro Light cigarette. The chief had

wanted him at the crime scene an hour ago, and he looked like he
was about to have an aneurysm.

"'Bout time, Doc," he growled, hands on his hips as he stretched
to his full height of six feet four inches, towering over the shorter
and slightly thicker doctor. "What the hell took you so long?" Eddie
Baxter was the owner of a particularly intimidating scowl, with
penetrating dark eyes that never missed a thing, and a well-honed
sneer. Over the years he had sharpened these traits to perfection
and used them to his advantage whenever possible. There weren't
many people who couldn't be intimidated by Chief Baxter's mere
presence, but the Doc wasn't one of them.

"You know what I always say?" Doc clapped the blustering
police chief on the back. "Heal the living first, then tend to the
dead, not the other way around."

"This isn't exactly a run-of-the-mill situation we have here,"
the lawman retorted. Then, kinder, "how's she holden' up?"

"She's a fighter, but you know wounds often run much deeper
than the surface, Eddie."

Chief Baxter nodded, slowly acquiescing.

"You know what would happen if I spent all of my time with
the dead, Bax?" Eddie and John were not only lifelong friends, they
were brothers-in-law.

"I wouldn't have high blood pressure," Chief Baxter grunted.

"No, Eddie, you'll have high blood pressure until you stop
smoking, drinking, and eating fast food." Doc Conway had been
after him for years to quit smoking, and his wife had recently been
harping on him about his diet, which was just enough to ensure
that he did neither, at least not until he was the one to make the
decision. Eddie Baxter hadn't become chief of police by doing what
other people told him to do, even if it was for his betterment.

"The reason I insist on tending to the living first is because the
dead can't get any worse," he said matter-of-factly. "Now, if you're
done scolding me, I'll go attend to Andre."

Dr. John Conway's lined, ruddy face became taught as he confronted Andre's bloody corpse. He had seen a lot of death during

his tenure in the Crystal Springs Medical Examiner's Office. Even in the most peaceful towns, people still died and not always in a pleasant fashion. But what he discovered when face-to-face with the bloodied remains of what used to be a dear friend made him reel; the savagery alone was unlike anything he had seen before. But then that wasn't exactly true. Years ago people had died; too many—but not like this. This was beyond horrific.

"Has anyone touched or removed anything from the body?" he demanded, feeling a sudden rush of heat throughout his limbs and in his face.

"What do you take us for, rank amateurs? Adam said with an exaggerated shrug to his shoulders.

"No, sorry, of course not."

"What is it?" Evie stopped what she was doing and stood at his side.

Without answering, Doc Conway knelt beside Andre, careful of the pooled blood around him, and more closely examined his right hand. Frozen post-mortem into the shape of a claw, it looked like he had been holding something. The inside of his palm was smeared with blood as if an object had been there and removed. Retrieving his own Blackberry from his belt, he held it next to Andre's inert hand. A perfect fit. The killer had still been here when Andre tried to warn Sadie.

Doc Conway said nothing else as he felt the sensation of hundreds of tiny malevolent spiders crawling up his spine.

CHAPTER 6

9:45 a.m.

Conde Nast and *Travel America* both described Crystal Springs as a quaint Missouri town, so named for the abundance of natural springs thickly lined with quartz crystal. It was these mystical springs around which the town had been long ago settled, first by Osage Indians, and later by hearty pioneers who, once seeing the springs, ended their westward push. The underwater prismatic light created by the sun's rays bouncing off the submerged crystals inspired many fantasies of myth and magic. Due to this, the town's main square, lined on all four sides with neatly laid cobblestone streets, was littered with cafés, sipperies, eclectic shops, and art galleries. It wasn't exactly the kind of place people expected to find hidden in the Midwest, but there it was, a glistening gem surrounded by rolling countryside, decorated occasionally with ancient red barns, and dotted with bales of hay. And it was Andre's shop, Rapture, that was by far the biggest attraction and what kept the tourists coming back year after year. To Andre the store hadn't been a thing but a living, breathing entity, with a heart and a soul all its own—one that was shared by its owner and now gone forever.

Still sitting in the back of the ambulance, her legs dangling over the edge, Sadie watched the jostling crowd beyond the hastily erected police barricade and felt sickened that to some this was better than the movies. Inside she felt hollow, as if a piece of her had been carved away with the madman's deadly dagger. Andre had been so much more than her boss; he had been her best friend. Even though they didn't always see eye to eye on everything and were decades apart in age, they always remained steadfast, each continually pushing the other to do their best.

Independent and headstrong Sadie enjoyed being in control of her own life and made no bones about it. She also kept herself, her true self, locked away from nearly everyone. True, she had more friends than most, but none of them really knew her—no one but Andre. He had seen through her façade as easily as if it were constructed of the finest tissue and done something no one else had ever done—he called her on it and then he challenged her to open up. And for him she had. Now that he was gone, she felt somewhat akin to a rudderless boat adrift on a turbulent sea.

The day, unusually warm for the first of November with its clear blue sky, seemed an affront to the happenings. To Sadie, it seemed roiling clouds filled with thunder and lightning would be more appropriate. Bile rose in Sadie's throat for the second time. Doubling almost in two, she placed her head back between her knees until this new wave of nausea subsided.

As she lifted her head again, a shadow fell across her line of vision on the sun-drenched sidewalk—someone was approaching. *What now?* She just wanted to be left alone. Looking up, she saw Dan St. James striding purposefully in her direction. A few years older than Sadie, Dan had left Crystal Springs right out of high school, only recently returning home after nearly being killed in the line of duty as a detective with the St. Louis police department.

In school all the girls had harbored crushes on him, and she was no different. Suddenly, Sadie found herself longing for such simple times. Dan was good-looking and friendly without being cocky like so many of the other jocks their town seemed to breed like cattle. Excelling in sports was one of the surest ways out of a small town like Crystal Springs, and their high school heroes were treated somewhat like royalty. But Dan never acted differently. At least from what she'd seen. Even though it was a small town, there were still cliques, and she was definitely not in his. Nevertheless, he had always been friendly toward her.

Since he'd been home they'd run into each other frequently, usually at Rapture where Sadie spent most of her time these days. Andre had teased her about being the *merchandise* Dan was truly interested in. She'd been flattered, but she'd also been busy, too busy with the showing and work to make time for serious flirtation, or dating, or at least that's what she'd told herself. Truth be told, Sadie shied away from forming intimate bonds with most people. Life was simpler and safer that way. But watching him approach now, the easy swath he cut through the crowd, self-assured, confident, she was glad it was he who was coming to interview her. She found it surprising that even though Dan was still a few yards away, his presence seemed to have a calming effect on her. Still, she didn't feel up to talking to anyone, and as much as she wanted him to stop, half of her hoped that he would pass her by.

"Hey, Sadie." He stopped in front of her.

"Hey, Dan." No such luck.

"Thirsty?" he asked, holding out a cold, unopened bottle of water.

"Thanks." Sadie took the bottle then fell silent again.

"How are you?" he prompted, leaning in close and removing the ice bag from her hand as he inspected her wound.

"Depends on which second you ask me. But I seem to be teetering somewhere between shocked mortification, profound sadness, and deep penetrating fear. Ouch." Sadie jerked a little as he parted her hair. Not one to let people get close easily, she was surprised to feel grateful for the company and comforted by his touch.

"Sorry." He replaced the ice pack gently, settling her hand around it with his own. "That's one hell of a lump."

"You know me. I never do things half-ass … er … way, half-way." Sadie rolled her eyes and groaned inwardly. She had never been comfortable talking to Dan. Where he'd spent his high school career quarterbacking the football team and taking them to state three times, Sadie preferred to spend her free time between the pages of a book. Even though high school had ended a lifetime ago, some habits proved hard to break.

"Are you okay? Otherwise—." He nodded at the bloodstains on her sweater and jeans and the bandage on her hand.

"Okay is a relative term. But yeah, I'll live. Just a bunch of cuts from the blown-glass collection I took out with my rear end."

"Those were your pieces, weren't they? The ones for your show?" Dan swung up next to her on the tailgate letting his legs dangle next to hers. If the circumstances had been any different, it would have looked to the casual observer more like a couple on a first date than a police interview.

"Yep, those were they. In mere seconds my butt destroyed my life's work. That has got to be some kind of record. Doc says I'm lucky to be alive."

"He's not wrong."

"I know," she said, shaking her head. Long blond strands from her loosened ponytail hung in her face. I can't wrap my brain around it. If I hadn't overslept this morning ... I would be ... I could be—." Suddenly a fresh wave of tears threatened her eyes, and she had to struggle to hold them back. "Sorry. I guess I'm not handling this very well."

"On the contrary, you're holding up better than most." Dan gently removed the strand of hair from her eyes, tucking it behind her ear.

"Thanks."

"I'm sorry you had to see this," he said. "I'm sorry anyone ever has to see things like this." Sadie could see that he meant what he said, that the words weren't simply platitudes right for the occasion.

"Who could have done this?" she asked, shaking her head as she spoke. "He didn't have any enemies."

"We don't know yet. But I promise you, I will find him."

"Why?" The question wasn't why would Dan make such a promise. It was *why did Andre have to die?*

"There's never a good reason. But it looks like an attempted robbery gone bad. We won't know anything until we get a thorough examination of the evidence." The words came out flat, and Sadie knew he was feeding her a pat line of bull.

"Robbery?" She set down her ice pack and turned to face Dan, fixing him squarely with her eyes. "Look, Officer St. James, I might not be a highly decorated police officer, but you can't make me or any other intelligent mammal believe for one minute that a person intent on robbery would stick around to mutilate his victim and not even bother to remove Andre's platinum and sapphire Rolex. There is no way you could miss it, for God's sake. That watch has its own gravitational pull." Although she kept her voice low, Sadie could feel her face grow red and her jaw clench as she spoke. Even though a part of her knew that she was overreacting, she couldn't stop the words from flowing once they'd started. Like a steam vent from a volcano, once the pressure was released, it had to continue until finished.

"Wow," Dan said, stunned, a half smile pulling at the corner of his mouth. "I'm impressed."

Sadie stayed silent, the look in her eyes hard, her lips drawn tight across her lightly freckled face.

"I'm sorry. I was just repeating what the chief wants us to tell everybody. He doesn't want a widespread panic on his hands. All we need is an old-fashioned lynch mob, equipped with pitch forks and micro-Uzis," Dan finished awkwardly. "I didn't mean to insult you."

Sadie nodded and slowly met Dan's eyes again. "I guess I over-reacted a little—a lot. I'm just so … I don't even know what I am. I'm scared, angry, sad, bewildered, and a dozen more unhappy emotions that I can't put into words."

"No apologies necessary. I didn't really think for a minute we would be able to sell the robbery angle anyway. Truce?"

"Truce." She nodded, attempting a smile that came off as more of a grimace.

"Good."

Sadie's face was still red, but the vein in her temple had stopped thrumming. The one good thing her anger had done was dry up her tears, and for that she was relieved. She hated crying in front of others.

"Ever thought about going into police work?"

"I shouldn't have taken it out on you."

"Hey, it's okay. I can take it." He flashed a winning smile that instantly melted the rest of her anger.

"You know what really spooks me?" she said, serious again, with no trace of her recent anger. "Not as if it isn't bad enough, but I'm pretty sure that whoever it was who did this called me from the store phone and waited for me to arrive before he ditched out the back door."

"Come again?" The last statement caught him squarely off guard. "Start at the beginning and don't leave anything out, no matter how insignificant it may seem to you."

Twisting the cap off the bottle of water, she took a healthy drink and a deep breath before reiterating her morning to him. Everything from realizing she'd overslept to the mysterious and now extremely disturbing phone calls. The smudge of what she had thought at the time was red paint on the doorknob, and finding Andre, grotesquely altered from a multitude of stab wounds, amongst the largest and most expensive pieces of her art.

"Which call do you think was from the killer?"

"The first one, on the house phone. No one calls that number anymore except telemarketers. I don't even give that number out anymore."

"Are you sure it wasn't Andre?"

"I can't prove it, but yeah, I'm positive. If you look on the list by the store phone, my home number is the one listed. Andre never got around to changing that; he just reprogrammed my cell number into the speed dial. Besides, he always used his Blackberry when placing calls."

"Then Andre called your cell, warning you not to come?"

Sadie nodded. "Why didn't I realize that he was in danger? I should have called 911 immediately." No longer able to control her tears, they slipped silently from the corners of her eyes, staining her cheeks. "He tried to warn me, but I'm too friggin' stubborn. I don't listen. I just react." Sadie felt the tight grip of guilt and remorse like a steel band constricting her throat.

"Hey." Dan took her chin in his hand, gently forcing her to look at him. "This is not, I repeat, *not* your fault. There is no way you could have known what was happening. And you could not have saved him. Even if you had called 911, he wouldn't have made it. He died trying to save you." This news only made Sadie cry harder, and for a moment the pair sat in silence.

"Hey, Danny, Chief's lookin' for you," Dan's partner, Mike Johnson, interrupted.

"Give me a sec," Dan said. "Are you going to be okay for a little while?"

"Is it okay if I just go home?" Sadie pointed to the looming Victorian and her third-story apartment across the street from where they sat.

"I'd feel better if you didn't. If you can just give me a few minutes—." Dan stopped, seeing the disappointment reflected in Sadie's weary eyes.

"Please. I just can't deal with this crowd any longer."

Dan eyed the apartment, looking for any signs that something was out of the ordinary. "Is Birdie still in Vegas?" Birdie was Sadie's landlord. An ex-Vegas showgirl, she still enjoyed traveling there several times a year to *soak it all in again,* as she always said.

"Yeah, she'll be there all week. Dan, look, I don't need a babysitter. I just need to be away from all of this," Sadie pleaded, waving her arm at the jostling crowd.

"How many boarders are living there right now?"

"No one. It's just me and Birdie." Still Dan hesitated, but in the end he could find no reason not to let her go. "Okay."

"Thank you."

"Give me your number so I can reach you later." He programmed her number into his phone then gave her his card and instructed her to call him if she needed anything or remembered anything else, whether it seemed pertinent or not. "I'll check in on you later, as soon as I'm done here. Cool?"

"Cool." Sadie nodded.

Dan looked uneasy about leaving her alone and was about to say something when Sadie interrupted. "Go, Dan, I'll be okay. Just find whoever did this."

"Deal." Then Dan disappeared with his partner through the throng of people toward Rapture and Andre.

CHAPTER 7

10:22 a.m.

Dan and Mike fell into an easy step next to each other. Even though they had only known each other since Dan's return home and were almost ten years apart in age, they moved more as if they were separate parts of the same organism, especially when on the job. Although different fundamentally they made an incredible team. Where Dan had a tendency toward brooding, Mike was fairly happy-go-lucky. He'd heard around town that Dan used to be the same, but something had happened during his tenure with the St. Louis Police Department, something more specifically on his last case that had soured him. Dan hadn't shared and Mike wasn't one to pry. Yet this secret that Dan kept didn't hamper their ability to work well as a team. The crowd fell away as they moved toward the front of the shop.

"You gonna tell me what's brewing in that brain of yours?" In the short time they'd worked together, Mike had never known Dan to keep quiet, especially when working a case, although he realized too that they had never worked a case like this before—at least Mike hadn't.

"I shouldn't have let her go."

"How's she holding up?"

"Better than most." Dan glanced back over his shoulder trying to catch a glimpse of Sadie, but she had already dissolved into the crowd. "She thinks the perp called her after stabbing Andre and waited for her to arrive or had some unfinished business to take care of before he left."

"What unfinished business? Andre was already dead, and he didn't rob the place—then what? Unless—"

"Let's not jump to conclusions. If he'd wanted to kill Sadie he had the opportunity. Why not take it?"

"Unless she's wrong about him still being there."

"No, I believe her. He was still in the shop when she walked in."

Mike nodded. He trusted Dan's judgment. "So far we haven't recovered either of the shop phones or Andre's personal Blackberry. But why use one of them—why not an untraceable cell?"

"My guess is he's already tried that and discovered that she only picks up if she recognizes the number," Dan said.

"It's beginning to sound like this is more about Sadie. Still, Andre's the one that's dead, not Sadie. If he'd wanted to kill her, why leave as soon as she got there? Why the whole cat and mouse?"

"It could be part of Andre's past catching up with him. I mean, no one knows anything about his life prior to coming here."

"True, he's never talked about his past more than to say *it's not really all that interesting.*" Mike did an impressive impression of Andre's accent. "Why call the cell? Was he trying to keep her away longer or—"

"Lure her there faster," Dan said through clenched teeth.

"You know what it means . . . if the perp did take Andre's phone."

"It means that he's got the personal contact information of practically everyone in town."

"Evie, you got a sec?" Mike grabbed his fiancée lightly on the elbow as they passed on the street. He could see from the furrows on her brow and the intense look in her mahogany eyes that she was deep in thought. She was always like this when she worked a case.

An entire retinue of dancing monkeys could descend upon her, and they wouldn't break her concentration.

"Mike, Dan. Hey. I'm on my way back to the lab. If you need anything else, give it to Adam. He's wrapping up." It was apparent that she was itching to get back to her white lab coat, test tubes, and microscopes.

"Cool, but one thing?" he asked, still holding onto her elbow to ensure that she didn't run off. "Can you dump Sadie's phone logs for—." He looked at Dan, his eyebrows raised.

"At least twenty-four hours, but we might as well go back as far a week just to be safe."

"Phone logs?" She turned, fully facing them, switching her gaze from Dan to Mike, realizing for the first time that they hadn't just stopped to chat. "What do you know that I don't?"

"We think he called Sadie sometime this morning," Mike said.

"From whose phone? You know we still haven't recovered any of them."

"Check them all, but also check for any unusual phone activity."

"You think he's stalking Sadie?"

"I don't know, maybe."

"Dan, no offense, but Sadie's the one that didn't get—." Evie didn't finish the sentence. She didn't need to. They'd all seen the grotesque condition Andre had been left in.

"I know, just please do it." Dan's request was clearly anything but.

"Okay. I'll let you know what I turn up." And with that she disappeared back into the crowd, once again fully focused on her work.

All Sadie wanted to do was disappear inside her apartment at No. 9 Main Street, away from the crowds and the sounds and the constant reminders of what lay just beyond the entrance to Rapture.

Her apartment was the top floor of one of the many historic homes that lined Main Street. Instead of tearing down the houses to make way for the rapidly growing business district, the citizens had voted unanimously to maintain the town's charming ambience. Sadie's apartment was actually an attic that had been refurbished and turned into a separate dwelling sometime in the forties. She loved the vaulted ceilings and deep window wells that gave her small set of rooms an open, airy feeling.

It seemed to take a Herculean amount of energy just to walk. Until now she had been protected by the police barricade, but as soon as she stepped across the barrier she was accosted by a mass of people—some she knew, and many she didn't—making her wonder if this was really what she wanted to do. Like vultures, people surrounded her on all sides, shouting questions and snapping pictures, all wanting to know what she'd seen inside. Asking her how she was seemed like an afterthought. It was all she could do to keep from screaming at them to leave her alone. Then suddenly she was alone on the sidewalk. Mayor Leona Banks had come out to give a statement to the press. Grateful for the reprieve, she crossed the remaining distance at a quick jog, thankful for the sudden burst of adrenaline.

An outdoor set of stairs that wrapped the side of the home allowed Sadie private access to her lofty set of rooms. Just as she hit the bottom step, she remembered that she'd promised to water Birdie's houseplants while she was on vacation. She also remembered that she'd forgotten for the past two days. She paused; they'd just have to wait.

Finally, she reached the small landing just outside her door—her haven mere seconds away. Key already in hand, she was just about to insert it into the lock when the door opened an inch on its own accord.

Sadie froze.

Her heart jumped then stopped for a second before resuming at a gallop. For several seconds she stood rooted to the spot, unable to move. Her nerve endings afire; they felt like hundreds of porcupine quills.

Never taking her eyes off of the crack of the open door, she slowly began backing away, trying not to make any noise that would betray her presence. She was certain that *he* was just on the other side of the door. She knew it. She felt it and she could feel him—his hate—radiating from within. Then, as if to confirm her fears, she heard, whispered from within, "Welcome home, Sadie." The words had been spoken so low that she couldn't be sure she'd really heard them. Images of Andre flashed through her head with sudden intensity. No longer frozen, Sadie took a step backwards, only to realize that there was nothing under her and began to fall down the steps.

D an was about to shoulder his way into Rapture when Chief Baxter appeared in the door, meeting them on the street just as the mayor raised her microphone, quieting the crowd instantaneously, everyone eager for an update. Leona Banks, with her light latte-colored skin and her melodious voice, never failed to captivate an audience. A former nightclub singer, she knew how to work a crowd and had just recently been unanimously re-elected for her second term.

Dan barely heard Mayor Banks as his thoughts stayed focused on Sadie. He sought her out, feeling instantly better when he caught sight of her bobbing ponytail as she picked up her pace putting distance between herself and the crowd.

The phone call bothered him; it was personal—too personal. It made him wonder if this was truly about Andre or if someone was toying with Sadie. But who and why?

He felt dirty. Having moved home just a few months ago, he thought he'd left the big bad behind. Silently, he hoped that something hadn't crawled out of the sewers and followed him home. The mere thought made him shudder. But that wasn't possible. He'd seen to it. His actions, the ones he refused to talk about, even to his family, had been heroic. In the end he had saved lives, but at what cost? He'd been called a hero. But words, no matter how nice, couldn't change the past. They couldn't bring the innocent back to life. No, he was no hero.

From where he stood, he could see Sadie cross the street and mount the stairs to her apartment. He watched her dig for her keys as she made slow but steady progress up the three flights to her loft, and then something caught his eye. Something, or someone, had cast a shadow across the window of her apartment. He couldn't be sure what he saw. The shadow could have been caused by a trick of light, but shadows didn't have depth and substance. Without a second's hesitation, he took off at a dead run, Mike close at his heels. He hadn't needed to communicate anything to his partner. Mike knew him well enough to know that if he was running, there was a good reason.

Dan took the stairs as quickly and quietly as he could. If the perp was inside, he didn't want to give his presence away too soon. As Dan climbed toward Sadie, Mike hung back, easing around the back of the house. The large shaded backyard was protected on all sides by a wooden privacy fence that opened onto an alley, offering a much more private exit for anyone not wanting to be seen.

Dan's eyes alternated between Sadie, who stood frozen on the edge of the landing, and the black inch of space between the door and the door jam. Just as he was almost to her, something startled Sadie out of her fear-induced inertia. She stepped back, not realizing how close to the edge of the landing she was, and began to fall, when he caught her.

"Dan!" Relief swept over Sadie when she saw Dan, and she clutched onto his strongly muscled arm.

"What happened." Dan kept a wary eye on the inch of open space as he helped Sadie find her footing and regain her balance. The door didn't open or close any more.

"Door was locked, now it's not, and something aside from my cat is inside."

Dan eased her behind him with his arm as he stepped in front of her, forming a barrier between her and the apartment door, as he drew his gun.

"Back across the street now. Fill the chief in and sit tight." Dan signaled Mike with nothing more than a slight inclination of his head. Mike, who Sadie hadn't noticed until now, immediately disappeared around back of the building.

Just then, three things happened all in succession—a door slammed, something fell with the sound of shattering glass, and a blurry shape hurtled itself through the gap in the door and shot past them down the stairs and under a car parked by the curb.

"George!" Sadie turned to follow the spooked feline down the stairs. Almost immediately, she heard Mike shout from the backyard, "Pursuing." With that, Dan soared past her down the stairs, vaulting the railing when he was still a good five feet from the ground, landing lightly. As soon as his feet touched terra firma, he was off and running, quickly catching up with his partner.

CHAPTER 8

10:34 a.m.

Sprinting, Dan lost little time catching up with Mike, whose fast pace had carried him through college on a track scholarship. The route the perp took was tricky and full of obstacles. It was obvious that he had practiced the course. Just as Dan thought they would lose him, the suspect turned into a blind alley, the backside of which was fenced off with ten feet of chain-link. Even if he tried to climb over the top, there was little chance that he'd make it before they caught up with him.

Careening around the corner, just a few feet behind Mike, Dan barely had time to see the suspect turn, raise his gun, and begin firing.

Dan returned fire over Mike's head as they lunged behind a large red dumpster, but not before several bullets whizzed by, slamming into the dumpster inches from where Dan's face had just been.

In those few seconds between securing themselves behind the dumpster and returning fire, the suspect managed to escape through a slit in the fence to a motorcycle on the other side, and in an instant he was gone. Both men fired after the fleeing suspect, who grew smaller and smaller by the second.

"That was close." Mike said.

"Too close." Dan said, fingering a tear in his jacket caused by a bullet. Grabbing his radio, he called Chief Baxter. "Chief, the suspect just escaped on a black Mercedes motorcycle down the alley behind Piccadilly Lane and turned left on Magnolia."

"Go!" Chief Baxter barked to others. "Bennett and Mackey are pursuing. I'll meet you at Sadie's," he said to Dan.

Dan clipped the radio back to his belt.

"He took a big risk parking all the way back here." Mike bent close to the hole in the fence, examining it. "I don't see any rust. This was recently cut."

"He didn't think he'd be chased."

"If he wanted to kill Sadie, why did he leave Rapture as soon as she got there?" Mike pointed to one of the clipped ends of metal from the escape hole in the fence. "We've got blood."

Dan didn't answer; in his mind he was reviewing his conversation with Sadie. It was something that she'd said before that hadn't seemed significant at the time but had suddenly taken on a whole new meaning. "Her alarm clock was new."

"Come again?"

"Sadie's alarm clock … she said that she bought it yesterday and checked it twice before going to sleep, but it never went off this morning."

"Well, if she didn't turn it off, and it isn't defective—"

"He was in her bedroom last night."

"Standing over her while she slept."

"Why not kill her right then and there?"

"Only he knows the answer to that, but my gut tells me he wanted her to find Andre—dead."

Dan's nerve endings seemed afire, not with fear, but with anger, pure unadulterated anger. He was angry that the creep existed. He was angrier that he had murdered someone, a friend, under his watch. And he was furious that while they had been picking up the pieces of his handiwork, the killer had been sitting across the street in an innocent girl's apartment, watching them, gloating. Dan realized that he was clenching his fists so hard they hurt.

It took Sadie several minutes to convince George to give up his hiding place under the parked car. Eventually he relented, slinking warily into her outstretched hands. After retrieving the terrified feline, she inspected him all over for injuries. His white fur was slick with sweat from being frightened, but otherwise, he was unhurt. "What the hell happened up there, George? What the hell happened?" Clutching the cat protectively to her chest, Sadie made her way back across the street, this time in the protection of a couple of uniformed officers who held back the seething crowd anxious for a news bite direct from the source. Just then she heard several shots fired in rapid succession.

CHAPTER 9

12:06 p.m.

Dan found Sadie standing in approximately the same place he'd found her that morning after she'd run out of the store and fainted, George wrapped protectively in her arms, secured against her breast and Chief Baxter standing guard a few feet away.

"Hey, Sadie, do you have somewhere else you can stay tonight? Well, for a few nights?"

"I … guess … I could stay with Doc, but he's allergic to George. I don't think Birdie would mind if I stayed downstairs while she's out of town, but it feels kind of—weird—too close for comfort."

"Hold that thought. I have a great idea," Dan said, disappearing back into the crowd. He was gone for only a minute. When he returned he wasn't alone. Rocco and Anna St. James approached with him.

"We understand you need a place to stay for a little while," Anna said, smiling.

"That's very generous, but I couldn't put you out. The motel outside town probably has a few rooms left." Sadie did her best to smile reassuringly at the concerned couple before turning to Dan and asking, "What happened up there?"

As Dan explained what they found, Sadie found herself shaking, cold with fear. She hadn't realized she was trembling until her legs grew wobbly beneath her. Sitting down on the concrete curb, she landed hard on her already-sore tailbone, dropping George in the process. Stunned, but okay, George curled up at her feet and batted at a rock in the gutter.

"That settles it. You'll stay with us for as long as it takes," Rocco said firmly. "God knows we have enough room, and Doc's got his hands full. And I don't think you should be alone right now." Bending down, he scooped up George, effectively ending the debate before it started. The St. Jameses owned an apple orchard situated a few miles of town.

"I…uh…thank you. That would be really great." Sadie breathed a sigh of relief before turning to Dan. "I need to get some stuff. When can I go up there?"

"We're still processing; it could be a while. Why don't you let Mom and Dad take you home, and I'll bring by some stuff later," Dan suggested. "Anything specific?"

"Some jeans, a few sweaters, socks, and you know, stuff." Though relieved that she didn't have to witness the destruction of her home quite yet, she suddenly found herself blushing at the thought of Dan selecting the more intimate portions of her wardrobe for her to wear. "If anything is left intact, that is."

"No problem. I'll ask Evie to pack up some stuff when she's finished processing."

"Good idea," Anna said. "Now let's get you home." She wrapped a protective arm around Sadie for the second time that day and gave her a little squeeze as Rocco, with George, took post on her other side. Then with Dan in the lead, they headed for the St. James's SUV. Dan only had to threaten a few reporters with jail time before they all got the picture and left Sadie alone.

CHAPTER 10

November 2, 12:33 a.m.

Rain came down in sheets. The storm, light at first, had grown steadily stronger and looked as if it had no intention of letting up any time soon. At 12:33 a.m., Anna St. James nervously paced the farmhouse's spacious kitchen. Though bright and comfortable, the room did little to lessen her worry. Sadie had been upstairs sleeping in fits and starts for hours, calling out and thrashing. Whatever frightening menace stalked her dreams seemed to grow worse by the hour. "Princess, why don't you go check on her?" Rocco moved in front of Anna, effectively stopping her pacing. Slipping their arms around each other loosely, they drew strength from one another.

"Princess" had been what he'd deemed her when he'd first seen her on the cargo liner where he worked as a deckhand a lifetime ago. She'd been wearing a bathing suit, sunbathing with a novel and a cold glass of iced tea. He remembered seeing the beads of condensation on the tall glass and how thirsty he was with only lukewarm water to satiate him. He decided then that she was just another spoiled little princess, with rich parents, who didn't know the meaning of a hard day's work. Now after many years of marriage, the name stuck; she was his princess, not because she was spoiled as he'd originally thought, but because she was precious.

"I'm sorry, sweetie; I didn't mean to wake you."

"You've barely been away from her door all night, and don't try to deny it. I don't sleep well when you aren't curled up next to me stealing the covers," he said lightly, although she could see that he was worried as well.

"I feel helpless. I wish there was something I could do."

"Have you tried to wake her?"

"I couldn't rouse her." Anna nodded. "She's out cold. God, I hate feeling helpless." She rested her head on her husband's chest, and he kissed her on the forehead, an act that always comforted her.

"You sit. I'll make some tea, and we can weather the storm together."

That's when the screaming started.

CHAPTER 11

12:45 a.m.

Sadie woke with a start.

Someone was screaming.

Frozen, she wasn't sure where she was. Then slowly the recollection came to her, and she relaxed a little; she was in the St. James' spare bedroom. Her brain felt slow and thick, and the T-shirt and shorts she'd worn to bed were soaked through with sweat and uncomfortable. Shivering, Sadie pulled the covers tighter around herself. The foreign room beyond was bathed in a coverlet of perfect darkness. Heavy drapes obscured the windows, making the room as black as velvet. In her mind's eye she saw the red velvet drapes of the store, and once again she could see her hand shaking as it reached out to part them. Vigorously shaking her head, she managed to clear the ghastly image. It felt as if something were watching her from somewhere in the darkness beyond the bed, and she knew it was more than nerves, or fear, it was something else … a knowledge. He was out there.

Her whole body tensed as she waited for an attack from out of the shadows. When none came, she relaxed a little and realized that the menace in the shadows was nothing more than the residue from a bad dream—a very bad dream. Just then the door swung open, flooding the room with ambient light from the hallway and chasing a few of the shadows into already darkened corners.

Anna came first, Rocco close on her heels. "Sadie, honey, are you all right?" Anna went immediately to Sadie's side while Rocco switched on a small light on the bedside table, sensing that darkness was not wanted just now. The worry on both their faces was evident.

"I heard someone screaming." Sadie struggled to sit up, blinking in the new brightness. Her voice was weak, barely audible, and her throat was sore; it felt as if she'd been gargling rocks.

"You were." Anna sat on the bed next to her and gently, reassuringly, grasped her hand. "You don't remember?"

"No, but that explains why my throat's raw. "I'm sorry I woke you." Relieved, yet embarrassed, Sadie immediately sought to make light of what had just happened. "I'm a little too old to be afraid of boogeymen and scary dreams."

"Stop right there." Anna immediately sensed what Sadie was feeling and put a stop to it. "You've been through a terrible ordeal, one that most people can't begin to relate to. I would be worried about you if you weren't having bad dreams."

"Am I that obvious, or are you that good?"

"She's really that good." Rocco picked up the coverlet from the floor where it had fallen during Sadie's nocturnal struggle and folded it before placing it neatly on the end of the bed. "It doesn't look like ole George here was having any trouble sleeping," Rocco said, picking up the cat and scratching him behind the ears. George purred his approval.

"Do you want to talk about it?" Anna smoothed a stray lock of damp hair back from Sadie's worn face, noting the pallor of her skin and the hollowness around her eyes.

"I don't remember it, except the feeling as though someone was here—in the room with me. It felt so real—like *he* was here." Sadie aptly avoided making eye contact by focusing on a glass of water next to her bed. It wasn't until she'd been staring at it for a time that she realized she was thirsty. The cool water tasted like ambrosia, and she quickly drained the glass. "I won't blame you if you think I'm certifiable." She mumbled into the empty glass, again trying to make light of the situation.

"Dreams can do that. I used to have night terrors as a girl, and even though they stopped when I was still young, I can assure you that I know how real they can seem." Anna made sure to find her eyes when speaking so that Sadie would know that she truly understood.

"You too? It's been a long time. I thought they were behind me." Anna saw a flicker of something behind Sadie's eyes, and she could tell that there was much more to the story than Sadie was willing to let on just now.

"You and George are safe here. I promise." Even though Rocco spoke softly as he continued to cradle George, Sadie could see the strength of his conviction behind his words, yet she doubted she would ever fell safe again.

"Thank you, again, for everything. I promise no more nightmares. Go back to bed and I'll make you breakfast in the morning—or something a little less toxic. My cooking is not quite Cordon Bleu material."

"I seriously doubt any of us are going to be able to get back to sleep right now." Anna assessed correctly. "You didn't eat a thing yesterday, did you?" Her tone knowing, and as if to answer, Sadie's stomach rumbled loudly.

"Why don't you come downstairs? We can have a late-night snack and weather the storm together."

"Really? That would great," Sadie said, greatly relieved at the prospect of not going back to sleep. "Do you mind if I clean up first? I feel gross." Looking around, Sadie realized that she didn't see any of her bags. "Unless Dan didn't get a chance to drop off my stuff yet."

"Absolutely, there are plenty of fresh towels in the bathroom and yes, you have clothes." Anna crossed the room to a large, veneered antique armoire and opened it to reveal Sadie's own things. "Dan dropped these things off hours ago. He was afraid that he wouldn't bring the right things, so he brought quite a lot. You were sleeping so soundly, I went ahead and unpacked for you. I hope that's all right?"

"Yes, that's fine. Thank you. I can't believe I slept through that."

"Is there anything I can get you?" Anna asked.

"No, thank you. I just want to freshen up and put on some clean clothes," Sadie said, impatient to strip off her sweat-soaked nightclothes.

"Come down whenever you're ready." Anna and Rocco filed out of the room, closing the door behind them. As soon as they were gone, Sadie hurried across the room and flipped on the overhead light, efficiently chasing all of the remaining shadows back out into the night. She hadn't needed a night light since she was a child, and now she wondered if she would ever be able to sleep alone in the dark again.

CHAPTER 12

12:55 a.m.

Stepping into the adjoining bathroom, Sadie found herself pleasantly awed. The tile floor, a beautiful shade of amber marble, was heated, she discovered as she stepped onto it barefooted. The tub, a spa, was inset in matching marble with many small, glass votive candleholders lining two sides. There were two different showerheads on either side of the enclosure and several other jets that shot water at the bather from all different directions. There was even a bench along one wall.

The shower's steaming spray felt wonderful, and soon she felt the streaming water begin to sluice away some of her tension. Caked layers of sweat from her long restless slumber made her skin itch. Using a fresh bar of delicately fragranced lavender soap, she attempted to wash away the lingering residue left by the horrible dreams that had held her prisoner for the past several hours. Disjointed images flashed through her mind's eye too quickly for her to make sense of them.

The wounds on her hand stung as lather from the soap found its way under the bandage where it had loosened a little from yesterday, causing her to wince. Gingerly she unwound the soaked gauze that wrapped her hand to thoroughly rinse the cuts. As she did this, her eyes fell on something that gave her pause, something that shouldn't have been there. Staring at the back of her hand she felt her heart catch in her chest then begin to beat wildly.

Twin puncture marks, raw and angry, now marred the back of her hand near the fleshy part between the thumb and the forefinger. Those hadn't been there yesterday; the back of her hand had been completely unaffected by the shattered glass. As if she didn't trust her eyes and needed tactile confirmation, she brought up her left hand to touch the marks. Afraid, her hand hovered in the air just above them for seconds. If the wounds were real, and not some horrible hallucination brought on by the horror of yesterday, it heralded something far more disturbing than a few bad dreams. A door to the past slowly began creaking open as she tentatively brushed the marks with her fingertip; feeling the raised edges around the welts, she quickly pulled her hand back as if it had been burned.

They were real.

The door swung open further still.

Sadie refused to become paralyzed by the past. Whatever the meaning behind the wounds, she could not, would not, let them control her. With the index finger of her left hand, she more slowly traced the contours of the wounds when suddenly a powerful image coursed through her mind. A bright strobe in an otherwise darkened room; the image, though short-lived was vivid and powerful. It was of a boy with black hair and striking blue eyes. Naked from the waist up, he wore only a torn pair of jeans. He was surrounded on all sides by several large hissing rattlesnakes as he cowered in an earthen pit, his back pressed firmly against a rough-hewn rock wall. The snakes rattled their long tails vigorously, sounding an ominous warning to the boy and those who surrounded the edges of the pit. Sadie couldn't see the others, but she could sense them surrounding the boy on all sides, breathless—excited.

With lightning speed and deadly accuracy, two of the vipers struck out, simultaneously biting the boy on the left side of his chest and on his right hand. As quickly as the image had come, it was gone. Feeling dizzy, Sadie slid down the shower wall, her legs too wobbly to hold her upright.

"Not real—just a dream. The snakes aren't real," she said out loud, softly at first and then stronger with more intonation in her voice, as if by saying it aloud, it would be true.

"Not real!"

This mantra, an old one from her childhood, had worked once, what seemed to be a lifetime ago. She hadn't thought about the nightmares of her youth for years. Terrible visions of snakes and other horrible things had haunted her dreams regularly when she was young, stopping inexplicably when she was thirteen. They were terrifying events the doctors called night terrors. She had been sent from specialist to specialist by her father in a vain attempt to stop the dreams.

Suddenly the roomy shower felt cramped, and Sadie hurried to finish her shower, anxious not to be alone any longer.

Outside the shower, a soft fog enveloped and obscured the room. Standing in front of the mirror, she used a hand towel to wipe away the steam that had turned the glass milky—although once she saw her reflection, she'd wished she hadn't. Hollow rings surrounded her eyes, matching the way she felt inside and accentuating the paleness of her skin. She was about to turn away, when she saw something else. Another set of puncture marks, identical to the ones on her hand. These marred her chest, her left breast. Frowning, she wiped more of the mirror clean and bent closer, examining the twin wounds identical in every way to the ones on her hand. They were small and equal in diameter. The skin around each mark puckered a little and stung. Then, as if by magic, she watched as they disappeared before her eyes. Once more, her skin appeared smooth and completely unmarred. Looking at her hand, she saw that those marks too had vanished. It was as if they had never been.

"Not again." Frustration mixed with fear as she pounded her fists on the hard marble counter. "Damn it! Why is this happening again? Why?!"

These were not the first "psychic wounds" as she called them, that she'd ever suffered. But they were the first she'd experienced as an adult. As with these, most of her earlier wounds had faded quickly, leaving no telltale residue except for the haunting images in her mind, making her wonder if she had imagined them, as her father had adamantly insisted years ago. Some marks lingered longer, hours even, but all eventually faded away and disappeared.

After a few minutes, she managed to convince herself that the dreams and the subsequent bites were nothing but residual ghosts from her childhood, brought on by the trauma, and that all she needed was food, people, and eventually some sound sleep. She made a decision not to tell anyone about the bites and only enough about the dreams to pacify them. Experiences from her childhood made her feel that no one would believe her anyway. They hadn't believed her then; why would they believe her now?

In his dream he relived the same nightmare he had lived as a child, again and again. Backed against the rough stone wall, the snakes surrounded him. Tentatively he opened his eyes, just a crack. That's when they struck. Two snakes, simultaneously, one sinking its fangs deep into the flesh of his right hand, the other striking his chest, on his left side. As the boy screamed in the dream, the man screamed in his sleep, and the woman screamed miles away, twin puncture marks appearing suddenly on her hand and breast.

CHAPTER 13

1:25 a.m.

The kitchen, though very modern and completely decked out with the finest appliances, somehow maintained the old farmhouse charm and style. It was a marriage that Sadie never would have thought possible, but here it was in perfect harmony. She remarked on this to Anna, who was stirring milk on the stove for real hot chocolate. Sadie also noted that Anna had traded her robe and slippers for a pair of well-worn jeans and what must have been one of Rocco's old flannel shirts, as it hung practically to her knees. Just then Rocco joined them from outside, carrying a pile of logs, which he stacked next to the already roaring fire in the brick fireplace.

Anna poured the cocoa into thick, earthenware mugs, adding a shot of peppermint Schnapps to each and topping them off with a dollop of whipped cream.

"Oh, I'm sorry, Sadie. I really should have asked you if you wanted the Schnapps. I can make you one without it."

"Don't even think about it." Sadie moved her mug closer to her, wrapping her arms around it protectively and dipping her tongue into the creamy whipped topping.

"Sometimes I forget that not everyone is a lush like you and I are, right, honey?"

"Speak for yourself. I'm as pure as the driven snow," Rocco said, straightening up and joining Sadie at the table.

"In New York maybe," Anna mumbled from inside the refrigerator as she removed a large platter of goodies. Sadie chuckled at their exchange, and she felt her mood begin to lighten a little. Even though she had only known the St. James' in a friendly, small town manner until now, she nevertheless felt right at home.

"Help yourself." Anna set down a platter piled high with sliced green and red apples, a saucer of peanut butter, and a variety of cheese chunks, whole-wheat crackers, and thin slices of dark chocolate.

"Wow," Sadie commented, smearing peanut butter on a slice of green apple and layering it with a sliver of chocolate. Biting into it, she shut her eyes, savoring the medley of flavors on her tongue.

"I didn't know what you liked, so I made you the St. James family favorite."

"Aren't you forgetting something?" Rocco said, eyeing the plate suspiciously.

"Oops." Anna crossed the kitchen to the microwave and retrieved a bowl of what turned out to be melted caramel.

"It looks like you've done this before." Sadie smiled, comforted by their easy exchange. Sadie's own family had never been demonstrative or overtly sharing of their emotions, and therefore she found it much easier to avoid what she was feeling than to talk about it. She sensed that the St. James family was the exact opposite.

"It's good to see you smile," Rocco said earnestly. "You had us worried. How are you feeling?"

"Exhausted and wired at the same time. I never did thank you for helping me after I fainted."

"Nonsense, no thanks are needed. You would have done the same thing if the situation had been reversed."

"You're right. But still, thank you."

"Do you want to talk about it—the dreams, I mean?" Anna asked, joining the others at the kitchen table.

"I don't remember much, except for the distinct feeling of being watched … or hunted, like a mouse knowing that the cat is out there but not able to see it. I used to have similar nightmares when I was young, but for years they've been ancient history. I don't know why they suddenly reared their ugly head now unless Andre's … what happened yesterday somehow triggered them again." Sadie looked from Anna to Rocco as she spoke, amazed that she had just opened up even that much.

"I think it would be a bit unnatural not to have nightmares after everything that's happened." Anna gave Sadie's hand a reassuring squeeze. "What can we do to help?"

"You're already doing more than you know. Just not being alone right now is really nice. I feel bad about keeping you up all night though." Suddenly Sadie had an inexplicable desire tell them everything, about the dreams, the strange marks—everything, but she didn't know how. She'd spent her entire life keeping these things a secret, and the fact that she suddenly wanted to share scared her. She reasoned that she couldn't tell them the truth, that if she did, they would think she was crazy.

Lifting the large mug of hot chocolate to her lips, Sadie blew on the surface, taking a tentative sip. The creamy cocoa at first tasted luxurious and smooth as it spilled over her tongue; then all of the sudden it turned thick and grainy, making her gag. Her heart racing, a cold sweat broke out on her forehead, and she craved something cold. She felt restless and angry, unable to sit still. The chair's legs squealed on hardwood floor as she pushed back hard, standing abruptly without her usual grace.

Anna noted Sadie's stark change in demeanor and exchanged glances with Rocco across the table. He looked as startled and puzzled as Anna felt. "Sadie, are you all right?" Rocco started to stand. Already pale, Sadie's skin turned white in a matter of seconds. She looked almost dead.

The presence from the bedroom was with her again—somehow controlling her. Sadie knew that the actions weren't her own, and yet even as she tried to fight them, she wasn't strong enough to stop them. Instead of seeing the shining chrome refrigerator in front of her, she saw a red cooler surrounded by darkness. Ripping the lid off of the cooler she saw herself—him—reach inside.

Sadie flung the door to the fridge open, her movements jerky as she fought for control over the invisible force that was controlling her. She felt like screaming, but she couldn't fight what was happening. She felt sick and thirsty, so desperately thirsty. Inside the refrigerator she saw the pitcher of cold water on the second shelf and below it several cold beers. The cold amber-colored liquid looked wonderfully refreshing. As if she were a puppet controlled by an amateur puppeteer, she grasped a beer in the same jerky movement and twisted the top off with her fist. Still standing in the open refrigerator, she drank it all in one long swallow.

He woke bathed in a cold sweat. Getting up, he walked naked across the room, moving easily through the dark with no need of light. He knew every inch of this forsaken place. Nothing had changed in the years since he'd fled it as a child. Except that now he was a man. Plucking a cold beer from the red Igloo cooler in the corner, he twisted the cap off easily and drank the cold amber liquid all in one long swallow.

As soon as Sadie finished drinking the beer, the presence left her, and she was once again in control. Confused and embarrassed by her erratic behavior and with no way to explain what had just happened, she quickly filled a glass with water and rejoined Anna and Rocco at the table, avoiding their questioning gazes. "Um … Sorry." It sounded lame even though she meant it, but she couldn't think of anything else to say. *Sorry, you let a loon into your home* didn't sound any better.

"Are you okay?"

"What happened?" Rocco, not being the kind to beat around the bush, asked, his electric blue eyes studying her closely. It was obvious he wasn't mad, just concerned.

"No, I'm not." The words flew out of her mouth before she could stop them. "I don't know what happened, and I'm scared." She tentatively met first Rocco's eyes then Anna's, and upon seeing both of their non-judgmental yet concerned gazes, she dared to venture on. "One second the cocoa tasted wonderful, and the next it … it turned to sand. Then I was thirsty, so thirsty I couldn't think about anything else. I saw … I was … I am very embarrassed. I won't blame you if you think I'm crazy." This was the closest Sadie had ever come to telling anyone about this aspect of her terrors. This particular nuance, where she felt controlled by another, she had kept completely to herself, not even sharing it with her childhood therapist. But then no one had ever witnessed an event before.

"I don't blame you—we don't," Anna said, grasping Rocco's forearm. "But I can't help feeling like you're holding something back. We just want to help you, Sadie. We aren't going to judge you or toss you out into the storm." Rocco nodded in agreement, never breaking his stare away from Sadie.

After a pause of several seconds, Sadie took a deep breath. Staring into her cocoa, she began to talk, letting the words out before she really had time to think about them.

"I don't know how to explain it. Suddenly I felt like I was inside a dream or someone else's. I could see and feel … I wasn't in control of my body, or my actions. I didn't even want a beer … but suddenly it was all I could think about … I know it sounds crazy. Maybe I am crazy."

"You're not crazy, dear. You, I believe, are exhausted, hungry, and trying to make sense of something that's senseless." Anna stood up and went to the refrigerator, quickly pulling together a turkey sandwich. "I should have realized that a few slices of apple weren't enough. Eat this." Placing the sandwich in front of Sadie, she left no room for argument. When Anna made up her mind it was set. Even though Sadie wasn't sure she completely agreed with Anna's assessment that she was just tired and hungry, she let the explanation stand. If only that could be the truth. If only.

"Don't I get one too?" Rocco eyed Sadie's sandwich hungrily.

"You don't need one." As strong as her resolve was, it was almost impossible for her to refuse her husband's playfully pleading gaze. "Fine, a small one." After making another sandwich and splitting it between herself and Rocco, the three of them ate in silence for a few minutes, listening to the crackling of the fire over the storm outside. "There's been more than one time when I've needed a drink. You're more than welcome to have another," Rocco said, after popping the last bit of sandwich into his mouth.

"I didn't even want it. And I would never do something like that, just take something that I hadn't been offered." Sadie cleared the dishes, loading them into the dishwasher. The mundane activity felt soothing, and she was glad that Anna let her help.

"Please feel at home while you're here. Help yourself to anything that we have," Anna said.

For a while the three of them sat in silence, a comfortable one this time, each of them saying a silent good-bye to their friend. As the night wore on, the storm eventually lost its power and died quietly away, while inside Sadie found herself bonding easily with Anna and Rocco.

"I ran into Andre yesterday," Rocco said, breaking the silence. "We literally ran into each other. He was focused so hard on something that he seemed oblivious to everything around him. He didn't even see me runnin' right at him, didn't hear me when I called out to him."

"That sounds like Andre." Sadie tried to smile at the memory but found it impossible.

Sadie could see where Dan got his good looks; his father, Rocco St. James, had to be one of the best-looking men she'd ever seen and in amazing shape for a retiree. Rocco was sixty-two years young, six foot two, and 185 pounds of solid muscle. His salt-and-pepper hair, more salt than pepper now, was cut short in a crew cut. It was his eyes, though, that were by far his best feature; a pure crystal blue, they sparkled with an intensity of warmth and genuine caring. Rocco was a man who had such a zest for life that he served as inspiration for many in town, young and old alike. He still worked out five times a week at the local gym. And he made the best lasagna this side of Italy.

"He was so startled when he turned the corner and saw me bearin' down on him that he nearly fell off the curb." Neither Sadie nor Anna tried to stop Rocco from reiterating his brief encounter with Andre, as it was most likely the last conversation that Andre ever had. "I kidded him about being a dull boy, all work and no play; I even invited him over for dinner last night. I was going to make lasagna." Rocco's voice choked with emotion, and he stopped talking.

Eventually the events of day and night took a toll on everyone, and they went back to bed. Although dubious about the prospect of sleep, Sadie quickly nodded off soon after crawling back into bed. This time her sleep was uneventful.

CHAPTER 14

7:45 a.m.

Dan stood in the shower, rinsing the shampoo out of his hair when the phone started ringing.

"Great timing," he said, shutting off the water and grabbing a towel as he headed for the phone, leaving a trail of watery footprints in his wake.

The caller ID read his folks' phone number. He picked up. "Hey, Mom. Glad you called. How's Sadie?"

"I've been better, but your folks are a Godsend; however, I wouldn't be surprised if they don't actively attempt to have me committed." Dan was shocked to hear Sadie's voice. Shocked but pleased.

"Why do you say that?"

"Let's just say it was a long night and leave it at that."

"Bad?"

"Bad, good, weird … I'll tell you about it later. I hope it isn't too early to call; your mom assured me that you would be up and … how did she phrase it again? … as hyper as a chicken on speed … that's exactly how she put it." Dan detected a hint of smirk in her voice and could picture her half-smile as she said it.

"Wonderful. Gotta love parents." He wished now that he hadn't told his mom that he liked Sadie, and he was really wishing he knew exactly what they'd talked about. Cradling the phone between his ear and his shoulder, he did his best to dry off and talk at the same time. "What's up?"

"I remembered something, and you said to call if…"

"Give me a sec, let me grab a pen." Sufficiently dry, Dan secured the towel around his waist and went in search of his coffee and something to write with.

"It might be nothing, but I've been getting a lot of prank phone calls lately. I figured it was just kids playing games and blew it off. It didn't seem scary, until now."

"How many is a lot?"

"One, sometimes two a day for the last week."

"What'd they say?"

"Nothing, but there was something—an odd sort of rattling in the background."

"Can you be more specific?" Dan scribbled notes into a small, flip-top notebook. "Was it static?"

"No, it definitely wasn't static. It sounded…" Sadie paused looking for the right words and Dan didn't try to interrupt. "…like a gourd or something, with dried seeds inside."

"Did you get a number?"

"No, it was always blocked. After the first call, I stopped answering, hoping they would stop. But it didn't matter; they left the same non-message on my voice mail."

"Were these on your cell?"

"No, house phone."

"Did you delete the messages?" Dan tried to keep the tension he felt out of his voice. Whoever it was had been stalking Sadie for at least a week, which led Dan to wonder if Andre had indeed been the killer's intended victim or just collateral damage. Maybe the reason Andre's murder had been so violent was because the killer had been disappointed. Was he anticipating Sadie being the first one in the shop that day? But then why not kill her when he had the chance? He knew he was missing something but just couldn't wrap his head around it.

"Actually I didn't delete them. In fact, I was going to report it, but I got so busy with the opening and Andre's party that I just forgot about it. Seriously, I didn't think they were a big deal."

"I'll need those, and I also need…" He found himself faltering, the words dying on his lips. Over the years he had seen the special hell victims have to go through when confronted with the destruction left after senseless violence enters their lives. Though it desperately needed to be done, he didn't want to put her through that.

"Help out with an inventory of my apartment and Rapture?" she finished for him.

"You're good. You sure you never wanted to be a cop?"

"No thanks. Who else can tell you if anything is missing? Look, it's definitely not something I want to do, but I also don't want to sit around with it hanging over my head or let that monster get away because I couldn't go back in there. If this helps, then I'll do it."

"Okay, I'll see you soon." After hanging up the phone, Dan headed back into the bedroom, pausing to sop up the wet marks he'd left on the hardwood floor.

Dan was pulling on his boots when the phone rang again. He looked at the caller ID skeptically—his number was unlisted. Hairs rose on the back of his neck when he saw the caller's name display. It read Andre Adington, and unless Andre had found a very good long-distance calling plan on the other side, this was the killer using Andre's stolen Blackberry.

Pressing a button on his phone that activated a micro-recorder, Dan answered, "St. James." His only response was dead air. He could hear someone breathing on the other end of the open line.

"Are you turning yourself in?" Again, the only response was a deep, controlled breathing; but there was something else, a noise, a faint rattling in the background. Just like Sadie had said, it sounded familiar yet he couldn't place the sound either. Suddenly he knew, without a doubt, Sadie's prankster and the killer were one in the same, and he felt hot adrenaline course through his body.

"Why'd you do it?" He was hoping he could draw the caller into any sort of a dialogue that might help them, but the caller remained silent, though the rattling in the background grew louder.

"The longer this goes on, the harder it's gonna be for you. Trust me, it will be better if you turn yourself in." Silence, but the background noise grew steadily louder and more agitated. Dan could almost feel the hate pouring through the open phone line, infecting him, making his hair stand on end and his blood run cold.

"You're not gonna win." By the time Dan finished, he realized he was talking to dead air. As soon as the line went dead, he disconnected and called Mike, who picked up on the first ring.

"You at work already?"

"Good morning to you too? And, yes, I was just getting our marching orders from the Chief." Mike said.

"Put me on speaker."

"Okay, done."

"What have you got?" It was Chief Baxter this time.

"See if you can get a GPS read on Andre's Blackberry."

"What happened?" Chief Baxter asked.

"The killer just called me," Dan said.

"Are you sure?" Mike asked.

"Positive." Dan said.

"What did he have to say?" Mike asked.

"Listen for yourselves." Dan pressed another button, playing the recording back for Mike and Chief Baxter.

"The good news is that the phone is still on. I should be able to get a read on his location," Mike said.

"That sound, the one in background—what do you make of it?" Dan felt like it was something he should be able to recognize, but the more he tried, the farther away he seemed to get from figuring it out.

"Hard to say. We'll hand it over to Evie and Adam. See what they can make of it." Chief Baxter said.

"Anything yet?" Dan could see the chief impatiently pacing the office, a cigarette—unlit—hanging from his lower lip. Smoking inside the precinct was strictly forbidden, and since it was Chief Baxter's own rule, he had to abide by it.

"Almost there," Mike sounded as if he were silently urging the machine to run faster.

"Right before he called, I talked to Sadie. She told me about a bunch of prank phone calls she received over the past week, all with the same strange rattling noise in the background."

"Why didn't she say anything about them yesterday?" Chief Baxter growled.

"She didn't think they were relevant at the time. How close are we, Mike?

"Hold on; it's coming through now. The call originated from— that can't be right."

"What?" Chief Baxter and Dan said simultaneously.

"According to the trace, the call originated from Sadie's place?" Mike said.

"He's taunting us."

"Mackey!" Chief Baxter barked storming out of the room. Although he was moving away from the phone, Dan could still hear him issuing orders to the other officers.

"Sadie volunteered to inventory both Rapture and her apartment today. But now I'm not so sure that's a great idea."

"We need that to happen sooner than later. Mackey and Bennett are on their way over there now. Dan, I'll have them call you as soon as we're sure it's clear."

"Okay," Dan said and hung up. Then grabbing a leather bomber jacket, he left his apartment. The morning was bright and chilly but certainly not cold. It looked as if it was going to be a beautiful day.

CHAPTER 15

8:30 a.m.

Sadie stared at her reflection. No amount of makeup would cover the dark circles beneath her eyes. She was drained. Deep down in her soul tired. As much as she tried to tell herself that Dan would catch the guy, that it would all be over soon, and that she could go home, she knew in her heart that it was a long way from being over and that her apartment would never feel like home again. In the marrow of her bones, she knew that she was an integral part of this mystery, and it terrified her. But for the life of her, she had no idea how or why. It wasn't logical or something she could explain. She just knew it. And that was why she had to go back into her apartment, back into Rapture.

She didn't know what she expected to find that Dan and the cops couldn't or wouldn't. She knew she wasn't qualified for detective work, but she also knew that she had to try. All her life she'd been a doer. She usually dove headfirst into whatever situation confronted her without looking back. Sometimes she hit her head pretty hard on invisible rocks lurking beneath the surface, but she'd always come out okay. She realized that she had never done anything like this before and hoped that the undertow wouldn't be too strong for her to fight.

Sighing, she put her makeup away. Resigning herself to the circles that wouldn't disappear, she went in search of Anna, determined to enjoy the morning for just a little while before heading back out into the proverbial storm. A part of her felt guilt over the fact that she wasn't completely despondent, that she was able to function, to wear a smile, even a small one. It wasn't truly happiness she was feeling; it was more a resigned stalwart front. She had to be strong. Even if she had to fake it for the sake of the investigation—for Andre. She had to help Dan and the police, and to do that she couldn't allow herself to fall into that black hole of despair that was waiting ever-so patiently just on the other side of her half-forced smile.

Sadie found Anna in the kitchen, brushing melted butter across the tops of homemade buttermilk biscuits before slipping them into the oven. They looked delicious. She had a feeling she was in danger of gaining weight if she stayed here too long.

"What can I help with?" Sadie asked, as she helped herself to a mug of cinnamon hazelnut coffee from the decanter on the table. After only a few hours with the couple, she already felt very much at home here, and in spite of her strange behavior during the night, the couple seemed to have accepted her entirely, which although strange to her, was more than welcomed. Sadie had spent the majority of her life a loner; although she was always surrounded by a plethora of friends, none of them really knew her. And though she had flirted with love before, she had always found a way to break off relationships just as they started becoming intense. She spent the majority of her waking hours either reading or sweating behind the large three-thousand-degree furnace in which she produced her blown-glass works of art. There were three places in the world she'd felt safe: her apartment, Rapture, and her studio. Now, in one fell swoop, two of them had been taken from her, and she feared that she would not have the heart to return to her work anytime soon.

"Nothing at all. I've got this completely under control. Rocco has a fire going in the stove on the porch, and he's taken the paper—and your George—out there. Why don't you take the coffee out? I'll join you in a few minutes."

Sadie, dubious at first about sitting on a porch in November, quickly changed her mind. A large wood-burning stove heated the porch beautifully, even though it was screened and somewhat open to the elements. There were several comfortable-looking chairs and a table long enough to seat at least eight. Rocco was sitting on a loveseat with George curled up next to him on top of the newspaper, defying anyone to move him.

"This is the most amazing house," Sadie said, offering Rocco a refill, which he gratefully accepted, holding out his almost empty mug as she poured. Choosing a chair next to the stove, Sadie found herself mesmerized by the beauty of the orchard in the daylight. She had been here several times throughout her life, but always as a paying customer and never as a guest. She'd never seen it from this side, and she found herself truly impressed.

"Did you know this house has been in Anna's family for over one hundred and fifty years?" Rocco asked, blowing on the steaming liquid in his mug before taking a sip.

"I knew that it had been here for a long time, but I had no idea it was that old," Sadie tasted her coffee. It was good and strong, just the way she liked it. Anna joined them on the porch shortly, and they took turns filling Sadie in on the history of the orchard while they waited for Dan to arrive and the biscuits to finish baking.

"The St. James Orchard has been in Anna's family for six generations, going back to the eighteen hundreds."

"St. James is my family name," Anna said and, seeing that Sadie was still confused, added, "My ancestors started the orchard over one hundred and fifty years ago. Anyone who marries into the family, men and women alike, always take the St. James name." Sadie could tell that Anna loved telling that part of the story.

"So you took Anna's name?" Sadie remarked as she sipped her coffee. She hoped that Dan took his time getting there, as she was really enjoying the story and wasn't looking forward to what was to come.

"Richard Joseph Barr," Rocco said, extending a hand across the table as if he were introducing himself to Sadie for the first time. "But my friends call me Rocco," he added with a wink.

"John and Suzie St. James settled here in eighteen fifty with a mule, two sapling apple trees, and Suzie already three months pregnant with the first of their five children. They worked side-by-side, day in and day out, and with the help of a few neighbors, managed to raise a house in short order," Anna added with obvious pride in her heritage.

"The original house was a one-room utilitarian structure, which did little more than keep the weather out," Rocco added.

"Over the generations the orchard grew and prospered until it became what you see here today," Anna said, sweeping her arm in a graceful arc. Just then they heard a car approaching on the gravel drive. Within a few moments, a black Jeep Wagoneer appeared, coming to a stop a few feet from the porch steps.

As Dan got out of the car, Sadie ran her hands through her hair, suddenly wishing that she spent a little more time in front of the mirror.

"You're beautiful." Anna winked, and Sadie felt a blush begin to rise in her cheeks.

"This looks like a motley crew," Dan said, opening the door and stepping into the porch and hugging both of his parents.

"Just waiting on the biscuits," Anna said. "Ah, that would be the timer now. I'll be right back. Sit down."

"We really need to go," Dan said without much conviction as the smell of the freshly baked biscuits wafted onto the porch. He had just heard from Officer Jen Mackey that Andre's Blackberry had been recovered from Sadie's and that both locations were secure and ready for the inventory to begin.

"Nonsense, I'm not letting you two run off with nothing in your stomachs but coffee," Anna said, and with that she disappeared into the house.

"Better listen to your mother," Rocco said, winking at Sadie.

"Okay, but we really do have to go soon," Dan acquiesced, following his mom into the house. "Can I help?"

After Dan left, Rocco excused himself as well. As soon as Sadie was alone, she took a deep breath and realized that she was suddenly nervous. *This is a murder investigation, not a date,* she thought, and then surprised herself by suddenly wishing it were something more than what it was; breakfast and then inventory, not exactly dinner and a movie. Dan had been flirting with her, albeit poorly, for months, and she'd enjoyed it but that's where she'd left it; telling herself that she didn't have time to pursue a serious relationship. A complete lie, and she knew it. Dating was messy, another lie.

Suddenly restless, she walked over to the far end of the porch. Watching the St. James family reunite filled her with mixed feelings of warmth and envy. She never remembered having affection like that with her own father. Her mother died giving birth, leaving an unspoken darkness over the family. Although in photographs of her parents together, before she was born, they always looked happy. Standing on the porch and staring out at the vast orchard, she wondered what it must have been like to grow up here.

Pictures of Dan growing up were everywhere in the house, and Sadie had found herself studying them more than once since her arrival. He was perfect in an imperfect sort of way. His brown hair had enough wave in it to keep it gently unkempt, and his smoky eyes, though bright, seemed to harbor some secret knowledge deep within them. Though this was not new, she'd noticed it had gained intensity over his years away from home. They seemed to betray a certain heaviness in his soul. So many times she'd wanted to ask him about it, but she'd never felt close enough to him to inquire about something so personal.

"Quite a sight, isn't it?" Dan said, coming up behind her, startling her. She hadn't realized that she wasn't alone on the porch any longer.

"I was just imagining what it must have been like to grow up here," Sadie said, turning around.

"Pretty great. Anyway, I'm sorry," Dan said.

"Sorry for what?" She turned to face him.

"Not saying hi when I came in a few minutes ago."

"You did."

"I did?"

"No, but I know you meant to."

"I did ... mean to."

"I know." Sadie was glad he was there. She felt safe and that felt good. Turning to look back at the orchard, she wished she could bottle this feeling and carry it with her.

Breakfast went smoothly, and Sadie found she was able to relax and enjoy the easy banter between the others at the table.

"Ready to go?" Dan asked as soon as they were done eating.

"Um, sure," Sadie said, looking at Anna. "Would you like me to help you with the dishes?" Sadie did not want to appear ungrateful or rude.

"No, no, Rocco can help me. You two get goin.' Just make sure you're home in time for dinner."

"Yes, Mom ..."

"Yes, Mrs. St. James." They said in unison as they stood up from the table. Neither one of them spoke again until they got to the car.

"We sounded like dorks," Dan said as he held her door open. He offered her a hand as she climbed into the passenger side of the Jeep.

"Huge dorks," she agreed. Dan shut her door and walked around to his side of the Jeep. Again they fell into silence as he started the car and began down the drive. Sadie stared at Dan as he drove and wondered if he would notice. It didn't take long before he glanced over at her, an eyebrow raised in question and asked, "Yes?"

"I'm just stunned and, I have to admit, impressed."

"By ..."

"I thought all of the gentlemen had died out with the dinosaurs."

"There are a few of us who escaped extinction, but don't let it get out," Dan said.

"Big secret society?"

"Exactly."

"So what happens if you're exposed? Would they hunt you tire-lessly until they caught you, take you to an old abandoned ware-house, duct-tape you to a La-Z-Boy recliner, and force you to watch dirty movies and drink cheap beer, all the while repeating phrases like 'women are the enemy'?"

"You know!" he exclaimed with mock surprise. "Damn. And I liked you too."

CHAPTER 16

9:47 a.m.

The day was beautiful, the storm of the night before having cleared off, leaving the sky bright and shiny, as if it had just had a thorough scrubbing. For the next few minutes, they settled into a comfortable silence, both of them still smiling from the recent exchange. Studying Sadie out of the corner of his eye as he drove, Dan detected subtle yet distinct changes in her demeanor the closer they got to town. It was a slight but constant rubbing of her middle finger on her thumb that first drew his attention. It was something he'd noticed before whenever she was nervous or upset. He doubted she was even aware she was doing it. Next he noticed her face, which just minutes ago had been relaxed and open, was now taut and strained.

The bright yellow crime scene tape across the entrance to Rapture and Sadie's apartment door stood out against the crisp November morning. Dan navigated the cobblestone street slowly, eventually coming to a stop at the curb across from Rapture, in front of Birdie's house. Putting the car into park, Dan left the engine idling. He was beginning to seriously doubt his own judgment. It was too soon. "You don't have to do this," Dan said, feeling like a jerk for dragging her out here. He was beginning to think he'd been a detective for so long that he'd forgotten how to be human.

"I don't want to go in there." she said, her long blond hair flowing freely as she shook her head. It was the first time she'd spoken in several minutes. "It's not *my* home anymore. *He* took it from me." Sadie wasn't looking at Dan; she was looking up at the window in which the brutal stranger had stood. "But I have to, whether it's today, tomorrow, next week, or next month. I have to confront it, and if going in there helps you catch him, I'll do it."

"Are you sure?"

"No, I'm not sure about much of anything right now. I'm walking an emotional tightrope. One second I feel like exploding and then crying until I completely dissolve. I seem to find little things that I wouldn't normally find funny, hysterical. I want to laugh until it hurts or all of the hurt goes away, but in the end I'm just left feeling hollow. I haven't really cried yet. I'm terrified that when I finally do break down and cry, that I'll never be able to stop, and to top it all off, I feel totally alone." Sadie spoke with her face toward the passenger-side window so Dan couldn't see what emotions she was wearing. But he could hear them.

As Sadie spoke, the world outside the Jeep evaporated for Dan. He was touched by her openness and honesty, and he felt himself drawn to her. This was the first conversation they'd ever had that hadn't been superficial, and he wasn't about to stop it now.

"Sorry," Sadie began to open the door, leaning away from Dan. "Let's get this over with."

"It can wait for a few seconds." Dan placed a hand on her elbow to stay her. "I'm not comfortable with you going back up there yet."

Sadie turned towards him, facing him for the first time since she'd began opening up. "First I lost my parents, and I dealt with that. Then Andre and Rapture became my family, and they have both been taken from me in one fell swoop." Then, so softly he could barely hear her, "I feel like an orphan." Though Sadie's voice was soft and her slightly slumped posture made her appear weak,

Dan sensed an underlying strength that was the very core of her and what he was most attracted to.

"You're not alone." Dan took her chin in his hand and turned her head so she was facing him, so that she could see the sincerity behind his words. "You have me." He paused until she met his gaze. "And I'm not going anywhere." Sadie didn't say anything but swallowed hard. Tears threatened her eyes. The laughter of the recent past evaporated.

"Come here." Dan surprised himself by pulling her close to his chest, wrapping his arms around her, and holding her to him. At first Sadie felt stiff in his arms, but soon she relented, and he felt her relax into him and allow herself to be comforted. The time he got to hold her was brief.

After a few seconds she straightened up, and running her hands through her hair, she said, "Come on, let's get it over with." With that she got out of the car.

Walking from the car to the building, they fell into an easy step beside one another. Mounting the stairs together, he felt her hand slip into his, and he accepted it without hesitation, although he had a feeling that it was more for support than romance. Walking side by side, they ascended the stairs. To any passerby on the street, they would look just like any other courting couple on a brilliant autumn day. The only thing breaking the illusion was the crime scene tape barring their way past the entrance.

CHAPTER 17

10:20 a.m.

At the top of the stairs Sadie stopped just short of the door. "Why is it that they chose such a happy color to be the herald of tragedy?" she asked, squeezing Dan's hand harder. She was amazed at the calming effect he had on her. "Why not puke green, or brown, or some other unfortunate color?" Ripping the tape off of the door she took a deep breath, opened it, and stepped inside.

The room was hardly recognizable. "My God, I know I'm not the world's best housekeeper, but this is ridiculous." It was obvious she was trying to put on a brave face. The sofa cushions had been slashed and torn; white stuffing bled out of the red fabric, like so many mortal wounds. The frame of a large mirror hung empty and broken on the wall above the couch. "I saved for months to buy that," she said, her eyes on the spot where the mirror now cast no reflection. "Where's all the glass?"

"Evie's got it at the lab. He cut himself when he smashed it."

"What are the chances his DNA will be in the system?"

"There's no way of knowing. But we can hope." Dan didn't

want to give her false hope, but he also didn't want to discourage her even more.

"How soon till you know?"

"Soon. Evie and Adam are the best, trust me."

And even though Sadie wanted to say that she did—trust him—she couldn't make the words come. Trust for her was difficult at best.

For the next few minutes Sadie circled the room in silence, absorbing the annihilation of her belongings. Dan did nothing to stop her, nor did he ask her any questions. She would talk when she was ready. Eventually, she stopped.

"Gone. Annihilated. He destroyed everything." Shaking her head slowly as if coming out of a daze, she finally looked up and into Dan's eyes. "These books," she gestured with her hand, "these things … my things, that he ruined," she said, biting her lip, "were all small parts of me. Nothing I had was expensive, but it was all I had and now it's gone." She could see Dan watching her closely, a worried look on his face. She knew he wouldn't stop her if she wanted to leave.

Turning in a slow circle, she took another moment to let the totality of the destruction settle in on her. Each little piece of ruin felt like an open wound on her soul. As she moved, fragments of her life crunched underfoot, much of it unrecognizable as the thing it used to be. "You know," she said quietly but firmly, "I thought I would be crying inconsolable, frightened, or bewildered … lost … but guess what?" Sadie turned and looked at Dan, her hands on her hips, one knee bent, and her head cocked slightly to one side.

"You're angrier than you've even been in your entire life?"

"Pretty much," she said with finality. Then dropping her defensive posture, she crossed the room back toward the front door, passing within a breath from where he stood, and stopped in front of the window, her back to Dan. "I don't think anything's missing from here."

"You're sure?" he asked, turning as she passed and following behind her across the small room.

"Positive," she said, nodding. "The only thing in here worth taking was the television, and it's still here. Decimated but…" She faltered, surprised to realize that Dan was right beside her, his hand pressed gently against the small of her back. Electricity seemed to pass directly from his fingertips and travel the length of her spine. Losing her train of thought, she stammered. All of her senses were filled with Dan, the subtle scent of his skin, the whispered heat of his breath on her neck. She was having trouble remembering what she'd been saying or why. "Um…it's definitely…"—she turned into him, her breath catching, his arm now encircling her waist— "still…"—her heart beat faster—"here." Their faces were inches apart. At first, Dan's arm felt good around her; then all of a sudden, it felt claustrophobic. This was too much. Breaking away from the almost embrace, Sadie made a hurried excuse, "I…uh…I'll be right back," and disappeared into the apartment's small bathroom, shutting the door firmly behind her.

Okay, what was that? Sadie leaned heavily against the bathroom door. The claustrophobic feeling dissipated as her heartbeat slowed. She'd been caught off guard by his closeness. The moment had been perfect or as perfect as one can get while surrounded by chaos. Things were happening too fast. Her emotions were on overload. *Get a grip, girl. You're reading too much into this. He was just trying to comfort you.* Somehow the bathroom had remained untouched, and it felt safe. Looking into the mirror above the sink, she took note of how the dark circles beneath her eyes made them look hollow. She wondered if she would ever be able to feel close, really close, to anyone ever again. Then she thought about what Dan had said in the car and wondered if he meant it. Everything Dan said, everything he did, felt right, but she honestly had no idea if her feelings were real or the misfiring of pent up grief. She hadn't responded to him back in the car, and then just minutes ago she'd almost, she'd wanted to…*I've lost too much already…* She didn't finish her thought. The thought of losing Dan and their relationship, whatever it might be, scared her too much to even think it.

She knew she could tell Dan she wanted to leave and he wouldn't object. The moment she'd opened the front door and stepped across the threshold, she'd already been there too long. But she'd come and she'd stayed to help Dan find whatever man-shaped demon had done this and send him back to the fiery pits of hell from which he'd so obviously been borne. Her hand on the doorknob, she took a deep breath before opening it and stepping back out into the hall. Finding Dan in the living room closely examining boot prints on her wall, she said, "I'll just check out my bedroom." She felt like an idiot.

"Okay. Are you okay?" Dan, still squatting, looked up at her, his face open and honest with no sign of hurt or anger.

"Yeah ... I'm just ... this place ... I'm sorry." And offering a half smile, she slipped back out of the room before he asked her any more questions.

CHAPTER 18

10:45 a.m.

I know I didn't imagine that. Dan said to himself, feeling conspicuously alone in the space that moments ago had held two. *You came on too strong, idiot.*

After Sadie escaped into the bathroom, Dan used the time to his advantage to look for anything that might have been missed earlier. He was glad to have the chance to come back without the noise, activity, and people that it took to process a crime scene. He needed time to be alone with the killer. To try and understand what he was feeling at the time of the crime. He tried to see through their eyes, the eyes of a criminal, not of a cop. Some people thought it was a waste of time. After all, how could he understand a criminal if he was a cop? But Dan had learned that people and their motives were not always black and white; it wasn't always as easy as playing cops and robbers. This was something he'd learned while working as a decorated homicide detective in St. Louis over the last nine years. He was the only member of the Crystal Springs police force with any practical experience with murder and the sociopaths that perpetrated the crimes. But unlike his buddies on the force, who thought he was some kind of hero, he felt dirtied by it, soured. He had witnessed the sick and the depraved at their finest, and it had almost gotten him killed. That was why he was back in Crystal Springs. He'd moved home to get away from murder.

Now, although he wasn't exactly alone, he had no trouble relaxing and opening himself to the subtle, often elusive characteristics of the crime scene. These often overlooked clues helped give him an insight into the killer. Many cops didn't possess the talent or the patience for this brand of detective work, thus making him a class above the rest. When he did this, he was able to devote his attention so thoroughly on the particular piece of the puzzle he was working on that he was able to block out every other sight and sound that was not related. It was a state quite similar to meditation. In fact, he'd taken courses over the years to help him relax and open his mind. Employing those techniques now, Dan felt everything else fall away as he connected with the crime scene.

CHAPTER 19

10:47 a.m.

The bedroom was a total disaster. It looked as though a tornado had recently blown through. This room, by far, had suffered the worst damage in comparison with the rest of the apartment. It looked as if it had been the epicenter of a violent storm, the remaining rooms having suffered only fallout after the tempest slowed, its fury already spent. Clothes had been ripped from their hangers and dumped from drawers. Many slashed and ripped beyond repair. They lay strewn about the bed and the floor, almost totally obliterating the surfaces from view. She realized that Dan had brought over only the few items of clothing that had escaped the frenzy.

At least she wouldn't have to be here long. It would be easy to determine whether or not anything had been stolen from her bedroom. Scattered around the room like so many pieces of confetti were what remained of the two hundred dollars in cash she'd left on her dresser, waiting to be deposited in the bank. The only other thing she had was her jewelry. A pair of diamond stud earrings that had been a gift from her grandparents, an amethyst pendant, and a star sapphire ring that had belonged to her mother were all that she had. From what she could see from her vantage point in the doorway, her jewelry box appeared intact and unmolested. Steeling herself, she focused her attention solely on the small black lacquered box that held her jewels and crossed the room swiftly. The box sat atop an antique oak dresser, which fell only a few inches below the top of her head. To see inside, she would have to lift the box down. For a fraction of a second, her hand faltered in the air above the box, suddenly afraid that instead of her jewels it might now contain something far more sinister, far less attractive. "You've gotta stop reading horror stories, girl," she said, letting out some of her pent-up tension with the words. The sound of her voice gave her comfort in the all too quiet room. Quickly, without giving herself a second chance to dwell on what psychotic maniacs might think were fun things to hide in girls' treasure boxes, she plucked the box down from its perch and opened it. Inside lay only her jewelry, no severed fingers or freshly plucked eyeballs—just jewelry. "I don't think anything's missing, and if it is, I'm not sure I could tell in this mess." Sadie was more than ready to leave this grossly altered mosaic of her life and hoped that Dan would be able to finish up without her.

"That was fast. Are you sure?" Dan called back from the living room.

"Yeah, I'm pos—." The rest of the sentence died on her lips as something on her bed, on her pillow drew her attention. "Dan, I think you better come see this," Sadie said, her voice barely resonating above a whisper. She felt drawn to the bed, to the pillow, and ultimately to the object that had been left behind for her to find.

Looking at the bed now, she felt her marrow turn icy in her bones. To say that what she saw frightened her would be a gross understatement. By far, out of everything she had seen here today, her bed was the most chilling, and she was shocked that she hadn't noticed it before. But then she had been so focused on getting out of there, fast. The bed, which she had left unmade had been made. The teddy bear from her childhood, which for years had enjoyed a comfortable spot on the window seat, had been carefully placed with its head on her pillow, its body tucked securely beneath the

covers. This in itself was not that disturbing; it was what had happened next that filled her with dread. The bear, lying in the exact
spot she rested her head every night, had been stabbed repeatedly
with a wickedly sharp instrument. It was difficult to see where the
bear ended and the bed began. But that wasn't all, and it wasn't the
worst. What held her attention was the small, innocuous object
lying atop her pillow.

It was a rattlesnake tail, the rattle.

It was about five inches long, and although inanimate, it seemed
to radiate sinister intentions. Instinctively, she knew she shouldn't
touch it, yet she found herself drawn to it—attracted and repelled
by it simultaneously. Mesmerized, completely unable to stop herself, she reached out toward it.

As soon as it touched her palm, Sadie was deluged by a wave of
dizziness that washed over her in a hot tide. The killer's thoughts
and feelings raged inside her. Her skin prickled and burned as if
thousands of angry fire ants swarmed over her naked flesh, biting
her again and again. In her mind's eye, she saw flashes of things, *her*
things, being smashed and slashed, thrown and stomped. Locked
within the vision, his thoughts became her own, and for a short
time she was completely at their mercy and living the tantrum herself. The visions came in bright bursts against a black background,
as though lit from behind by a giant, malevolent strobe light. Her
head pounded in time with these bizarre flashes. She felt the white-
hot fury that had driven the uncontrollable fit of rage, mixed with
hatred and loathing.

CHAPTER 20

10:55 a.m.

When Dan found Sadie, she was standing over her bed looking down at something on the pillow. Something that made his heart stop and chilled him to the core. Something that had not been there yesterday when he'd left and locked her apartment himself. In that instant he knew instinctively that the call he'd received this morning had been placed from this room.

While the killer had been leaving his calling card behind, he'd called Dan to rub it in, as if to say, "I can move amongst you—through you—and you can't stop me." Everything next seemed to happen all at once, yet in slow motion at the same time. He saw Sadie reach out to pick up the rattle. But even as the objection reached his lips, it was already too late. The evidence was already cupped neatly in the palm of her hand.

That's when Dan's world went from bad to weird. As soon as she touched it, Sadie's entire body went rigid, as if she were being shocked by some unseen electrical current. Dan rushed forward, catching her in his arms just before she fell backwards. Sadie's body was taut like piano wire and seemed to vibrate. Her limbs shook and her back arched as her head fell backward. The expressions on her face changed like quicksilver, each one melting into a different emotion—rage, pain, horror, rage, pain, horror—over and over again, until suddenly it stopped and she sagged heavily in his arms, barely conscious.

CHAPTER 21

10:56 a.m.

The whole episode had taken less than a minute, even though it had felt unending while locked in its horrific grasp. Dizzy from the overpowering psychic experience, Sadie felt her knees turn to jelly as she sagged backwards, only then realizing that she was already safely in Dan's arms. Her heart beat fiercely as a cold sweat made her shiver uncontrollably. Her head pounding, she felt a trickle of something on her upper lip that tasted like copper. A nosebleed.

"Hold on," Dan said, helping her sit on the bed while he grabbed a box of tissues from the bedside table.

"It's okay, just a nosebleed. It'll stop soon," she said, holding a wad of tissues to her nose as she held her head back to try and staunch the flow. As soon as the nosebleed stopped, she walked silently into the bathroom and washed her face. For the second time that morning, she found herself taking refuge in the cramped bathroom of her apartment. She wondered how Dan would react. Would he think she was a freak and steer clear of her from now on? Or worse, would he think of her as a cool novelty but tire of her when she revealed that she couldn't command the powers to locate the winning lottery numbers? Defensiveness from the past welled up inside of her and wrapped itself around her like invisible armor. To make it worse, she discovered that her right hand was bleeding and again she saw in her head a vision of the killer smashing the mirror in the living room with the palm of his hand—his cut in the same place as hers. *How am I going to explain this?* Sadie thought, thoroughly panicked. But then before her eyes, the wound dissolved back into unbroken flesh; the only evidence remaining, she watched swirl down the drain.

When she returned to the bedroom, she found Dan gathering the pieces of the shattered rattlesnake tail from the carpet and depositing them in a small plastic bag. She didn't remember crushing it, but that must have been why the vision had stopped so abruptly.

"Sadie? Dan rose and began moving toward her. "Are you okay? What happened?"

"I'm sorry I crushed your evidence," she said, taking a step back for every step he took forward.

"You didn't answer my question." Dan stopped moving and so did Sadie.

"I...it was nothing." She looked like a scared rabbit tensed to run.

"Bull." Dan reached out, grabbing her lightly by the elbow.

"I don't know what you want to hear, I..." She pulled back from Dan. A sudden defensiveness overtook her, and he saw a hard determination settle behind her eyes as if a steel curtain had just come crashing down. She was shutting him out.

"I want the truth," he said, letting her go. "And don't tell me nothing happened. I was here. I saw you. I felt it happen to you. You looked like you were being electrocuted."

"Look, I can't explain it," she said softer, relenting a little. Dan was the last person she wanted to be fighting with now or ever.

"Can't or won't?"

"Can we just leave now, please?"

"Not until you tell me what happened." Dan was adamant.

"Fine." Sadie was angry now. "You want to know what happened? I saw *him*, here, destroying these things, my things. I could feel his hate, his loathing, his rage searing me from the inside out. I knew his thoughts and I felt his emotions. I could hear the breaking of the glass under his boot as he drove his size thirteen foot—yes, that's his shoe size; don't ask me how I know that—into my face again and again, and I know why he did this. " She was practically yelling as she gestured emphatically around the room. "He did this because I stole the show from him. I was getting the attention he felt he deserved, and he went crazy." Her anger spent a little, she lowered her voice. "Satisfied?"

"I ..." She could see that Dan was shocked, and she expected to see that same look of cynical disbelief wash over him as it had her father before she had learned to keep these experiences to herself, but the look never came. Still Sadie refused to let go of her defensive shield.

"Don't bother. I knew you wouldn't believe me. Let's just go." Sadie said, turning to leave.

"No," Dan said, gently catching her firmly by the arm and turning her around to face him. "Are you saying you had some sort of a psychic ... vision or something?" Dan's tone was open, not accusatory. Sadie just looked at him. She wanted to trust him. When she didn't respond, Dan said, "I have no way of knowing what just happened to you, but whatever it was, it was big ... huge ... and it physically affected you. I don't know if I believe in psychics ..."

Sadie pulled her arm out of his grasp and started again for the door.

" ... but I don't know that I don't believe either."

She stopped walking, although she kept her back to him. She didn't want him to see the tears forming in her eyes.

"What I do know is that something potentially devastating just happened, and I also know that for some reason you don't trust me enough to tell me what that was." He was behind her now, one hand on either side of her waist, preventing her from walking out of the room.

"It's not that I don't trust you, Dan," Sadie said, turning and looking him in the eyes as she spoke. "It's that I don't know how to trust anyone with this." Seeing that he wasn't about to give up any ground, Sadie relented a little. "Look, I promise, I'll answer all of your questions. I'll tell you everything, but not here and not now." The look in her eyes had gone from one of defiance to one of pleading, and Dan could see that whatever she was hiding, she was hiding as much from herself as she was from him.

"I'll hold you to that," he relented.

"I know," Sadie said, turning toward the door.

S adie felt better as soon as she traded the apartment for the clean, crisp air outside. However, she still needed a few minutes alone, to clear her head, before moving on to Rapture. Instead of holding his hand this time, she kept hers shoved deeply in her pockets, keenly aware of her fear that he would never want to touch her again. As they made their way down the stairs in silence, she remembered that she had yet to water her Birdie's plants.

"Do you mind if I stop downstairs for a few minutes? I promised Birdie I would water her plants while she was away, and I haven't done it once. She'll kill me if they're all dead." Although she tried to make her tone light, it sounded anything but.

"Do you want some help? I've got a fairly green thumb."

"No, I need . . . I'll meet you across the street in a few minutes."

"Okay. See you at Rapture in five." It was clear that Dan wanted to reach out to her, but Sadie just couldn't deal with that just now. If he truly was interested, he would have to wait for her to come to him. Backing down the stairs from him, she smiled. "In five." Then she turned and continued on ahead of him.

CHAPTER 22

11:20 a.m.

Deep inside the shade of the Victorian's front porch, Sadie felt thankful for the few moments alone. Since there were no other tenants now, Sadie was the only other person who had a key to Birdie's front door, and she was the only other person who had a key to Birdie's personal residence on the first floor. Over the years boarders had come and gone, but Birdie had only ever trusted Sadie. The key was more for emergencies than anything, and Sadie had only used it a few times on occasions such as this when Birdie was off in Vegas reliving her golden days as a highly acclaimed dancer.

Using her key now, Sadie unlocked the front door and let herself in. The door opened into a good-sized foyer lit with a modest crystal chandelier. Just ahead of Sadie and a bit to her right stood the grand staircase, which led up to the other tenant apartments but not hers. The pull-down stairs that led to the attic had been sealed over during the renovation, leaving only the outer stairs and a secret staircase that ran from Birdie's kitchen pantry to the house's upper levels, including the attic. No one but Sadie and Birdie knew about those stairs, and out of respect for her tenants' privacy, she never used them. She had only shown them to Sadie late one night after one too many scotches.

Running along the master staircase and beyond was a narrow hallway that ended abruptly at a pocket door, which was pulled tightly closed at the moment and locked. This led into Birdie's apartment and the rest of the house.

Sadie selected another key from her ring and unlocked the pocket door, sliding it back just far enough for her to slip inside. No sooner had she opened the door than she was accosted by the stench of sour milk, spoiled fruit, and something more insidious that she couldn't place.

Birdie, although eccentric, was a fastidious woman and always kept her home sparkling clean and smelling like gardenia, her favorite scent.

Wrinkling her nose, Sadie hesitated in the doorway. The usually bright room was shrouded in a blanket of gloom. All of the heavy drapes had been pulled, making the room appear as black as night inside.

Sadie couldn't remember a time when Birdie had ever pulled those closed. As her eyes adjusted to the gloom, she noticed other things that were out of the ordinary. There were plates of half-eaten food on the sofa and on the floor and spilled milk on the coffee table.

Instinctively, she stepped back outside.

R eaching through the car window for the phone, Dan replayed the last few minutes in his head and surprised himself a little when he realized that he believed her completely. Psychics, visions, and other supernatural mumbo-jumbo were definitely outside his comfort zone, and if it had been anyone else telling him the story, he wouldn't have believed it. But he couldn't deny what he'd seen— what he'd felt. Sadie had experienced some sort of attack, and even though his logical mind kept trying out words like *epileptic, seizure, stress, breakdown,* he knew innately that none of them were right.

He'd had enough experience dealing with people to know when

someone was lying. She was telling the truth, of that he was sure He also felt a good deal of wounded pride over the fact that she hadn't trusted him enough to tell him everything at once. All that aside, there was something much more significant about the find, and a great deal more disturbing than psychic visions. The rattle that they found was the calling card of a vicious serial killer who, until now, had been stalking the citizens of St. Louis, over two hundred miles away.

"Coincidence." Dan tried the word out on the morning air. It rang hollow. As a rule, he didn't believe in coincidences. Pressing the speed dial for Chief Baxter's cell, he paced alongside the car.

"Baxter," the chief answered before the phone finished its first ring. "What have you got for me?"

"We've got a problem."

"You want to be a little more specific?"

"It's him. He's here."

"Who him? Who's here, Dan?" The chief wasn't a patient man.

"The Rattler." It chilled him to use the nickname given to the serial killer by the St. Louis PD, a name that bothered Dan to no end. It made it seem as though whoever dreamt up the name fancied himself a denizen of Gotham, expecting Batman to rescue them in a moment's notice.

"You sure?" the chief asked, his voice taking on a harder edge than usual.

"I just bagged the evidence myself."

"Where?"

"On Sadie's pillow. I'm sure that's where he called me from this morning."

"That's where Mackey found Andre's Blackberry, and she didn't report finding anything else." the chief pointed out.

"He must have come back. There's no way she would have missed it. And not only did he leave the rattle, but he also changed the scene."

"What are you talking about?"

Chief Baxter let out a low whistle as Dan described the bear. "You're right; I was there too and think that was something I would have remembered. Still doesn't make sense why he left his signature at her place and not at the murder site. Previously the rattles were always found on the victims. Sure this isn't a copycat?"

"It can't be. That's the one piece of evidence that hasn't been released to the press. No, it's him. He's evolving." Ice water ran through Dan's veins as he stared at the remains of the rattle that lay on the front seat of his Jeep. "And I don't think he failed to leave one at Rapture," he continued, "I think we failed to find it."

"Don't come back until you do."

"Tell Mike to get his ass over here. I've gotta go." Dan hung up suddenly, just as he saw Sadie backing slowly out of Birdie's front door and down the wooden stairs that led to the street. He had a feeling this was going to be a very long day.

CHAPTER 23

11:32 a.m.

Sadie leaned against the hood of Dan's Jeep, watching Dan disappear around the back of Birdie's house and felt a distinct chill settle deep into her spine. The scene was familiar—too familiar. Though much quieter than yesterday, it was nevertheless unsettling. Anna was on her way to pick her up, so for now there was little she could do but wait and try to get in the way as little as possible.

Shutting her eyes, she tilted her face toward the sun, hoping its powerful rays would somehow have a healing effect on her, but instead jagged images from her vision danced before her eyes like evil marionettes accosting her and forcing her to open her eyes. She shook her head a little, hoping the sudden movement would act to clear the unsettling images from her mind like a broom sweeps away unwanted debris. It worked, though she feared only temporarily. Now, though, she was faced with the fact that Dan wanted, deserved, answers and she had no idea what to tell him.

It startled her that she hadn't lied to him back in her apartment, but then she knew he would have seen through it. In truth, she wanted desperately to convince herself that she had simply freaked out at the sight of her mangled bear in her bed, but she couldn't.

His words, *I don't know if I believe in psychics… but I don't know that I don't believe in them either,* played over and over in her head. At worst he would think of her as a lunatic, a freak at best. For better or for worse, she had to tell him the truth. He deserved it. Yet the prospect of sharing this secret that she'd kept so closely guarded for so many years unnerved her. She didn't even know why she'd said what she had. Suddenly she'd felt an overwhelming desire to tell him everything. She wondered if she wasn't trying to scare him away, as she'd done to so many others in the past in one way or another. If he decided that she was a flake or weird, she could at least safely keep the rest of her secrets hidden behind the wall that life's unfortunate events had helped her erect. Until recently its mortar had seemed like iron, and she'd secretly feared that it would never be breached, until Dan had moved home and started hanging around Rapture.

Ever since he'd moved home, she'd felt the stirrings of something more than friendship whenever he was around, which recently had been quite a lot. Then today, in the apartment, when she'd found herself in his embrace, it had been too much. If she ever had hopes of having a relationship with him, or anyone for that matter, she would have to be able to trust them, and she couldn't trust them if she had to lie to them.

"Dan tries to comfort you, and you freak out and tell him that you had a psychic vision of a deranged madman. Good going," she said to the sun. "He must think I'm certifiable." Her stomach felt like she'd swallowed a rock, a whole river of them.

Sadie didn't consider herself a psychic. But she knew she wasn't "normal" either and that her dreams—some of them—were much more than random firings in her brain while she slept. For years she had fought to put meaning to the odd and often inexplicable things that happened to her. Once she had made the mistake of telling her father; instead of helping her, he admonished her for "acting out" and trying to get extra attention. Early on, Sadie learned not to talk about the visions, or the odd marks that appeared on her body for no reason, and the other strange things that happened to her regularly as a girl, no matter how bad they got. Although she never spoke about them again, her restless night terrors constantly betrayed her secret.

Eventually her father had sent her to the Sleep Institute in Ontario for an entire summer to see if the doctors there could fix her. He instructed her to tell her friends that she was going to a special summer school for gifted children. The institute ended up being a wonderful place filled with caring men and women who listened to her and helped her. After a few days there, the night terrors stopped completely, and after a month she was free and sleeping soundly throughout the night.

However, once she was back home, the problems not only returned, they increased in their ferocity and intensity.

These events were part of her earliest memories. She'd grown up with them and become accustomed to them. Then, inexplicably, when she was about thirteen, they just stopped. Now after almost twenty years of being free from them, they'd started again. Looking back, she thought of the nightmare she'd had nearly a week ago. At the time she'd chosen to ignore it. But now she couldn't—not with everything that was happening.

She'd been immersed in water, a hand grasping her hair tightly from above, keeping her down as she struggled to break free. In the dream she could feel strands of her hair pull free from her scalp as she fought to break her attacker's iron-like grip. Around her in the depths of the pool, she felt and saw rattlesnakes swimming all around her bare legs as she kicked, intertwining themselves with her flailing limbs, biting her again and again. The dream was an old one, and though she hadn't thought of it in many years, it still brought with it a chill of gooseflesh and the fear that this was how she was going to die.

The sight of Anna in Rocco's old red truck was never more welcomed, and Sadie was thankful when Anna began a light conversation about the finer points of baking the perfect apple pie.

CHAPTER 24

11:56 a.m.

The discovery of the rattlesnake tail bothered Dan a lot more than he'd let on to Sadie. It was disturbing how something so small and fragile could carry with it such menace. It was the last thing he'd expected to find. The tail of a mature rattlesnake had been found previously on five other victims, all in the St. Louis area, and all within a fairly short period of time.

The victims, which so far included a lawyer, a florist, a member of the Forest Service, a librarian, and a recluse, had not yet offered up any satisfactory clues as to the identity of the killer. What was more disturbing was that there seemed to be no pattern, no method to his madness, which made it even more terrifying, because the killer was random and unpredictable.

Anyone could be next.

The rattle was the one piece of evidence that had been kept from the press and public, zealously guarded by the men and women in blue. Dan thought about his ex-partner, Doug Covington, who was the lead detective on the Rattler's case in St. Louis. During the last few months since moving back to Crystal Springs, he and

Doug had kept in touch, talking on average once a week, but since the appearance of the Rattler, Doug hadn't been calling; he was too busy working the case. Last week Doug had called late one night, waking Dan up.

"This wacko is a real freak," Dan remembered Doug saying.

"Aren't they all? What makes this one so special?" Dan yawned as he shrugged on his hunter green bathrobe and headed for the kitchen in search of refreshment.

"Snakes, poisonous ones."

"That's new." Dan selected a Dos Equis from the variety of beer in his fridge and opened it.

"This guy has a real love of vipers, and I'm not talking about the car. So far we've found a rattle on each of the victims. That's the only way we know the cases are related."

"A rattle?" Dan asked doubtfully.

"Yeah, a rattlesnake's tail," Doug said. "Then today we found the place he's been holing up, until recently that is, and consequently his fifth victim. It was the residence of a Mary Doyle, a reclusive woman, who lived alone, no family or friends to speak of."

"Recluse. Easy mark."

"She was a recluse, but she wasn't exactly alone," Doug said.

"Pets?" Dan fished in his pantry for something to munch on.

"And lots of them."

"Don't tell me—crazy cat lady. How many did she have?" Dan settled on a can of mixed nuts.

"About fifty, but not cats—snakes, poisonous ones."

"That's just wrong. Are you sure they belonged to her and not the perp?"

"No, they were hers. You should have seen the set-up she had for them. It was impressive. Each snake had its own temperature-controlled habitat, which were nicer than my apartment."

"Almost everything is nicer than your apartment."

"Touché."

"Is there really that big of an underground market for poisonous snakes?" Dan shuddered, chilled by the thought of so many reptiles. He didn't hate snakes, but as a rule, he thought it wise to keep a safe distance from them, especially ones that required trips to the emergency room.

"You don't want to know, suffice it to say that there are a lot of snake lovers out there."

"Just the same, I'll stick with dogs."

"We found a variety of poisonous snakes, over fifty cages in all, her favorite being pit vipers. From what we can estimate, she had over twenty mature rattlesnakes, all of which are now missing."

"Missing?"

"Yeah, all the other snakes were there, loose, all over the house. It's amazing that none of them got out into the neighborhood. Anyway, once the handlers from the zoo got them all back in their respective cages, the only ones left empty were labeled as rattlesnakes."

"How was she killed?"

"He left her tied up on the floor of the room, opened all of the cages, and left. According to the ME, she suffered over a hundred bites."

"Sounds like they had a grudge against her."

"Doesn't it, though? But I haven't told you the seriously weird part yet."

"This gets worse?"

"It wasn't the venom that killed her. In fact, the ME said that if she hadn't dehydrated, she would have lived. Looks like she was somehow immune to their venom."

"No wonder they didn't bother her. You ought to consider moving here, man. The most dangerous thing I've come across in Crystal Springs so far was last week when Art Franklin accidentally blew up his still." Dan finished his beer and considered opening a second one, but opted against it.

"Is he okay?"

"Yeah, but he's missing a couple of fingers."

"Best we can figure, he kept her captive." Doug turned the conversation back to his case. "We found the room he'd kept her in while he lived upstairs. It was more like a storage area, tucked under the stairs in the basement with nothing but a soiled mattress, and one thin moth-eaten blanket. "

"Do you have any leads so far?"

"Not one, but I don't think he's done."

"Well, he's not gonna get far toting a bunch of snakes around. That would kind of make him stick out a little." Just then Doug's other line rang, and he'd hung up with Dan, promising to call back soon.

Letting the memory fade into the bright sunlight, he waited now for Mike to arrive. Dan wondered if it was too late to switch professions and become a train conductor like he'd wanted to be in the fifth grade.

CHAPTER 25

12:02 p.m.

While Dan waited for Mike to arrive, he studied the exterior of Birdie's house, looking for something that had been missed previously. They would start here and then move on to Rapture. He needed to ascertain the original point of entry. *How the hell did you come and go with such anonymity?* Dan wondered, not for the first time. From the brief look he'd had inside, the guy had been living there for days, and no one had had any clue. Sadie had told him that Birdie had left five days ago for Vegas and was not expected back for another few days, so that meant that he could have been there since last week, eating, sleeping, and watching every move Sadie made.

Since Sadie lived in the attic and Birdie on the first floor, that left the second and third floors empty—a perfect buffer zone to conceal the movements of someone who didn't want to be noticed. The thought that this guy had lived under his very nose (under Sadie) made him shake with rage. "I will put you in your grave. That's a promise from me to you," Dan vowed aloud.

"I'm not that late," Mike said, coming around the corner of the house into the backyard.

"Just venting. Chief fill you in?"

"About what?"

"Guess not."

"I won't know unless you tell me."

"Has anyone ever told you how annoying you are?"

"All the time. You'll learn to love me."

"That'll be the day. The Rattler's in town and until recently living here."

"Doug's Rattler?"

Dan just nodded, raising his eyebrows slightly.

Mike ran a hand through his hair. "That explains how he knew Andre's movements but not how he was able to slip in and out unnoticed. This is still a small town, and I would think that someone would notice a strange man living at Birdie's."

"But no one did. In fact, I didn't even know she didn't have any other boarders until Sadie confirmed it."

"Which means the neighbors probably didn't either. Who would really notice another stranger coming in and out of a boarding house?"

"Exactly. Besides, I think he kept his movements to a bare minimum, only coming and going if he had to. I don't think he used the front door or even the back."

"Then how did he get in—tunnel?"

"Maybe the fruit cellar."

At first glance, nothing looked amiss. It wasn't until he'd actually tugged on the padlock securing the fruit cellar's doors that he realized it was nothing more than window dressing. It had been disabled. The doors that it pretended to secure were the kind that opened on an angle, from the ground, revealing a staircase below that led into the fruit cellar and basement beyond.

"This could be our man's point of entry." Dan pointed to the lock.

"Lock's busted; looks brand new though," Mike said, producing an evidence bag from his jacket. Quickly, they had the lock bagged and tagged, both of them hoping that it would turn up at least one viable fingerprint.

"Why would Birdie have needed a new lock?"

"Maybe someone broke in?"

"You remember getting a call about it, or seeing a report on it?" Dan asked earnestly.

"Nope, and until very recently that would have been big news around these parts."

"It would explain how he would have been able to come and go without being seen.

"These holly bushes provide a perfect screen."

"Age before beauty." Mike drew his gun, as did Dan. Neither one actually believed the boogeyman lurked in the bowels of the building, but neither was willing to take any chances either.

As soon as Dan pulled the doors open, the smell hit him in the face. It was ten times worse than it had been upstairs. "Oh man, that's ripe." It was the unmistakable perfume of the dead—decay.

"Maybe it's just a dead raccoon."

"Yeah ... a raccoon," Dan said without conviction.

There were ten narrow concrete steps that led down to another door immediately at the base of the stairs, which stood ajar. Dan could see a pull chain for a light just inside. Descending the stairs quickly, he kept his back to the cool cellar wall, shining his flashlight's bright beam into the gloom when he reached the bottom. The only things that moved inside were dust motes stirred into activity by his boots. Nudging the door open, Dan shone the light into the far reaches of the room. Everything remained quiet. Boxes, crates, and some discarded furniture draped with dusty white sheets took up most of the space in the cellar. Moving swiftly into the room, Dan heard Mike follow behind him on the stairs and soon stood at his side. Dan moved to the left as Mike went right, checking behind anything big enough to conceal a man.

"Clear," Dan said when he finished his sweep. Aside from the spiders that raced from his path, the room was void of life. Turning off his flashlight with one hand, he pulled the chain on the bulb dangling from the ceiling with the other. The single bulb swayed a bit in its ancient fixture, casting its light in a jittery pattern around the cellar, until it lost momentum and finally hung still.

"Definitely not a raccoon," Mike said from the other side of the cellar. Dan felt his stomach clench as he walked to where his partner stood. Lying not two feet from Mike, in a congealed puddle of blood lay Bernice Louise Prentice—Birdie—or what was left of her. Dressed in a fashionable suit and high heels, she was a long way from Vegas.

"It looks like he caught her on her way out. She always dressed to the hilt when leaving for Vegas."

Her body had been covered in some sort of a white powder that had had the corrosive effect of acid where it touched the wounds in her flesh. A hammer matted with blood and hair lay a few feet from her.

CHAPTER 26

12:27 p.m.

After spending almost the entire night at the morgue, Dr. John Conway had almost canceled his standing golf date. But now he was glad he hadn't. To John, the day couldn't have been a more perfect antidote for yesterday's tragedy. The sky was as clear blue as a jeweler's prize blue topaz. The temperature was crisp, yet not cold, and he was about to make a birdie on the sixteenth hole of the Crystal Springs Country Club golf course. This hole, a particularly long one with numerous bunkers and a pond the size of a lake smack dab in the middle, had been his arch nemesis since he'd taken up the game over thirty years ago. Now, for the first time, it looked like he was going to walk away from the hole the victor; unfortunately, fate was not in his corner this day.

As soon as he heard the solid thwack of the driver hitting the ball, he knew it was going to be a decent shot. Even as he watched it soar straight and true, he had no idea that he would clear most of the ground in one excellently executed shot, the ball landing just a few yards from the water trap, in the middle of the fairway.

"Great shot, John!" his buddies said, repeatedly slapping him on the back as each man passed him on the way to finding his own errant ball.

"Thanks," John said again and again, hardly registering the praise as he was a bit in shock and petrified that he would sink the next shot in the lake or in one of the many treacherous sand traps that lay in wait along the rest of the approach to the hole.

"Relax, head down, eye on the ball," John coaxed himself through the next shot, almost afraid to look up and follow the ball's course across the heavens after it left his club.

"Across the water in two, you're on fire today," Manny Peterson said excitedly. Again, John's back was slapped, but not wanting to give into the excitement until he'd sunk the last putt, he accepted the praise quietly.

He was one putt away from finally championing his nemesis when his pager vibrated insistently in his pocket. He almost ignored it, positive it was something that could wait, but being the consummate professional, he checked anyway. It was a 911. Excusing himself for a moment, he fished his phone out of his golf bag and called the police chief.

"Bax, John. This had better be better than good, because you just interrupted the best golf game of my life," John half joked.

"John, it's Birdie." As soon as he heard his brother-in-law's voice, he knew it wasn't a social call. "The boys found her a few minutes ago."

"Birdie? What are you talking about? She's in Vegas."

"Not this year."

"Where is she?"

"At her house," Chief Baxter said resolutely.

John was already in the cart and heading back toward the parking lot, leaving his golfing buddies bewildered and without a ride back to town.

CHAPTER 27

1:11 p.m.

A serpentine set of bloody footprints wound their way across the cellar floor, in and around boxes and crates, from the body to a set of stairs at the opposite end of the room. These stairs led to a door that opened into Birdie's kitchen above. The smell in the subterranean room was thick and cloying; it seemed to have a life of its own, clinging greedily to Dan's clothes and hair.

"Why doesn't it smell worse down here?" Mike asked, holding his own shirt over his mouth and nose and breathing through it.

"Are you saying you don't think it smells bad?"

"No, but after a week, shouldn't it be a lot worse?"

"You're right. The smell would be a lot worse if the temperature were any warmer outside," Doc Conway said, joining them in the cellar with Chief Baxter close on his heels.

"Since when do doctors wear cleats to a crime scene?" Dan nodded toward the other man's feet.

"Don't ask," Doc said. "Back to the matter of the smell"—he moved closer to the body—"I'll have to run some tests to be sure, but if I'm not mistaken, she's covered with lye. That would explain the corrosive nature of the wounds and would also help retard the stench. I'll be able to tell you everything you want to know after I finish the autopsy. If you're done here, why don't you boys let me do what I do best now?" Doc Conway knelt next to the body of the second close friend he'd lost in as many days. It wasn't until he began photographing the body that something caught his eye, a strange lump in her right hand. "Looks like she's got a hold of something, but I can't make out what it is." Doc backed up, making room for Dan to move in closer.

"Have you already photographed the hand?" Dan asked.

Mike nodded.

"Okay, can I get a—oh, thanks." Mike had anticipated his needs and had an evidence bag at the ready and was holding it open.

Carefully, Dan removed as much of the obscuring white powder as he could until the shape in the dead woman's palm began to take on form and shape; as it did, he felt a surge of dread course through his body. "Anyone have any doubts now?" Dan said moving back so everyone could see the three-inch-long rattlesnake tail in the dead woman's upturned palm. "The Rattler is in Crystal Springs."

"I don't get it," Mike said shaking his head. "Why would he come to Crystal Springs?"

"I doubt it was a random decision," Chief Baxter said.

"Andre was just in St. Louis on a business trip," Mike said.

"And this wacko fixated on him and followed him back here?" Dan caught on to Mike's thought train.

"Yeah, why not? It would explain why he moved in on Birdie and how he knew when Andre was alone in the shop."

"And also how and why he decided to fixate on Sadie next," Dan said, nodding slowly at first and then more vigorously as the idea grew on him.

"It's a great theory, but I'm afraid it doesn't hold up. For one thing, the business trip was in Chicago, and it got canceled at the last minute."

"It's still a valid theory though. Andre travels to St. Louis all the time." Mike wasn't ready to give up on his idea.

"I don't know how well you boys remember the Sister Jane investigation. It was years back, when I was a rookie myself," Chief Baxter said.

"The snake lady?" Dan looked from the chief to Doc Conway, who seemed unnaturally pale in the dim light of the cellar.

"Story has it she was killed by the townsfolk and her ghost now haunts the woods outside of town," Mike said. "We used to scare the crap out of ourselves as kids daring each other to go sit alone in the Springs and wait for her. Kind of like the Blair Witch, only with snakes."

"Man, you youngsters are dorks; we used it to make out with girls." Dan rolled his eyes.

"I have to agree with Dan on that one. Seriously, I've heard all the stories," Chief Baxter said, shaking his head. "They all make her out to be some sort of misunderstood monster in a modern day fairy tale. The truth is, she wasn't nice, sweet, or good; she was pure unadulterated evil."

"You're kidding? I thought she was an urban legend or something, but I never thought the stories were real," Mike said, taken aback.

"She was real all right, and now…"

"Don't go jumpin' to conclusions, Bax," Doc Conway's voice took a harsh tone. It was the first time Dan could remember Doc talking to anyone, especially Bax, that way.

"Conclusions about what?" Chief Baxter said very matter-of-factly. "Twenty years ago Crystal Springs had its very own snake cult, which culminated in the unexplained deaths of several people, and now people are getting killed by a lunatic with a rattlesnake fetish. For me, that's too close for comfort."

"Slow down," Dan said. "What are you talking about? I was in high school then, but I don't remember any murders."

"That's because all of the deaths were ruled either accidental or suicide, not murder," Doc Conway said with finality. "I should know; I performed the autopsies."

"Those cases are still open for investigation." It was obvious Chief Baxter was agitated.

"Refresh my memory." Dan glanced between the two older men, noticing a palpable tension rising between them. In his whole life, Dan had never once seen Doc and the chief so much as argue, not even when Doc's marriage to Eddie's sister ended in divorce.

"Three people died within six months of each other: an attorney, his wife, and the Johnsonville town physician," said Chief Baxter.

"My mentor," Doc Conway added. "At that time he was the county coroner. It wasn't until he died that I took that over as well. His autopsy was my first," Doc said quietly, a tired, drawn look on his already weary face. "What good is this doing except dredging up all sorts of unpleasant memories?" Doc asked the chief.

"All three appeared to be suicides, but then we discovered that all three could be linked to Sister Jane's group."

"Snake handlers," Dan tested the words.

"I thought that sort of thing was … well … fiction," Mike said, a bit dubious.

"You would have had a leg up on me; twenty years ago I'd never heard of snake handlers and probably still wouldn't have if she hadn't moved into town. Anyway, after Tobias died, rumors flew around town like birds in a hurricane, and they were equally as hard to pin down. She had airtight alibis for all three deaths, and we were never able to get any of her loyal members to turn on her." Chief Baxter wasn't letting Doc win. And for reasons yet unknown to Dan, this case bothered both men more than they were letting on.

"Have you told the St. Louis PD about your theory?" Dan was intrigued; instinct told him that there was something to this.

"Yes, and they nicely told me to hasten my retirement."

"I can't believe Doug would have …" Dan started, shocked and a little indignant.

"He didn't, but everyone else did. They don't have time for small-town cops and outlandish theories—and that's a direct quote."

"Did you at least send them the old case files?" Mike asked.

"Can't. They went missing during the course of the investigation. One night they up and disappeared from a locked room at the station. Everything we had—which, granted, wasn't much—is gone. All I have to offer is my memory and my gut," Chief Baxter said. "And apparently that's not worth much outside of Crystal Springs."

"Forget them," Dan said with unabashed disdain. "It's our case now. Let's do what they obviously couldn't and stop him." Everyone could see the light of a new vigor shine behind Dan's gray-blue eyes.

"It's been, what, almost twenty years? Maybe people will be more likely to talk about the cult now," Mike said.

"Not likely," Doc said quietly. "Her group was loyal then, and I'm sure they are embarrassed and disgusted by their own actions; besides, there is nothing overtly linking these murders with her or her church. The longer we stand here talking, the longer this maniac is on the streets. Please move aside and let me do my job. Have Evie and Adam see me as soon as they get here. I would like to get the body processed so I can get her back to the morgue and begin my autopsy as soon as possible." Doc snapped.

"You're sure there's nothing left?" Dan asked the chief as they made their way out of the cellar.

"If I've looked once, I've looked a hundred times over the years. Even my own notes managed to disappear from my home office. All I have is one thin notebook where I tried to capture everything I could from memory after the theft. But it's nothing that would hold up in a court of law."

"One thing I've learned," Dan said, "is that instincts are rarely wrong."

CHAPTER 28

1:33 p.m.

Alone in the cellar with Birdie, Doc Conway heaved a heavy sigh and let a few tears wash unrestrained down his tanned, lined face. Birdie had been a close friend, closer than Andre. A sense of the unreal settled down around him as he stared at the corpse of the once-vibrant woman on the cellar's earthen floor. Breathing a sigh of resignation, he began his preliminary investigation. Using a small handheld tape recorder, he began.

"The day is Sunday, November second; the time is one thirty-three p.m.," he said, consulting his watch. "This is Dr. John Edward Conway, county coroner, examining the remains of..." He found he couldn't go on, his finger sliding off the record button. As much as he desperately wanted to deny it as a possibility, he feared Bax was right—that part of Crystal Springs's dark history had come back to haunt them—to kill them. And he couldn't help feeling that in a very real sense, it was his fault.

CHAPTER 29

2:28 p.m.

Birdie's bedroom, more so than the rest of the normally immaculate apartment, looked like it had been hit by a freight train. "From the looks of Birdie's bed, I'd say our boy doesn't enjoy sleeping very much," Dan observed.

"Evie and Adam are on their way!" Mike yelled back from the kitchen. "I just got a call from the chief."

"How long do we have?" Dan asked.

"Not long. As soon as we see them walk through that door, he expects us to hightail it across the street."

"Hightail, who says hightail?" By now Mike had joined Dan in the bedroom.

"I think I've seen about as much as I need to, for now anyway. How about you?"

"I see what you mean about not sleeping well," Mike commented, looking at the bed. The sheets were twisted and thrown aside, the comforter lay crumpled on the floor, half shoved under the bed, and the bottom sheet was turned up at all but one corner.

"I found a couple of bloody towels in the bathroom hamper.

Looks like that's what he used to clean himself up with after he killed her. Doesn't look like he took a shower until later, which means…"

"Which means," Dan finished for him, "that Sadie must have been home when he killed Birdie."

"And he couldn't take a shower, because Sadie would have heard the water running and would have known that something was wrong, since she thought her landlady was out of town."

"I found an estimate from Ploughman's Plumbing in the basket on the kitchen counter. Apparently the old pipes rattle when the water is running."

Dan's blood ran cold in his veins, not for the first time since yesterday morning. "He's been living under our noses, for days, and no one noticed." Dan was now sure he knew where Sadie's mysterious calls had originated. He felt sick. "He's been watching Andre and Sadie come and go day and night, keeping track of their every move." Dan surprised himself and Mike by punctuating his sentence with a fast right hook to the wall. He cringed when the wall failed to give and brought his bloodied knuckles up to his lips. "Ow."

"Good old fashioned architecture." Mike patted the wall. "Plaster, not dry wall. This house was made right."

Dan acknowledged him with a glare, and then laughed. "Man, that was stupid."

"You said it. When you're done taking out your anger on the walls, I've got somethin' else."

"Yeah?"

"I know how he got into Rapture and Sadie's without having to break in," Mike said, capturing Dan's full attention. "The only keys missing from the pegboard in the kitchen are labeled 'Sadie's spare set.'"

CHAPTER 30

2:47 p.m.

Evie and Adam showed up just as Dan and Mike were wrapping up. It was lucky that they were in town, since they spent the majority of their time traveling far and wide, working crime scenes, and bringing the evidence back to their lab to be processed for districts with too much crime and too little time, manpower or money to do the evidence justice. Their state-of-the-art lab had been the generous gift of a wealthy businessman in St. Louis, who was eternally thankful for their assistance in identifying the man who'd murdered his brother in cold blood and securing the evidence that would send the killer to death row. He had tried to seduce the pair away from Crystal Springs originally, but when they'd refused to leave, he'd relented and built the lab here. As a result, Evie and Adam were very busy people.

"We really have to stop meeting like this, Officer," Evie said, passing close behind Mike, brushing lightly against his arm. "Somebody's going to start talking."

"They're already talking," Mike said, kissing his girlfriend lightly on the cheek.

"Hey, what did I say about public displays of affection." Evie swatted him half-playfully, half-seriously, but beamed at him all the same.

"It's just Dan and Adam. They aren't public; they don't count."

"Thanks," Dan said with mock hurt.

"The place is yours, girl. We're out of here. See you tonight." Mike kissed her quickly on the other cheek and then ducked out of the way before she could swat him again.

"Come on, Casanova; we've got work to do," Dan said, leading Mike out by the shirt.

With Evie and Adam upstairs and Doc Conway in the cellar, there was nothing left to do but cross the street and find what they had previously overlooked. After the scene in her apartment and finding the remains of the squatter at her landlady's apartment, Sadie had asked Dan if she could put off going back into Rapture, giving him the passwords to access the store's detailed inventory on the shop computer, but he doubted seriously if they would need them. This case was definitely about anything but robbery. Looking at the ashen color in her cheeks, Dan had agreed instantly.

"Doesn't feel right in here," Mike said as they stood inside Rapture. "It's too quiet."

"Yeah, I know what you mean, this place was never quiet. It was always so full of life."

"Just like Andre," Mike commented.

"Just like Andre." Heading in different directions, the men didn't need to discuss who would look where. They worked together as two halves of a whole. Dan never failed to realize how immensely lucky he was to have had two great partners on the force, both men he trusted with his life, and he knew the feelings were mutual.

With Mike poring over the window display, Dan looked around the room. Every nook and cranny was filled to overflowing with things—small things, big things, colorful things. It made it difficult to separate them out, and he wondered, not for the first time, how women do it. Then something caught his eye. In the middle of the store, on top of a medium-sized table was a large, red glass vase. It stood about a foot and a half tall and housed an amazing array of flowers and decorative grasses. Among them were a few dried cattails. Only one of them was different from the others.

"Mike, come here and tell me if you see what I see."

"I see a bunch of flowers."

"Is that all? Look closely." Mike circled the table looking at the arrangement from all angles. Finally he said, "Well I'll be a son of a monkey's uncle. That boy - he's gettin' creative on us."

There in the middle of the bouquet, secured to the stalk of a cattail, was the missing evidence.

"A son of a monkey's uncle?" Dan looked up at him raising an eyebrow. "Really?"

CHAPTER 31

3:30 p.m.

Bright sunlight streamed through the bay windows of Sadie's room in the St. James' farmhouse. Exhausted, Sadie wrapped herself in a warm afghan that lay neatly folded on the foot of her bed and curled herself around George, hopeful that the bright sunlight would serve as a shield against the predatory night terrors that had recently begun stalking her nighttime hours.

In the dream, she stood over Dan as he lay mortally wounded on the ground, blood rushing out of a vicious wound in his chest, and she asked him how it had felt to shake the hand of death. Just then the phone rang on the stand by her bed, jolting her back to consciousness.

Covered in sweat, she lay impossibly twisted in the afghan; with every turn of her body, it grew more and more constricting. Panicking, she almost yelled out, before getting a grip on herself. Employing a tactic that she hadn't used in what felt like a lifetime, she found a spot on the ceiling and focused all of her attention there until her breathing was normal again. She had just managed to free herself from the constricting blanket when Anna rapped gently on the door, opening it a crack. "Sadie, are you awake? Dan's on the phone."

"Okay, thank you." Sadie took a deep breath before picking up the extension; she hoped she didn't sound as shaky as she felt.

"Hi," she said.

"Sadie, I'm truly sorry to have to...Oh hell, Sadie, Birdie's dead."

Sadie was silent.

"I'm sorry," Dan continued. "I hate having to tell you this way, but it couldn't wait. I need to know if you know when and why she purchased the new lock on the cellar doors."

"She didn't buy it. I did, about a week ago, right before she left town. She woke up in the middle of the night and smelled someone smoking down there. Whoever it was ran when they heard her open the door. She figured it was just neighborhood kids; she'd caught a couple of them down here a few months ago drinking beer and smoking pot. I told her to file a police report. I guess she never got around to it."

Staring at the phone in her hand, she didn't remember saying good-bye to Dan or hanging up the phone. She was in a haze. She had to get out of the house. She had to move. Putting on her shoes and grabbing her jacket, she headed out into the orchard.

CHAPTER 32

5:17 p.m.

It was already dark when Dan finally arrived at the orchard. Chief Baxter had ordered him to take the night off, fearing correctly that Dan would work straight through the next several days without sleep. Tired cops were careless cops, and Chief Eddie Baxter wasn't going to have any of that on his watch. Dan knew he was right too; exhaustion was often a cop's worst enemy. It wasn't that he hadn't been successful; he'd found the other rattle. It was easy to see, but also easy to overlook. Dan likened it to searching for starfish in the ocean at low tide. At first you can't see any. Then suddenly you find one, and then another and another. It wasn't that they weren't there before; you just didn't know how to see them. He'd found it so easily that it made him wonder how they'd missed it earlier. Had it been there? Or had their resident snake lover come back, planting the evidence later, saying, "Ha-ha, I can come and go right under your nose?" Or had he been so distracted by Sadie that he hadn't done his job? That thought bothered him a lot.

Over the years he'd had a couple of girlfriends, flings that lasted a couple of months, none of them ever amounting to anything, and all of them unhappy about his chosen line of work. He'd always been the consummate detective, focused to a fault, until recently, until Sadie Mozart. Looking up at his parents' home, he felt relieved to know that all of the people he cared about most were safely ensconced inside. He sincerely hoped the depravity of the outside world never darken this doorway.

The big old farmhouse looked warm and inviting. He was glad to have the night off to spend with his family and Sadie. Suddenly impatient, he hurried through the thickening darkness into the brightly lit farmhouse.

Anna was in the living room sitting next to a cheerful fire, George curled up in her lap, sound asleep. She was reading a mystery novel by one of her favorite authors, a cup of hot tea on the small mahogany table next to her. He noted the cat did not appear to be any worse for the wear from yesterday's excitement and, in fact, seemed quite at home in the large farmhouse.

"Hi, Mom." Dan exchanged kisses on the cheek with his mother, slipping his jacket off.

"Hi, sweetie." Anna put her book down.

"Where's Sadie?"

"She went out for a walk right after you called. She was very upset. Actually, I was expecting, hoping, you to be her just now." Anna sighed. "I know she is quite capable of taking care of herself, but she's been gone for a few hours, and you know how confusing the orchard can be at night..."

"I'll go find her." He pulled his jacket back on.

"Thank you. At least four times in the last hour, I've convinced myself to do the same thing and then changed my mind. I don't want it to seem like I am crowding her, but for heaven's sake, I've been on the same page for the last half an hour and I couldn't tell you what's happening."

"Don't worry; I'll find her."

"I know, honey; it's just that—if you could have seen her last night, heard her...Well, if I didn't have any white hair, I do now." Anna could see by Dan's expression that he was confused. "She didn't tell you about the nightmares or the … other incident, did she?"

"No." Dan's stomach clenched as he remembered the strange event that had taken place in Sadie's apartment, at the same time visualizing the destruction that followed in the killer's wake.

"The nightmares … she said that she didn't remember. That they were probably about Andre, but …"

"But she's a terrible liar," Dan finished for her.

"Horrible. Why couldn't you have been such a bad liar? It would have made my life so much easier." She winked and Dan rolled his eyes playfully.

"What about the other incident?"

"I'll let her tell you about that." Anna had never been a gossip. "She needs to know that she can trust you."

"Will you tell her that?"

"Just be you—she'll come around."

"Don't worry, Mom; we'll be back in no time."

Dan was more determined than ever now to get to the bottom of Sadie's disturbing behavior.

He hoped Sadie hadn't wandered too far. The orchard was large, and it was easy to become disoriented among the endless rows of trees. Rounding the farmhouse, he opted to follow the most logical route and take the service road that led deep into the orchard. About fifty meters down the road, he came upon the barn. A golden light shone through the window of the loft above. If it wasn't his dad up there, it would have to be Sadie; and if indeed Sadie was in the loft, she now knew him better than most people. The loft was his special place, keeper of many of his favorite memories, and where many of life's mysteries were revealed to him. It was the one place in the world that was truly his, and the thought that Sadie had found her way there and might be somewhat comforted by his presence through his things, made him feel good.

When Dan turned eight, all he'd wanted was a tree house fort, but since all of the trees on the property were apple trees, and thus unavailable, Rocco converted the loft into Dan's own *Mission*

Impossible headquarters (after one of Dan's favorite TV shows). Rocco could never be accused of doing anything halfway, and by the time he was finished with it, the loft had a full bathroom (including a shower), heat and air conditioning, a mini-fridge, bed, couch, antique roll-top desk (that Dan loved because of all of the secret compartments), and a whole wall full of shelves for nothing but Dan's things. When he was eight, the shelves had held his extensive comic book collection, baseball card collection, model car collection, and various other gizmos and gadgets that were so imperative to have as an eight-year-old boy. In the center of the room Dan had painstakingly constructed a full-size electric train track equipped with bridges, station houses, and passengers, each piece paid for by money he earned helping out in the orchard.

As childhood gave way to adolescence, the comic books were traded for contraband *Playboys*, and the train track was dismantled to make room for a weight bench, free weights, and a bag for boxing practice. By the time he was seventeen, Dan had moved out of the farmhouse and into the loft. Even though he now lived in town, he still maintained the loft, keeping clothes and toiletries there. Anna had long since turned his bedroom in the manor into a guest room; in fact, it was the room Sadie was sleeping in now. Today the loft was a mishmash of Dan's life, everything except the train still there, each piece of his past living harmoniously with the others.

What he heard upon entering the barn wasn't at all what he'd expected. He stood quietly listening for a moment, perplexed at first, then relieved. He'd anticipated he would find her crying inconsolably or in a state of shock, but he had not expected to find her cussing like a sailor, while beating the hell out of his old punching bag. From upstairs he could hear the familiar thuds, coinciding with forceful cursing. Greatly amused, he had to stifle a laugh as he made his way up the stairs to the loft, stopping when he reached the uppermost steps and watching her. She looked beautiful to him; her hair, tied back in a high, tight ponytail, accentuated her lovely face and neck. She had on a pair of faded blue jeans, and a simple white men's T-shirt, which he recognized as one of his own. Her own sweater lay crumpled on his bed. On her hands she wore a pair of his boxing gloves. Obviously too big, they hung absurdly on her tiny wrists. Even though she didn't have enough power in her punches to move the bag, she was still hitting it with everything she had, and he could tell that she'd been at it for a while because the T-shirt was sticking to her, accentuating her breasts. He thought it looked better on her than it ever had on him. Every time she punched the bag, she screamed another curse.

"Your form could use a little work, but you've got the cussing part down," he said, coming all the way up the stairs and joining her in the loft. Startled, Sadie swung around so quickly that one of the gloves flew off her hand, barely missing Dan as it soared past.

"And an A-plus for glove tossing."

"How long have you been watching?" She panted.

"Just long enough to hope that I never piss you off." Dan walked over to the minifridge and retrieved two cold beers, opening hers first and handing it to her. Sadie accepted the beer, a St. Paulie Girl, and drank deeply. "God, that tastes good," she said. "Since when do people keep refrigerators full of cold beer in their barns?"

"Cool, huh? Welcome to Dan's world." He swept his arm in an arc around the room. Sipping their beers, they stood a few feet apart, and for a moment there was the beginning of an awkward silence until Sadie broke it. "I hope it's okay that I borrowed your gloves and your T-shirt." She bit her lip, a nervous habit that Dan found irresistible. "My sweater got too hot." She hoped that he wouldn't press her about what had happened earlier; she needed more time.

"It's more than okay," he said, moving a step closer to her. "I was worried that I'd find you curled up in a corner bawling your eyes out. I never once dreamed that I'd come across you doing a damn fine impersonation of Ali, though I don't think he cussed quite that much." Dan was having trouble concentrating on anything. The planned interrogation fell away.

"Therapy."

"Cussing therapy. It's a new one on me. Does it work?"

"Wonders." She was no longer breathing as hard; however, Dan couldn't help but notice the steady rise and fall of her chest. He found it difficult to look away. He was having trouble concentrating on the conversation. He took another step toward her; she didn't back up.

"I could give you boxing lessons, if you want." He moved closer still, his heart beating faster with every step.

"Sure." She tugged at the front of the shirt self-consciously, as if she just realized that it was sticking to her. "I guess I worked up a pretty good sweat." Dan thought she looked adorable when she blushed.

"It looks good on you." He finished closing the gap between them. Setting his beer down on the little worktable next to her, he set hers down as well. Putting his arms around her, he drew her close, wondering if she would break away from him as she had this morning. Her body felt wonderful and right pressed against his; he could feel her heart beating against his chest. Instead of backing away, he felt her press against him. Slowly, he lowered his head as she raised hers and for a long moment they stood in silence, staring into each other's eyes, their bodies speaking for them. Her eyes, green with flecks of gold, were wide as she searched his for signs of reassurance. In that instant he knew that she felt the same about him and kissed her, tentatively at first. He still half-expected her to pull away from him, but instead she returned his kiss, wrapping her arms around this neck. With one hand on the small of her back, pulling her close, Dan loosened her ponytail with the other; her hair felt like delicate strands of silk against his palm. Just then Dan's cell phone started ringing.

"St. James," Dan answered, sounding annoyed.

"I found something." It was Mike.

CHAPTER 33

6:15 p.m.

Sadie went upstairs to shower, and Anna went to join Rocco in the kitchen, leaving Dan and Mike alone.

"What have you got?" Dan settled himself into the chair Anna had just vacated.

"This." Mike held out a small black leather book tied shut with a strip of leather the same color. "Evie found it in Birdie's bedroom; looks like it fell off the nightstand at some point and lodged between the stand and the wall. From the looks of its contents, I imagine our boy is going to be pretty upset when he realizes he's lost it."

"What is it—a journal of some sort?" Dan turned the book over, inspecting it from all angles before opening it. It was old and worn, the leather soft and dulled from years of handling.

"Less journal, more a scrapbook of sorts," Mike said between sips of his beer. "You're not gonna like it."

"It looks like it's been around the block a few times. Let me guess, it's a detailed accounting of the life as a psycho-killer?"

"Not exactly."

"A poor-me story, explaining why he's so deranged?"

"Just open it." Mike gestured impatiently with his beer.

"Okay, okay. You're in a mood." Dan grinned at his partner as he deftly untied the knot.

"Same could be said about you." Mike raised a questioning eyebrow.

Dan's grin and all traces of his recent happiness burst when he opened the book. The first page was titled *The Life and Times of the Wholly Undeserving*, and on the opposite page was a picture of a newborn baby girl, wrapped in soft blankets and sleeping peacefully. The caption under the photo, in neat, careful printing, read "Sadie Elizabeth Mozart, 2 weeks." Astonished, Dan flipped the page. This one bore a picture of a much older girl riding a tire swing high into the air, pigtails sailing out behind her as she screamed with laughter and joy. The caption on the adjoining page read. "Sadie's 5th Birthday. She got a party, cake, and presents." Dan didn't say anything as he turned one page after another until he finally dropped the book as if it had burned him. "This is Sadie's entire life."

"Whoever this guy is, he's obsessed with Sadie, and not in a good way."

"How did he get these pictures of her childhood and college?"

"That's the million-dollar question, isn't it? Those pictures are too yellowed and worn to be new copies. I bet those are the originals."

"The ones in the beginning are, but this one..." Dan turned silent as he quickly thumbed through the book to the last entry. "This one was taken at Andre's party two nights ago." Dan held up a photo of Sadie looking radiant and happy, wearing a black cocktail dress with spaghetti straps and a simple empire waist. The picture had been cut in half so that the only portion of the other person in the original photo was of an arm, which was draped loosely around her waist.

"How do you know?" Mike hadn't been able to attend due to a suddenly violent but short-lived case of food poisoning.

"Because that's my arm around her waist."

"Who took the picture?" Mike leaned in with interest, hoping that they had suddenly caught a break.

"Mom."

"No help there, unless Anna is living one hell of a double life."

"If Mom were going to kill someone, she would guilt them to death."

"It's not likely she's in the habit of handing out pictures of you and Sadie to strangers with violent tendencies."

"Doubtful."

"So, how did he get the picture?"

"Hold on, let me go ask her when she dropped them off." Dan left and was back within what seemed like seconds. "She dropped them off yesterday at Wilson Photo. When she went in today, he said that he'd misplaced the copies and would have to run them again. She's not supposed to pick them up until tomorrow after three p.m."

"I'll stop by on the way home and see if he can get them for me a little earlier," Mike said.

"He's been following Sadie, following her for—what—her whole life."

"Which means he's from here."

"This handwriting is too neat to be a kid's. Maybe he fixated on her in college and did some backtracking."

"That means she's got a stalker, and one that's been around for a long time. That's not good."

"No," Dan agreed. "That's not good at all. But if he's been obsessed with Sadie all along, why the other killings? Why not just come after her?"

The questions hung in the air.

"There's one last thing I wanted to show you. This was loose inside the book, but not really part of it." Mike passed Dan another black-and-white photo, this one larger than the others, about six-by-eight, and it looked like it had been to hell and back. It had been handled so many times that it had fallen apart and been taped back together. It was a group shot of a bunch of adults, standing in a clearing surrounded by woods on either side. The women all worn ankle-length dresses and had long hair, some falling to their waists. The men wore long-sleeved shirts and slicked back hair. What was similar to each person in the photo was the look of grave severity on each of their faces. No one was smiling. In the center of the picture was a youngish woman, beautiful and lithe. Dan didn't recognize anyone in the photo. "Do you mind if I keep these for the night? I'd like to go through them."

"Do you really think it's a good idea to keep that here—what with Sadie living here and all?"

"Give me some credit." Dan slipped the small journal inside his jacket pocket. "I'll see if I can't sweet-talk Doug into sending his files from St. Louis overnight."

"It obviously means a lot to this guy. From the looks of it, he carried it with him at all times—like a reminder." Mike nodded toward the photograph.

"A list."

"A kill-list." Mike nodded. "But so far, neither of the people he's killed in town are in that picture. Andre was still living in London when this picture was taken. He didn't move to the US until the eighties. And Birdie—well, this looks like a group of religious high-rollers—"

"And Birdie was anything but." Dan nodded in agreement. "This picture had to have been taken in what—the late sixties, early seventies from the looks of the clothes."

"Your guess is as good as mine. I wasn't even a gleam in my mother's eye in those days."

"I wonder..."

"What?"

"Nothing—well, something...I need to check on something first before I...just give me until tomorrow."

CHAPTER 34

6:58 p.m.

As soon as the door closed behind Mike, Dan called Doug. He answered on the second ring, somewhat out of breath.

"Did I catch you at a bad time?" Dan fingered the mysterious photo.

"Just finished a run. What's up?" Dan could hear Doug opening a bottle of something and taking a long drink.

As Dan filled Doug in on the events of the past couple of days, his ex-partner sat in silence on the other end of the phone, not once interrupting him. When Dan was finished telling him everything, he said, "Sounds like he's escalating, two murders in as many days."

"Yeah, I know. How easy do you think it will be for me to take a look at the case records now that he has jumped jurisdiction?" Dan knew that often cases were botched and criminals escaped due to stupid human pride on the parts of the people investigating and prosecuting the cases. Everyone wanting to play the part of the hero, often loath to give up crucial evidence, feeling a proprietary right over it somehow, but Doug was not one of these. "I've got it sitting right here. I'll send the courier first thing in the morning."

"I owe you one."

"You owe me more than one, but I'll settle for one of your mom's apple pies."

"I'll see that you get two."

Just then Sadie appeared in the doorway, looking fresh from her shower and beautiful in a pair of jeans and a V-necked green sweater that conformed to the curves of her body. Dan found himself at a loss for words and, managing a hasty good-bye, hung up the phone.

"Sorry, I didn't mean to interrupt you." Sadie hesitated a little in the doorway, then seeing the picture on the table, she froze. "Where did you get that?" Sadie crossed the room grabbing up the photo before Dan could stop her.

"It's what Mike called about," Dan told a half-truth. "Evie found this at Birdie's, along with a few other items that belong to the killer."

"I've seen this before." Sadie's hand started to shake.

"Where?"

"I don't know." Her voice was barely above a whisper. "But I know I've seen it."

"Do you recognize anyone in it?"

"No, sorry, but…" She cocked her head to the side. "Who is she?" She pointed to the attractive woman in the center of the photo.

"I don't know. I don't recognize any of the people either, but the picture was definitely taken up at the springs."

Taking the picture into her hands, Sadie studied the woman more intently before turning it over. "There's writing."

Dan couldn't believe he hadn't turned it over. "Let me see that. They're names. That's helpful."

"Why are they all scratched out?"

"That's a good question."

Just then Anna called out to the porch, announcing that dinner was being served.

CHAPTER 35

7:25 p.m.

Adjourning to the dining room, they found Rocco pouring the Chianti he favored when serving his legendary lasagna.

After dinner, as they enjoyed coffee and dessert, strawberries covered in dark, white, and milk chocolate, Dan related to the others what he could about the case, showing them the photograph that Sadie had already seen but leaving the journal out of it.

"Sister Jane and the Church of Jesus and Life Everlasting," Anna said, a distinct look of distaste on her face.

"What a nut job. She was a real piece of work." Rocco rolled his eyes. "Those *deaths* were big news back then. But it's funny, once she left town, the talk about her, at least in public, died almost instantly."

"After she was run out of town, no one wanted to admit they had associated with her," Anna said.

"Until the chief brought it up today, I'd totally forgotten about it," Dan said.

"You were in high school then. You didn't care about much aside from sports and girls back then," Rocco said.

"Where did she come from?" Sadie asked quietly.

"That's another one of the big mysteries surrounding her. One day she just showed up in town, nearly starved to death, with no name and what she said was a bad case of amnesia," Anna said, pouring more coffee all around.

"You didn't buy it?" Dan asked.

"Most of the town didn't and steered clear of her," Rocco said.

"Chief Baxter seems to think that the current murders are somehow connected to her group back then."

"I don't see how, that group disbanded years ago." Rocco picked up the picture, scrutinizing it. "I don't even think any of them still live in the area. As soon as she left town—"

"Was run out of town," Anna interjected pointedly.

"The case dragged on for months, and then one day they just dismissed the charges. No one ever really knew why either."

"Chief says that all of his case files up and disappeared from the station house as well as his home one night, and without them the case fell apart," Dan explained as he helped himself to gigantic strawberry covered with dark chocolate. He noted silently that Sadie had chosen the dark chocolate as well. He wasn't sure why it made him so happy, but it did.

"That woman and her so-called church were a disgrace, but she had a loyal following," Anna said.

"Do you remember anything else about it?" Dan asked.

"Hold on for a minute; I'll be right back," Rocco excused himself from the room, leaving everyone puzzled, but not for long. When he returned to the table, he had a box of newspaper clippings that he called his "idea box." Every time he read something that gave him an idea for a book, he clipped it and set it aside, always intending to write the next great American novel but never actually getting started. After shuffling through the contents of the box for a minute, he found what he was looking for.

"There you are."

"What have you got there?" Anna asked, getting up and reading over her husband's shoulder, her wine glass in one hand. After finishing the brief article, she kissed Rocco on the top of his head and resumed her seat.

Rocco read in silence for a moment and then handed the article to Dan, who read it through from start to finish twice before looking up.

June 22, 1991—Crystal Springs Gazette
Sister Jane, Pentecostal preacher and leader of the Church of Jesus and Life Everlasting, located somewhere outside town in the heart of the Springs, was questioned today in the suspicious deaths of several of her followers:

Tobias Smith—age 35—lawyer, found dead in his bathtub six weeks ago; both wrists slit, originally ruled suicide. The case has recently been reopened, although the police have declined statements as to why or how they have connected him to this case.

Nancy Smith—age 33—wife of Tobias, found dead two weeks ago of an overdose of sleeping pills mixed with vodka, in the same bathroom where her husband died. The investigation surrounding her death, originally ruled suicide, has been reopened. Police decline to comment on new evidence.

Jackson Black—age 52—Johnsonville town physician, whose body was just discovered yesterday floating downstream in the East River in what originally looked like an accidental drowning but has now been ruled suspicious. Dr. Black suffered from over twenty rattlesnake bites prior to drowning.

Each victim was found clutching the tail of a mature rattlesnake. Reliable sources inform this reporter that evidence has been discovered linking all three deaths to Sister Jane and that she and her mysterious church are being investigated. Police urge anyone with information related to this case to come forward.

"This article doesn't give a lot of details," Dan said. "The first two could very easily be suicides, and the doctor … I guess he could have somehow wandered into some sort of a snake den, but …"

"That's a lot of bites," Sadie said.

Anna shook her head. "It's odd really, but as much as she was big news back then, no one really seemed to want to talk about her, or it. In the proper sense, I mean. Sure, people gossiped like crazy in private, but if asked to provide proof behind their words, they fell mute. She was so outside the norm and removed from town, that even while this was going on she seemed like more of a made-up character from a Grimm's fairy tale than a real living, breathing woman."

"I think she was really only real to her followers," Rocco said.

"Yes, only to them, and I still can't figure out what her draw was."

"I wonder," Sadie said almost to herself.

"Wonder what?" Dan asked.

"My dad was her attorney. He was the only defense attorney in town," Sadie said almost apologetically. "Until he fired her as a client."

"What happened?" Dan asked, picking up the wine bottle and refilling everyone else's glasses before filling his own.

"One night, late, I remember overhearing him screaming at a woman named Jane. I'd never met her and didn't that night either, but I always assumed it was her—Sister Jane."

"What were they fighting about?" Anna asked, leaning in.

"I'd had an accident that day after school. Apparently, I fell into the river and hit my head on a rock pretty hard. The strange thing is, I don't remember going to the river that day; in fact, I don't remember anything about that day until waking up in bed at home, with bandages on my head, legs, and arms and sore all over. I woke to the sound of angry shouting. Dad was screaming at someone— a woman—and she was yelling back. I wasn't used to hearing the sound of a woman's voice in our house at all. Dad never expressed interest in remarrying after Mom died and I'd never known him to date, so I was shocked to hear a woman's voice. He had also always made it a point not to bring his work home. So, I found it doubly odd. He said, 'You've got to control that monster before he destroys everything. How can you be so nonchalant about it?'"

"It definitely sounds like she at least knew who the killer was." Dan said.

"It certainly does." Anna nodded. "What happened next?"

"No idea. Just then my father saw me and very quickly ushered me back upstairs and admonished me for eavesdropping."

"Did you see her?" Dan pointed to the mesmerizing woman at the center of the photograph.

"Just from behind. But I can't think of who else it would have been. Later, after she was gone, he brought me the biggest bowl of rocky road ice cream imaginable and then proceeded to help me eat it while we watched late-night reruns of *The Three Stooges*. It was one of the best nights I ever had with my father. He dropped the case the very next day."

"Do you know why?" Dan asked.

"No, I asked him once, but he just shook his head and walked away. But I still might be able to help—I bet I could get you his old case notes."

"You have them?" Dan asked, thinking about the state of things in her cramped apartment.

"Well, they're still at home. At Dad's house, I mean. I never sold it. I've only been in it a handful of times since he died. I can try to find them for you—I mean, if you think it would help."

"That would be great. If you want to wait until I get home tomorrow night, I can go with you," Dan said.

As the others around the dinner table continued talking, Sadie let her mind wander back to the childhood visions she'd had of the little black-haired boy with blue eyes who was always surrounded by snakes and terrified. "Was there a little boy? Did one of the church members have a son with dark hair and blue eyes?"

"I have no idea," Anna said, shaking her head and looking at Rocco. "Honey?"

"Not that I know of."

"Why?" Dan asked.

"Because I... never mind. I just thought I remembered something but I must have been wrong." Sadie had never known if the boy in her dreams was real. In a sense he was and always had been alive to her. But her father and the doctors had adamantly refuted his existence, insisting that he was a product of her imagination.

After dinner the men moved from the table to the porch by the fire continuing their talk, while Sadie, thankful for the excuse to distance herself from the conversation, insisted on helping Anna clear the table.

CHAPTER 36

11:15 p.m.

Later in her room, Sadie sat on the window seat, looking out over the orchard. A full moon hung pregnant in the sky. It was stunning, and she wished she could properly appreciate it. After helping Anna with the dishes, she'd said a quick goodnight to Dan and Rocco. Feigning sleepiness, she slipped away upstairs, leaving the St. James men still heatedly discussing Sister Jane, the odd, enigmatic woman who had haunted her father until his death, and was now haunting her as well.

Sadie had no idea how long she'd been sitting on the window seat, when she realized that the house was silent and had been for a while. Looking at the clock, she saw it was after eleven. The memories stirred up by the dinner conversation had left her feeling empty and alone. She had a feeling that she wouldn't be sleeping much that night and wished for someone to talk to. She wondered what Anna and Rocco would say if she knocked on their bedroom door and suggested another late-night pajama party. She figured they would think she was off her rocker and ask her to have her bags packed at first light. Just then she noticed a faint glow coming through the trees and realized that she'd never heard Dan's car leave. Without a second's hesitation, she pulled on her shoes, grabbed a jacket, and headed toward the door.

The old farmhouse was quiet. A faint light glowed under the door to Anna and Rocco's bedroom. She could hear them talking softly to each other. She envied that type of closeness in couples.

Walking softly down the stairs, she felt like a teenager sneaking out after curfew and had to stifle a laugh. Once outside, she walked quickly through the chilly night air to the barn and Dan, or what she hoped was Dan. When and if she found him, she hoped he wouldn't press her for an explanation for today, but if he did, she decided, she would tell him, maybe not everything, but enough.

Halfway down the road, she realized she could no longer see the light through the trees and began to wonder if this was such a good idea after all. She'd been so excited that she'd left without really thinking it through. For one thing, she couldn't even see the barn from that window; the light could have been a reflection off any number of things. Still, her feet kept moving steadily forward. *What if it wasn't him but someone else?* Just then the moon disappeared behind a large cloud, bathing the trees around her in darkness. The orchard seemed to have taken on a life of its own, and Sadie found she wasn't having any difficulty envisioning monsters and madmen behind every tree and in every deep pool of shadows. *I shouldn't have come out here.* She was feeling very much like Dorothy in the haunted forest, but without the faithful sidekicks. She was about to turn back when she heard the crunching of gravel on the road right behind her.

Dan thought about Sadie as he climbed the stairs to the loft. He opted to stay over instead of getting behind the wheel right now. Exchanging the sheets on the bed for a fresh set, he thought about Sadie and the kiss. He wished she'd given him a chance to say goodnight to her, instead of rushing off the way she had. He sincerely hoped he wasn't in any way responsible for her hasty departure.

With the bed made and ready for him, he opened the small leather journal and went through it one more time, page by page. There wasn't much there to give away the identity of the stalker. He left his comments short and often scathing. The photos were all in chronological order and closely followed Sadie's life. Dan felt a sense of intrusion as he studied the stalker's invasive chronicle of her life. He would have to study it later in earnest—later, but not tonight.

After closing the book, Dan turned off the light and sat in a comfortable old chair by the window, gazing up at the full moon that loomed large over the orchard. It was an amazing sight, and even though he'd seen it countless times, it never failed to take his breath away.

Shadows played among the trees in the orchard like ghostly dancers carried on the wind and illuminated by the glow of the moon. Dan sat and watched them. As a boy he'd been frightened by them, then fascinated by them, and finally comforted by them. But tonight something in the shadows seemed off. One of them, he knew, shouldn't be there. Instinctively he knew that something bigger than a jack rabbit was lurking outside the barn. Grabbing his jacket and his gun, Dan headed down the stairs.

Sadie's heart couldn't decide whether to stop altogether or do a jitterbug in her chest. Visions of Andre's mutilated corpse danced in her head, and suddenly she was convinced that the killer was out here, that the source of the mysterious light had been him and not Dan. "You're imagining things," she said aloud, trying to calm herself. "Just turn around, and you will see that no one is there."

"I wouldn't call myself a nobody," Dan said, causing Sadie to jump and scream.

"Shhh … Mom'll call out the militia." Dan laughed.

"You scared the crap out of me." Sadie hit him on the arm, relieved and a little embarrassed, her heart still running a marathon.

"What are you doing out here?" Dan asked. "I thought you went to bed."

"I couldn't sleep. I ... um ... I saw a light through the trees, and I was hoping it was you."

"You came looking for me?" Dan asked, raising his eyebrows a little. Sadie didn't know what to say.

"I'm glad you did," he said, pulling her close to him and kissing her. "Hey, you're shivering. Let's get inside." Arm in arm, they walked through the night and into the barn.

CHAPTER 37

11:32 p.m.

They walked through the night and into the barn in silence, the orchard no longer seeming scary but instead full of magic. They sat together in a big comfy chair by the window. Sadie was on Dan's lap with her back against one armrest and her legs draped over the opposite one. Dan had his arm around her back. This way they could share the chair and still face each other while they talked.

"So what was it you wanted to see me about?" Dan asked, kissing her neck lightly and brushing an errant hair off her face.

"I wanted to explain why I left so abruptly after dinner." Sadie didn't look at Dan; instead she gazed out over the landscape. "The memory of my father and learning about that woman overwhelmed me. It was the last thing I was expecting, and it totally threw me for a loop. I'm sorry."

"No need to apologize. I'm just glad it was only something I said and not something I did," Dan half joked. He wondered if she was going to follow through with her promise to tell him what had happened this morning or if she was going to see if he would let it slide. At this point, he was just glad to be with her, listening to her;

he had no intention of interrogating her tonight. Tonight he'd let her direct the course of the conversation.

"It's all been rough these last few days." The understatement of the century.

"I know; I'm sorry. I know how much they both meant to you."

"It's not just that." Sadie paused. Dan didn't rush her. "It's seeing you and your family, and being invited in to share in a few pieces of it makes me realize how truly alone I am. How much I miss—I've always missed—being part of a real family. What you said in the car today, that I had you and you weren't going anywhere, really meant a lot to me. I hope you meant it." She turned to look at him now, searching his face for clues in the light cast by the moon to how he felt about her.

"Every word." He kissed her hair. "You were in college when your dad was killed."

"Finals week, freshman year." Sadie turned back to looking at the landscape. "I was getting ready to pick up the phone and call home. I'd just aced my archeology final, and I was bouncing off the walls. I couldn't wait to tell him. We must have placed our calls at exactly the same time. I swear the phone never rang. I just picked up the receiver and there was Doc Conway on the other end, and he told me that my father had been killed the night before by a tourist who'd had too much booze and thought it was cool to speed through the country without headlights. He never let me see him when I came home. I never got a chance to say good-bye." Swallowing hard, she choked back the emotions that threatened to overwhelm her and fell silent.

"I'm so sorry. I didn't even hear about it until I came home for break myself. I tried to call you that summer a couple of times, but you were never home."

"You did?" Sadie stopped, looking out the window. "I didn't know. I never came home that summer, except for the funeral. I stayed at school year-round, until after graduation, and even then I only intended to come back long enough to sell the house."

"What happened?"

"Andre and Rapture; and the rest is, as they say, history. Why did you call me?"

"Why did you take archeology?"

"I asked you first."

"Because I wanted to see if there was anything I could do. And because I've sort of had a thing for you since high school."

"You have?"

"Guilty."

"I have a confession too," Sadie whispered, kissing him softly. "I sort of have a thing for you too."

Picking her up, Dan carried her to his bed, laid her down gently on the soft down comforter, and then lay beside her. Looking deeply into her eyes, he searched for any sign of hesitation, and when he saw none, he kissed her.

CHAPTER 38

November 3, 3:15 a.m.

In her dream he crept stealthily between bushes and a brick wall, his big boots crunching on the fallen leaves yet to be raked. It was part of a building. It was Dan's apartment complex. Somehow she knew this, although she had no way of knowing that. She had never been to Dan's apartment before. The man's heart raced with anticipation, and Sadie could feel it as if it was her own. His breath quick and shallow. She could see the ghosts of vapor that escaped his mouth each time he exhaled. She saw what he saw, felt what he felt. An uninvited participant, she witnessed the actions of the person in the boots, unseen and unbidden and unable to stop him. At the corner of the building, he stopped and looked both ways. The night was still and quiet. There were no other people on the narrow, earthen path. Rounding the building, he opened the basement door and slipped inside, smug that no one had spotted the tape he'd placed over the lock earlier in the day, rendering it ineffective. He doubted that any of the tenants had even noticed. Creeping upstairs, he made sure to avoid the stairs that, earlier in the day, he'd discovered squeaked. He stopped outside the door to Dan's apartment. Sadie screamed at him to stop, but she was not really there.

She had no voice. No power to stop him. She watched helplessly as he deftly picked the lock and let himself inside. The rage in him that had been building the whole time was stronger now. She felt him fight to keep it under control. He went straight to Dan's bedroom. After opening a few drawers, the intruder found the one he'd been searching for, the one containing socks and underwear. Quickly and carefully, he lifted the crate he'd been carrying and emptied a large rattlesnake into the drawer, swiftly shutting it before the agitated viper could attack.

Just then the dream switched, and daylight streamed through the windows; the intruder was gone. She watched Dan enter the bedroom from the bathroom. He was dressed only in a hunter green bath towel, his hair still wet from his recent shower. Sadie grew panicky watching Dan cross the floor to his dresser and the drawer where the snake lay in wait. Tossing and turning in her sleep, she tried to call out to Dan to not open the drawer. But she could not make herself be heard. Helpless, she watched as he opened the drawer and the viper lunged at him, striking his face just below his right eye.

A sharp pain in the ribs woke Dan suddenly and painfully. Sadie lay beside him thrashing and moaning in her sleep. Her hair was wet with sweat and her breathing was quick and shallow. Dan remembered his mom mentioning nightmares earlier this evening. He had totally forgotten about it.

In her sleep Sadie twisted first one way then another, tearing the bedcovers loose from the mattress. Dan thought of the shape of Birdie's bed and shivered. Worried, he wasn't sure what to do. Were you supposed to wake up a dreaming person or let them be? No, it was a sleepwalker you weren't supposed to wake up. Just as he was about to rouse her, she screamed, "Dan! No!" Sadie sat up in bed, eyes wide, shaking.

"Dan!" Sadie turned to him. "I saw ... there was a snake ... he put a snake in your sock drawer."

"Come again?" Dan laughed. He was fully awake now, but he wasn't sure Sadie was. That had to be one of the strangest things anyone had ever said to him.

"A snake. The killer put a rattlesnake in your sock drawer, and it bit you in the face," Sadie repeated. She was wide awake and deadly serious.

"Slow down. It was a dream. You were having a bad dream, that's all. I'm fine. See? I'm right here," he said, taking her hand and putting in on his bare chest as if to prove that he was whole and uninjured.

"No, not here, at your apartment. I saw him do it," Sadie insisted.

"How could you? You were sleeping in bed with me." Dan reached over and switched on the lamp by the bed, hoping that a little light would help chase the dream away, but instead it brought the nightmare to life. On her face, under her right eye were two wicked-looking puncture marks that looked remarkably like a snakebite.

"Listen." She looked him square in the eye, her tone quiet but serious. "You keep your socks in the fourth drawer down from the top of an antique cherry highboy. The socks are on the left, and your boxers are on the right. You have prints of M. C. Escher lining your hallway, the middle one is skewed a little to the left. Your bath towels and your robe are hunter green. The robe's left pocket is missing." Dan just stared at her. Everything she'd said was exactly right, only she'd never been to his apartment.

"I believe you," Dan said, unable to look away from the marks on her tender cheek, so close to her eye.

"No, I ... what?"

"I said I believe you. I don't understand any of it, but I believe you."

"You do?" Sadie didn't know what to say.

"Just one question, if the snake bit me, how come you're the one bleeding?" Dan asked, touching the bite. His finger came away smeared with a drop of her blood.

"I..." Sadie hadn't even realized she'd been marked again. Raising her hand to her check, she tentatively explored the wound with her fingertips. Then taking a deep breath, she began to explain, "I call them psychic wounds." Sadie's voice was so low Dan had to strain to hear her. Gathering the afghan from the bed, she stood and walked to the window wrapping herself in the warm, soft blanket. "I have no idea how or why it happens to me, but sometimes the things I see in my dreams hurt me—physically."

Sensing that this topic scared her for many reasons, Dan followed her out of bed and sat in the chair they'd occupied earlier, gently urging her to sit on his lap. At first she resisted, staying at the window for a few seconds longer. Eventually, she relented and joined him in the big chair. Slowly, over the course of an hour, she told him things that she'd never shared with another person. Things that scared her and hurt her, that had caused her to feel different and distant from every person she'd ever met. She even told him about the dark-haired little boy—the one always surrounded by snakes. Dan realized as she spoke that he'd never felt closer to another person than he did to her right then.

"So," she said finally, "do you think I'm crazy?" Although the question was masked with a false bravado, Dan knew that she was seriously scared he would reject her.

"No, I think you are brave and strong and beautiful."

"You do?"

"I do."

"You aren't sorry we..." She trailed off as if afraid to finish her question.

"Are you crazy?" Dan joked, lightening the mood. "No way, you're stuck with me now."

"Good." Sadie fell silent then and stared out the window, finally relaxing against him for the first time since they'd sat back down.

"Be careful when you go home, please. It's kind of funny, though, a sock in your snake drawer."

"Don't you mean a snake in my sock drawer?"

"What you said."

"Don't worry. I'll be fine."

They sat together in silence for a little while, how long, Dan didn't know. Eventually, he realized that Sadie had fallen asleep. Careful not to wake her, he picked her up and carried her back to his bed, tucking her in and then slipping in next to her. In her sleep, she rolled over, and he moved next to her. Forming the perfect spoon, they stayed that way until dawn.

CHAPTER 39

7:25 a.m.

Dan woke before Sadie and slipped quietly out of bed, trying not to wake her. He had to get home and take a shower. He had a long day ahead of him and a lot of puzzle pieces to figure out. Just as he was about to sneak down the stairs he heard, "Hey, don't I get a kiss good morning?"

"I'm sorry. I didn't mean to wake you. It's early." Dan crossed the room and sat next to her on the bed. She put her head in his lap.

"What time is it?" she asked sleepily.

"Almost seven thirty," Dan said as he stroked her hair.

"I should probably get inside before your parents wake up and find out what a hussy I am."

"You're probably safe for a little while longer. Mom and Dad don't usually wake up for a few minutes yet."

"Good. I'll see if I can find those records of my dad's for you today."

"You don't have to. I don't want you to do anything that makes you uncomfortable."

"I've been meaning to go there for a long time. I've just always managed to find an excuse to put it off before. But now since I can't go back to my apartment, I guess I have to go home again."

"If you want to wait for me, I'll go with you tonight," Dan offered.

"Thanks. But I think I need to do this alone."

"I better get going. I have to be at the station in less than an hour." He leaned down to kiss her.

"I probably have dragon breath."

"I probably don't care."

After a brief kiss on the lips, Dan kissed her on the cheek, where the mysterious bite had been only a few hours before, and then on the forehead.

"The bite?" Sadie asked.

"Is gone, just like you said it would be." He traced his fingers over the unblemished skin under her right eye.

"Be careful, Dan. I mean it."

"I will." He gave her hand a squeeze before getting up to leave.

Lying in his bed, Sadie listened to him make his way down the stairs and walk across the barn floor. She felt like she could easily stay wrapped in these sheets forever; last night had been by far the most magical night she'd ever had. Even the dream hadn't managed to spoil it. Well, not all of it anyway. Trying not to think any more about the dream, she got out of bed and dressed quickly in the same clothes she'd had on the night before at dinner. It wasn't that she doubted Dan about the time his parents rose, but she didn't want to take any chances.

The air outside was cold, and the sky still dark as she walked through the orchard back to the house. She had just about made it all the way to her room, when the door to Anna and Rocco's door opened, and Rocco stepped out into the hall.

"Morning," Rocco said cheerfully, as he walked down the hall and disappeared down the stairs.

"Morning," Sadie replied, turning a thousand shades of pink. "Shit," she said closing the door behind her.

"Maybe he didn't notice that I am wearing the same clothes I had on at dinner last night." Sadie went directly to the bathroom and turned on the shower. As she waited for the water to heat up, she surveyed her face for any lingering trace of last night's dream; there was none. This one, as the ones before, had faded completely away.

F reshly showered and dressed in a pair of jeans and a comfy navy blue hooded sweatshirt, the kind that zipped up the front, Sadie found Anna in the kitchen.

"Coffee's on the stove," Anna said brightly, putting a tray of homemade cinnamon rolls, the size of a giant's fist, into the oven. "Would you mind slicing the fruit while I take a shower?" she said after straightening up. Sadie was positive she detected a new glint in the other woman's eye but decided she was just being paranoid.

"I'd be happy to. Is there anything else I can help with?" Sadie deftly avoided eye contact as she selected a mug from the rack above the pot and helped herself to a cup of the obsidian brew; she detected a trace on cinnamon in the coffee.

"Not a thing." Anna took her apron off and crossed to the same door Sadie had just come from. Just before leaving, she looked over her shoulder and said with a wink, "I think you two make a wonderful couple." And with that she was gone, leaving Sadie with her mouth agape, happily amazed.

Slicing the apples, melons, and berries into bite-size pieces, Sadie thought about the dream and what she'd told Dan. She'd never intended to tell anyone even half of what she'd told him just a few hours ago. But once she'd gotten started and he didn't mock her or bristle toward her, she'd found everything she'd bottled up for so long spilling out of her like water out of a freshly opened dam. Last night's dream scared her more than any of the ones from her childhood. It was more potent and somehow more real. It had felt like she was actually there, living it instead of just bearing witness to it, and she hoped against all hope that she hadn't been prophetic.

CHAPTER 40

7:45 a.m.

Nearing home, Dan used speed dial to call Mike, deciding that it would be faster if Mike met him at his place instead of the station house.

Mike answered on the second ring. "Evie's got evidence for us."

"What is it?" Dan turned down his street and parked outside of his building. Looking at the bushes along the side of the building, he felt a chill.

"She didn't say. You know how she is—she prefers more show than tell."

"When can we get the results?" Dan got out of his car and locked it. The street looked peaceful, quiet.

"As soon as we get there. I'll pick up some coffee and bagels and be over in about twenty minutes. Does that give you enough time?"

"Plenty," Dan said and hung up. In the light of the day, Sadie's dream seemed impossible. He couldn't deny what he'd seen, though, that somehow her dream had manifested outside of her subconscious and drawn blood. But bad dreams and psychic experiences aside, how likely was it that she actually witnessed an act of vandalism by telepathy? Not very, he guessed. More than likely, she'd just had a very bad dream brought on by the events of the last couple of days, and her sixth sense, being as strong as it was, manifested the bite mark. Although he wasn't sure whether or not he bought it, he decided it was more plausible than the other explanation.

Walking up the path to the front door, he was tempted to circle around the building and check for fresh boot prints in the dirt. But then he reasoned that even if there were prints, it wouldn't necessarily mean anything. Any number of people could have used it for a cut through.

Using his key to let himself in the building's main door, he paused—everything was quiet. At his front door, he checked his lock and door for any signs of forced entry. He found none and the lock was in perfect working condition.

"It was just a dream." Dan decided, walking down the hall, disrobing along the way. As he walked, he noticed that one of the three M. C. Escher prints on the wall was hanging askew as if someone had bumped it. He felt his mouth go a bit dry.

He had just finished toweling off when he heard the buzzer to the building's outer door. "Who is it?" he said in a high, little-girl, sing-song voice, into the intercom.

"The big bad wolf," Mike said through a mouthful of something Dan assumed was a bagel. "Let me in or I'll drink your coffee."

"Don't ever threaten a caffeine junky on too little sleep like that." Dan pushed the button, allowing Mike access to the building.

"Nice towel," Mike said, sitting down at the kitchen table and opening Dan's morning paper.

"Be right with you." Dan grabbed his coffee and headed for the bedroom. Crossing the floor to his dresser, an antique highboy made of cherry wood, he counted the drawers down from the top. His sock and underwear drawer was the fourth one down from the top. His heart sped up a little, and he hesitated with his hand on the pull.

"Oh hell." Dan thought about all of the other "coincidences" of Sadie's dream and wondered if they were really coincidences after all. What if there really was a snake in his sock drawer?

"My God, man, open the drawer already," Mike said, coming into the room. "You've been standing there for half an hour," he exaggerated.

Feeling sufficiently foolish, Dan started to pull the drawer open then stopped. *What if?*

"What is it?" Sensing tension, Mike crossed the room.

"I think there's a rattlesnake in there."

"A what in where? And how do you think it got there? Last I checked, snakes hadn't evolved opposable thumbs."

"I'll explain it to you later, just back the hell up," Dan said. Seeing that he was serious, Mike took a few steps backward. He began to wonder if his partner had completely lost it as he watched him loop a leather belt around the metal pull and stand back out of the way.

Taking a deep breath, Dan realized that he would never live this down if there was nothing in the drawer but skivvies.

"Here goes nothing." Dan gave the belt a swift tug. The drawer flew open and crashed to the floor as a three-foot rattlesnake flew out like a demented jack-in-the-box. Dan immediately noticed that the snake was missing its rattle.

"Oh shit! That's a frickin' rattlesnake." Mike jumped up on Dan's bed. The snake lunged at him but missed, then slithered under the bed, disappearing out of sight.

Unable to see where the snake had gone, Dan jumped on the bed too, loath to be on the floor wearing nothing but a towel with an angry pit viper.

"Well, this is just dandy," Mike said. "You realize we are never going to live this down as long as we live."

"Not if anybody sees us standing on top of my bed like this, especially with me nearly naked," Dan said. The enormity of what had happened was still settling on him. The dream had been prophetic. Sadie had foreseen this.

"Keep the towel on," Mike said, scanning the floor on his side for the snake.

"Don't worry."

"Where'd it come from?"

"Three guesses."

"The snake fairy?"

"What kind of a warped childhood did you have?"

"Don't look at me. You're the one with the snake in his underwear drawer," Mike said.

"Where's your gun?"

"It's in the kitchen. Where's yours?"

"On the chair," Dan nodded to the chair by the bathroom door. His shoulder holster with his gun was hanging off the back. "I think I can get to it." Dan scanned the floor at the foot of the bed.

"What are you gonna do? Shoot it?"

"You have a better idea?"

"No."

"Okay then." Dan was just about to step off the bed when the snake slithered out from under it, effectively blocking his path.

"What is the thing, psychic?" Dan asked, incredulous.

"Psychic snakes, great, that's just great. What now?"

"I have an idea." Dan retrieved the afghan from the end of the bed. "As soon as I throw this over it, get out of here. Maybe we can trap it inside."

"How do you know there aren't more of them out there?" Mike asked.

"Sadie only dreamt about this one."

"Huh?" Mike was looking at him like he had suddenly grown an extra head.

"Never mind," Dan said.

"Gladly." Mike crouched, poised to jump.

"On the count of three. One … two … three." Dan gently tossed the folded afghan over the snake, covering it and rendering it harmless for the moment. Jumping off the bed, they raced through the door and slammed it shut, the snake safely inside.

"Do we have to call this in?" Dan was not looking forward to the plethora of practical jokes this would set him up for.

"You wanna keep it as a pet?"

"Good point. We are never gonna live this down." Dan groaned, picking up the phone.

"We! Who we? I'm not the one in the towel."

This was one of those mornings when Dan was glad he'd gone against everything his mother had taught him and left his clothes strewn everywhere. As they waited for animal control to show up, Dan moved across the living room, snatching up and putting on last night's clothes. As he dressed, he told Mike about Sadie's dream.

"Okay, now that's just weird—cool, but weird," Mike said. "You think she's somehow connected to this freak?"

"No way. She was terrified." The truth was, Dan told Mike only enough to get by. He left out the majority of what Sadie had shared with him in confidence, explaining only that she'd had a nightmare, which had somehow managed to come true.

"I didn't mean his accomplice or anything, but everyone he's killed in town has been connected to her in some way. And what about the journal?" Mike said.

"I don't know, but I'm damned sure I'm gonna find out." Just then the buzzer at the front door sounded.

Opening the door, he found a petite redhead with bright blue eyes and a pixie nose holding a cage in one hand and a long pole with a loop on one end in the other.

"Hey, Lana," Dan said. "Animal Control to the rescue! I'm glad you could come so fast."

"No problem. Hey, Mike," Lana Grainger said, stepping through the doorway. Lana looked around. "So where is the poor little thing?"

"Poor little thing's in the bedroom," Dan said. "But I'm not exactly inclined to feel sorry for it." He led the way through the apartment.

"As a rule, snakes are afraid of people," Lana lectured. "And contrary to popular belief, they do not attack without provocation. If it lunged at you, it must have felt threatened," Lana stared pointedly at Dan. "Now if you gentlemen will excuse me, I have a snake to rescue."

"Brave girl," Mike said. "What do you think she would say if she could have seen us standing on your bed like sissies?"

"Let's never speak of that again."

"Definitely."

Once Lana was gone, Dan turned his apartment over to Evie and Adam to search for fingerprints or anything else that might have been left by the intruder. Without telling them about the dream, he asked them to check the lock on the back door for tape residue, simply telling them that he was following a hunch.

The majority of the ground between the bushes and the building was covered with leaves, effectively providing a barrier through which no telltale footprints could be recovered, except in one bare spot where Dan found a single perfect boot print. As Adam made a mold of the print, Evie reported that the basement door did indeed test positive for tape residue. There were no fingerprints in the apartment aside from theirs and Lana's, but they did find a black hair that was not a match to anyone Dan knew and that matched several found at Birdie's. Looking as exuberant as someone who'd just won a prize, Evie hustled out the door, anxious to get back to the lab with her new evidence. "Give me a couple of hours, guys. Come by this afternoon." She gave Mike a quick peck on the cheek.

"Good luck," Mike said, walking her to the car.

"Thanks." And with that, she and Adam headed back to the lab. Just as they were pulling away, a courier van pulled up. The driver got out, carrying a thick package for Dan. It was from Doug.

"What now partner?" Mike asked.

"Interested in a little light reading?"

CHAPTER 41

9:42 a.m.

Breakfast that morning with Anna and Rocco was a leisurely affair and seemed less like Sadie's second day staying with the couple and more like … family. It was the only word she could conjure that conveyed what she felt. After Sadie sliced the fruit, Rocco engaged her in a lively debate over the best comic strips of all time: he was a defender of *Calvin and Hobbs* while her vote came down squarely in the corner of Burk Breathed's masterful creation *Bloom County*. The breakfast conversation flowed seamlessly, and for a brief pocket of time she was able to put the ugly events that had brought her here on the back burner.

"Cinnamon roll?" Rocco said, basket in hand, preparing to help himself to another of the delicious breakfast pastries.

"No thank you," Sadie said, patting her stomach. "If I try to fit one more thing in, I might burst."

"You don't need another one either," Anna said, confiscating the basket from her husband. "The rest are for Dan. Besides, weren't you just complaining that your pants were fitting a little tighter these days?" Anna set the basket down next to her, out of Rocco's reach.

"See what I put up with around here? Rocco said dramatically, throwing his hands into the air. "They starve me," he winked at Sadie.

"It's true, dear," Anna said, taking on a serious tone. "Since we've been married, I've starved him up three whole pant sizes."

"I see scales work differently around here." Sadie laughed, loving the couple and their playful banter.

"Would it be all right if I borrowed a car? I need to go to my dad's house and look for those files for Dan." Seeing the couple glance at each other across the table, Sadie mistook their meaning. "Of course, I should probably move over there and get out of your hair." She felt her heart start to plummet into her already overly full stomach.

"Are you sure that's a good idea?" Rocco said, his face suddenly serious. "I'm not sure you should be alone right now."

"Not that you aren't capable," Anna said, seeing the pained look on Sadie's face. "It's just that...the killer, he's still out there, and you have lost so much lately."

"We would feel more comfortable..." Rocco continued.

"And we know Dan would too..." Anna interjected.

"...if you would stay here a while longer, at least until this situation is resolved," Rocco finished.

"Please stay," Anna said, smiling and covering Sadie's hand with her own and squeezing gently.

"I..." Sadie hesitated, relieved. "Thank you. I would love to stay. I just thought you...well, when I asked about the car and...oh never mind, it's nothing."

"When we glanced at each other, you thought we expected you to say you were moving out because you have a place to go to." Anna correctly assessed the situation.

"Well...yes, I just don't want you to feel like I'm taking advantage."

"Nonsense, you didn't ask us to take you in. We invited you here, and we would like it if you and George would stay."

"Okay. Good, we will." Sadie smiled, relieved.

"The reason we glanced at each other is because your car has been here since yesterday," Anna added.

"It has?"

"I guess we forgot to tell you. Dan had a couple of the junior officers bring it by, so you wouldn't feel stranded," Rocco explained.

"Oh," Sadie said, her face flushing pink with embarrassment.

"Good. Then that's settled," Rocco said. "I'm not sure I like the idea of you going off alone."

"Why not wait for Dan?" Anna agreed.

"It's something I have to do myself." Sadie could see they were about to object and spoke again. "If there is even the slightest thing out of place or wrong, I'll turn around and call Dan."

"I'm still not sure it's a great idea," Anna said, relenting a little.

"I'll keep the doors locked. I'll be fine." Sadie smiled.

"You're going to go, no matter what we say," Rocco surmised.

"I need to do it alone. I'm sorry," Sadie apologized. She hated worrying them.

"Don't be. We understand completely; we're just worried." Anna smiled.

"Now if you ladies will excuse me, I have firewood that needs chopping, an orchard that needs tending—and apparently, I have a couple of cinnamon rolls to burn off," Rocco said, getting up from the table. He winked at Sadie as he grabbed his coat and a third cinnamon roll out of the basket as he scooted out the back door.

After helping Anna with the dishes, Sadie collected her car keys, purse, and jacket.

"You're sure I can't persuade you to wait for Dan," Anna tried one last time.

"It's not that I don't want him to come with me, but I really think this is something I have to face myself, alone. At least the first time," Sadie said, hugging Anna before walking out the back door.

In her car, a black Jeep Wrangler with a soft-top, Sadie took her time on the back country roads, admiring the beautiful display of autumn colors that still graced the trees. The long, graceful, back roads that wound over and around the numerous rolling hills that made up the geography of Crystal Springs. The narrow country road, a continuous black ribbon of tar that had always given her a thrill of excitement as she drove, now gave her a different kind of chill as she noted how much its sinuous curves resembled a snake. Pushing the chill aside, she thought about Dan and how perfect the night before had been. However, as she neared her parents' home, she felt the glow of last night and this morning start to wane, and more than once she considered turning around and going back to the orchard. Turning off the road into the driveway, she realized that she was holding her breath.

CHAPTER 42

10:15 a.m.

After a rather long call to Chief Baxter explaining the events of their morning, during which Mike sorted through the contents of the numerous files sent by Doug, Dan put on a pot of coffee and joined Mike at the table, adding the worn leather journal to the mix. "I read it through last night—"

"And?"

"There's some pretty disturbing stuff in there."

Dan picked up the book, untied the strings, and opened to the pages he'd already seen. Staring up at him from the page was a gap-toothed, smiling girl he had never known, but it was unmistakably Sadie. He could see it in her eyes, even as a child she'd had the most amazing eyes. This was going to be hard—harder than any piece of evidence he'd had to study before. When the coffee finished brewing, Dan set the book down, not relishing picking it up again.

"This feels like a waste of time." Mike waved his hand over the files. "If there was something here Doug would have found it. We know all this already, five victims from different backgrounds all without a common denominator to link them."

"Except for the rattle." Dan set two steaming mugs of coffee on the table and sat across from Mike. Mike was already poring through the information from Doug, taking notes—dissecting it. Even though he was frustrated with the lack of progress in the investigation and the looming presence of the killer, Dan knew Mike would not stop until he had devoured every single shred of evidence in the files. While that information was no doubt invaluable, Dan knew the key to finding the killer was in the evidence Mike had brought him last night, but it had thus far eluded him. *You can't hide any longer.* Dan picked up the journal once again.

"You think the chief is right? That this is all somehow connected back to that crazy snake lady and her cult?" Mike took a tentative sip. The coffee was still too hot, so he blew on it, savoring the exotic aroma. "This smells great. What is it?" Mike asked.

"Chocolate hazelnut, Hawaiian macadamia nut, and cinnamon, equal parts of each and voila, perfection. I'd be willing to put money on a member of a snake cult, considering my little coming-home present this morning. You know, the one that tried to kill me."

"If all of these people were members of some off-shoot, not-so-accepted church, it stands to reason that the cops would have had a difficult time finding a connection between them. I don't imagine that they socialized much outside of their—what would you call them—services, which I'm sure were held in secret. By the way, tell me your mom gave you this coffee, and I don't have to start calling you Martha."

"It's Dad's concoction, and I would love to see you call him Martha. You're assuming that they were even still meeting."

"Well, given the number of snakes found in—who was it..." Mike flipped through some pages until he found what he was looking for. "They found over fifty poisonous snakes in the residence of one Mary Doyle who had been tied to a table and left for dead in her own basement."

"So, this guy is searching out the members of an old snake-handling church and killing them—why? Did they refuse him membership?"

"Maybe he was more into it than they were, and he's become some sort of avenging angel—messenger of God sort of thing," Mike suggested. "Damn, Martha, but this coffee is good. If this whole cop thing doesn't work out, you could—"

Mike stopped when Dan threw one of his shoes at him.

"So, you're saying that he's exacting some sort of personal vendetta?" Dan lathered cream cheese on an everything bagel and took a bite. "That's a solid theory until he gets to Crystal Springs, but then it falls apart. I have trouble believing that Andre and Birdie were secret snake worshipers or handlers—whatever."

"Not to mention Sadie."

"Except that this all seems—at least the part here—to be about Sadie."

"You think Andre and Birdie just got in his way?" Mike got up and helped himself to a glass of water.

"No, he's had plenty of opportunities to kill Sadie already and he hasn't."

"He's toying with her."

"He's trying to destroy her."

"Hey, hold on," Mike said, leafing through the files and pulling out pictures of what looked to be hand-drawn sketches. After studying them for a second, he shook his head and passed them to Dan. "Take a look at these."

The pictures were two of a series of remarkably well-rendered sketches in charcoal. The first showed a girl of about thirteen at the edge of a pool or some other body of water. In the next she was in the pool being held underwater by the hair by an oversized hand as she kicked and fought to survive. The third and final rendering in this set showed a mass of snakes attacking the girl from all sides. This picture was marked with writing. It said, *First attempt—failure.*

The second group of sketches depicted a woman standing at the edge of a pit of rough-hewn rock. The next frame showed her unconscious and bound at the bottom of the pit. But the last was by far the worst, sending tendrils of fear throughout Dan. It showed her surrounded by snakes—dozens of snakes, all biting her. The woman was Sadie, the likeness undeniable.

"First attempt failed? That makes it sound like he's tried to kill her once before," Mike said when Dan set the pictures aside. "It also makes sense that the St. Louis PD couldn't make heads or tails of these, they don't know Sadie."

"And without a victim to draw a direct link they probably hoped they were nothing but sick fantasies." Dan laid the sketches next to each other on the table. Then said, "I think he did try to kill her once." Mike listened as Dan related Sadie's story from last night, about her falling into the river in junior high.

"And her dad covered it up? Why would he lie? It sounds to me like he knew a lot more than he was letting on."

"Doesn't it? It also sounds like he was a lot closer to Sister Jane than just attorney and defendant. The fight Sadie told us about sounded personal."

"And she had no idea?"

"No, she still doesn't. I only started to put it together last night. But I'm not about to accuse her dead father of what—being a snake handler and covering for a murderer? Not until I have proof, solid proof."

"Good call. That information could be potentially devastating. Girls don't have a tendency to date men who destroy the only happy memories they have of their fathers."

"That's why I'll let the evidence do the talking. I just have to find it first. Mom and Dad told me a lot last night—mostly the small-town gossip, but it might be useful."

"Gossip has to start somewhere, and the strangest fiction usually comes from fact. So okay, spill." Mike poured another cup of coffee, leaned back in his chair, and propped his feet up on Dan's kitchen table. "I'm all ears."

It didn't take Dan long to bring Mike up to speed on what he'd learned at dinner the night before. "Sadie offered to dig through her father's files for us and see if she can find something, but I'm not sure I want her going anywhere, especially alone."

"No, she shouldn't. You sure she'll wait? Sadie's pretty headstrong."

"She ... actually she said she wanted to go alone. Give me a sec." Dan hit the speed dial for his parents and waited for the phone to be answered. "Mom, can I talk to Sadie? She did? When? Okay, thanks." Then turning back to Mike, he said, "She already left. She promised to turn around or call if anything felt the least bit off." Dan briefly contemplated going to get her but then changed his mind. He didn't want her to feel like he was hovering, which is exactly what he would be doing and he knew it. He wanted to protect her, but he knew she was too independent to ask for it. He also had a feeling that if he pushed too hard he might just push her away. As vulnerable as she had been lately he knew that underneath was a core of iron and that she was used to doing things her own way and on her own. Begrudgingly Dan sat down again and returned to the files.

"Hey, let me see that picture again. The group shot?" Mike said, suddenly sitting up straight, the front legs of his chair landing hard on the floor with a resounding thud shaking Dan out of his worried revelry over Sadie.

"What have you got?" Dan slid the picture in front of him.

"Well, I was thinking ..." Mike looked hard at the picture and then rooted through the case file until he found what he was looking for, another picture, and silently compared them for several long seconds side by side. "What do you think? Do we have a match?" He slid the pictures in front of Dan. Even though the pictures were a lifetime apart in years, there was no doubt that Mary Doyle, the murder victim in St. Louis, was one and the same as Sister Jane.

"Good work, but we still don't know why he's targeting Sadie?"

"Give me a break; I can't do all the work," Mike complained good-naturedly.

"According to her social security number, Mary Doyle died a long time ago," Dan continued reading from the file. "Looks like a little case of identity theft." One of the muscles above Dan's left eye started twitching, and he massaged it a little. This always happened when he became stressed.

"I seriously doubt that Sister Jane was her real name either," Mike said. Neither man had expected to find the missing clue in these pages, but the more roadblocks they incurred, the more frustrating it became.

"According to the tox report, along with the venom in her system they found strychnine, and shoved down her throat they found a page from the Bible. Whoa, this is just not right." Mike read silently for a moment.

Dan narrowed his eyes. "Your life expectancy is growing shorter by the second."

"Listen to this quote from Mark."

"Mark?"

"As in from the Bible, not Mark the used car salesman from Johnsonville. Mark 16:18 of the King James Bible says, 'They shall take up serpents; and if they drink any deadly thing, it shall not hurt them; they shall lay hands on the sick, and they shall recover.'"

"I'll stick with Mark the used car salesman. He's chatty, but no snakes. I wonder why Doug didn't mention this when Chief Baxter called?"

"Maybe he called before they found her. If he did, there would have been no way to connect the dots."

"Yeah, but what about after they found her. Don't tell me they all forgot about the chief's call. It just doesn't seem like Doug." Dan was visibly upset by the inconsistency.

"Call him."

"Partner, you're readin' my mind." Dan dialed Doug's cell number from memory and paced while he waited for an answer.

"Doug, it's Dan. Yeah, I've got it right here. Thanks again. Look, I've got a question for you..."

"So?" Mike looked at Dan expectantly when he rejoined him at the table.

"Doug says hey."

"Hey back."

"And that he did take what the chief told him to heart, but it looks like he was the only one. By the time they found the quote and figured out what it meant, the killer had already left town, so basically..."

"Basically, they're dumping him in our laps. Good riddance and Godspeed," Mike finished for Dan.

"Not Doug's call," Dan added.

"But it's why they were so willing to share all of their files."

"Probably, plus they are really busy," Dan sounded less than convincing. "And we have more man power to devote to the case on a full-time basis."

"Okay, so they have washed their hands of it completely, and we have a lunatic on our hands. What do we do now?" Mike smiled sarcastically.

"We connect the dots—fast," Dan said, putting on another pot of coffee.

"Who do you think this guy is? A fellow snake handler?"

"Or a snake handler's kid."

"The dark-haired boy from Sadie's dreams?"

Dan hadn't shared everything, but that seemed too important not to share. He hoped Sadie would forgive him if she ever found out. "Exactly."

"Well, he'd be about your age, maybe a little younger. Do you remember any kids like that in school?" Mike asked.

"No, not ever remotely, but I had the same thought. Last night I looked through my old year books back as far as first grade. Nothing."

"What about birth certificates?"

"It would be like looking for a needle in a haystack without at least a little more information to go on."

"Let's hope we find it soon."

"I've got a call into Doc Conway. I'm hoping maybe he'll be able to shed some light on it."

"Anything else on Sister Jane?"

"Not much," Dan said, refilling both mugs with fresh, steaming coffee. "Dad remembers she was a beautiful woman, a girl really, when she moved here. In the beginning she was seen as a delicate, homeless waif, and many people felt sorry for her, bought her clothes, and gave her food and money. Then she started preaching from some rundown old shack at the far end of town. Mom and Dad said they even checked out her service one night, but it was too full of hellfire and brimstone for them, so they left and never thought about it again. At that point, she hadn't picked up snakes yet, or if she had, they weren't part of the sermon that night because Mom and Dad would have remembered something like that."

"So what happened?"

"From what Dad could remember, as soon as she introduced the snakes, most of her regular following got spooked and stopped going. She was no longer seen as harmless by the community. Eventually, she moved out into the woods, only showing up in town when she needed supplies, and then not at all. It seemed she became something of a town pariah and was considered a first-class outcast. If people continued going to her services, they did it in secret because attendance at St. Michael's went back up."

"I can't believe this happened here. Crystal Springs just doesn't seem the type of place to breed a cult of any kind, unless it involves shopping and caffeine."

"Bear in mind that all of this 'information' is basically small-town gossip at its best. There's no real way of knowing what really happened in that church unless we can find someone who actually attended the services."

"What's the chance of that?"

"Finding someone who went to the church? Possibly. Getting them to talk...well, I doubt that would be as easy."

"Why do you say that?"

"Apparently, after she left town, people stopped speaking of her altogether; it was as if she had never existed."

"Small towns have a great way of doing that with things they don't want to acknowledge, but what about the suicides?"

"She was questioned but had airtight alibis for every one."

"How did they die?"

Dan pulled out the newspaper article from Rocco's "box of ideas" and passed it to him.

Mike skimmed the page. "Not a lot to go on. Without more proof, there is no way to know that all of these weren't suicides."

"That's an awful lot of suicides for a small congregation," Dan said, raising an eyebrow.

"Not when you compare it to Jim Jones."

"Good point. I might buy that theory if there wasn't a lunatic on the rampage leaving a snake's rattle behind as a calling card."

"Well, if we are going to make a real connection, we're going to need a lot more to go on than one inflammatory piece of journalism."

"Yeah, I hope we find it fast."

"You don't sound hopeful," Mike said.

"I'm not."

CHAPTER 43

10:21 a.m.

Sadie stood deep inside the columned porch of her father's Greek revival home—her childhood home—for what seemed like ages, working up the courage to go inside. As a child she'd always loved standing here amongst the many Doric-topped columns that graced the front of the house. But now the house seemed sad and austere, and she longed for the whimsical fancy of Birdie's Victorian. Or was she just afraid to go inside? There was only one way to find out. It wasn't fear, she reasoned, as much as a deep penetrating sadness that made her hesitate. By opening that simple red door, with the graceful curve at the top and the lion-head doorknocker, one that she had picked out at the age of eleven, she would be opening a door in her heart that she had managed to keep closed for what seemed a lifetime. Inside these walls lived a lifetime of memories— memories of a girl, and memories the woman wasn't sure she was ready to face. As soon as that door opened, she would have to face all of the emotions she'd kept tightly bottled up, and she was afraid to do that. She was afraid that once she started crying, she would never stop. By never coming home and never selling the house, she'd managed to keep this part of her life in a sort of stasis, never having to truly deal with it.

"I'm home," she said, her voice hollow with sadness and choking back a wave of grief as she opened the door to her past.

Sadie expected to feel overwhelmed with emotion and deeply, tragically sad as she stepped across the threshold, but to her surprise she felt something completely different. She felt comforted.

Although the house smelled musty after a decade of inertia, when she walked into the kitchen, she could almost smell the sweet scent of homemade coffeecake fresh out of the oven from a recipe she had struggled over to please her father. The cake had been dry and not so sweet, but her father had loved it, or said he had. Sadie smiled at the memory. Her father had been an excellent liar; she could still taste the terrible cake today, but he ate every last bit of it.

In the breakfast nook she could see herself sitting at the sunny kitchen table reading a Nancy Drew/Hardy Boys mystery and her father across from her reading the paper. It had been a Sunday tradition, breakfast around the table, no television, and no talk of work, bills, or chores—just them. Her father had called it "The Church of the Family." For reasons never truly explained to her, they had never gone to church on Sundays with the rest of the town, instead spending the time together alone, as a family. "Why didn't we go to church?" Sadie said, breaking the spell and dissolving the memory that for a few seconds had seemed so real.

Walking from room to room, she stopped to look at photographs. Most of them were of her, smiling and laughing. There were many more of her mother, pictures that Sadie knew by heart. Even though she had never met her mother, she knew every line of her face intimately. Over the years, Sadie had studied these pictures, trying to find similarities between them. Her mother had long hair, dark like her father's, with deep soulful brown eyes and a thin athletic body and a hint of mischievousness behind her eyes and in her smile. But she looked nothing like Sadie, and this had always bothered her. Her father had explained that she looked exactly like his grandmother, although he was never able to produce a single photograph of her.

Over and over, her heart swelled to the point that she thought surely it would burst inside her chest. Long-forgotten memories came flooding back, washing over her, each of them a like a gigantic hug from the past. Instead of being overwhelmed with grief, she was overcome with a feeling of love, and she couldn't believe she'd waited so long to come home again.

He slept fitfully on the bare, moth-eaten mattress, an old sleeping bag thrown over him for warmth. In his dreams he saw her in a house—one that he remembered from childhood—one that he had never been allowed inside. She was happy. He could feel it. She was happy and she was in love, and at that moment he hated her more than he'd ever hated her before. "Laugh now, because soon you die," he promised. Soon his demons would be hers, and she would know each and every one intimately before she died.

CHAPTER 44

10:35 a.m.

Across town Dr. John Conway pushed the remnants of his breakfast around on the plate with his fork. Before he had been ravenous; now the look of the food made his stomach churn relentlessly. He'd been up almost all night, restless and unable to sleep, then when he had finally slept it had seemed as if he'd been drugged. He woke late, and that irritated him, but he had nowhere to go, not this morning, so he'd decided that a feast would help. It had been a mistake.

He was anxious, restless, and scared. Those feelings gnawed at him as if they had somehow manifested into something more, something real and dark, and something that might eat him alive from the inside out. Cooking and eating had produced a sort of cathartic effect, and for a short time the angry worm in his gut had been satiated, but already he could feel it stirring again. For the first time in a very long time he considered adding a healthy shot of bourbon to his morning coffee.

It had been well after two o'clock in the morning before he'd dragged himself, heavy of mind and heart, through the front door and upstairs to bed. After leaving the crime scene the previous morning, he'd gone directly to his office where he'd performed an autopsy on the second close friend that week. Once home, he laid in bed awake, the disembodied voices of the victims, past and present, shouting accusations at him from all sides. He'd tossed and turned in a vain attempt to lose his accusers. To make them stop. But the voices kept raging in his head until finally he'd awakened more tired than he'd been before lying down. John sat on the edge of his bed, his head in his hands and rubbed his temples against the pain. He couldn't quite grasp the tenuous dreams that had plagued him throughout the early morning hours, their unrelenting anguish had left him feeling hung over. Now showered and fed, the large breakfast he'd felt that he wanted, needed, and deserved sat heavy in his stomach.

Dishes done, he took his coffee and sat in his favorite chair in the living room. The house was quiet, save for the noises of the furnace. It was too quiet, and not for the first time, he thought about adopting a dog.

Finally alone with his thoughts and nothing to distract him, he allowed his attention to focus on what was really bothering him. Staring out the window, but not seeing the scene beyond, instead seeing the faces of friends—of the victims—he knew what the voices were trying to tell him: these murders were in a way his fault, as were the deaths that had plagued their peaceful little town so long ago. Even though he had never lifted a finger to harm another, even though he had lived his life as a healer, he couldn't help but feel responsible.

He hadn't thought about Sister Jane in years, and he hadn't wanted to. Now racked with guilt, he picked up a picture of his ex-wife Sally and cried. It had been his act of adultery that had caused her to leave him. But it wasn't just the adultery, and he knew that. The memories of his past life were almost too painful to bear. He was a different man now than he had been then, but he knew that no amount of atonement would ever make up for his mistakes.

CHAPTER 45

12:00 p.m.

"The second victim was one Alice Brown, fifty-three, lived in St. Louis, a librarian for the last thirty years, and never married. There's nothing remarkable here, except that, hold on ..." Dan scanned the paper again quickly.

"Well," Mike prompted.

"It fits. She spent the first thirty years of her life about twenty miles from here off Route Z, and looky here." Dan pointed to the woman to the right of Sister Jane in the tattered photo found in Birdie's bedroom. "That's her."

"Does it say exactly when she made a break for the big city?" Mike stood up and stretched a little while Dan continued to look over the file.

"No, but that doesn't necessarily mean anything. How many people don't leave the area for greener pastures?"

"That aren't filled with cow manure," Mike added.

"Yeah."

"The third victim," Mike read from the file, "was Charles Lafayette, a lawyer who lived and practiced in St. Louis. He was fifty-six years old at the time of his death. He left an ex-wife, two kids, and a girlfriend young enough to be his daughter in the middle of a heated legal battle over alimony and wills. Says here he wanted to amend his will to leave everything to his new girlfriend, and his wife was contesting it in court."

"Sounds like she had plenty of reasons to want him dead. Are they sure he was done by our guy?"

"They found a rattle, so unless there is a leak in the St. Louis police, there is no way it's a copycat."

"I guess the girlfriend will have to find another sugar daddy," Dan said. "Is there anything in there connecting him to the area?"

"He was born and raised just outside of Johnsonville. He didn't move to St. Louis until 1991."

"Funny, that's exactly when Sister Jane's little cult went kablooie."

"And if I'm not mistaken, he's in the picture too. Look."

"Add a full head of hair and take away fifty pounds, and you've got a dead ringer."

"Okay, number four, come on down," Mike said without humor. "What have you got?"

"Michael Dallas, a lifer with the Forest Service, divorced, no kids."

"Mickey Dallas?" Mike looked as if he'd been slapped. "Let me see that."

"You know this guy?"

"Maybe, is there a picture?"

"Yeah, here ya go." Dan handed the photo to his partner.

"That's him, that's MD," Mike said.

"How could you possibly know him? He's, what, fifteen years older than you are?"

"My dad was a Forest Service ranger, and he ran the station up at the Springs. MD worked for him for a while. I hung out there all the time and thought he was pretty cool, kind of followed him around a lot."

"What happened to him?"

"MD had a penchant for—of course—rattlesnakes. It seemed so cool then, but now—"

"Not so much," Dan said.

"Not by a long shot. Anyway he was showing off one day in front of me and a couple of the other kids that hung out up there. Looking back on it now, I guess he was ... er, snake handling. Dad walked in, caught him, and fired him on the spot." Mike shrugged at the memory. "Makes me wonder what exactly Dad knew."

"You mean if he fired him for putting you in a potentially deadly situation, or because he found out MD was part of Sister Jane's group of fangy friends?"

"Or both," Mike said.

"Would your mom know?" Mike's dad had died of cancer a few years back.

"No, we never told her about it."

"Is MD in this picture?" Dan indicated the group shot.

"No, but that doesn't surprise me. Mickey hated having his picture taken. He told me that it was because he was wanted by the cops down in the Caymans for something and he had to keep a low profile."

"More likely he was wanted a lot closer to home. Good role model, Mike."

"What can I say, he drove a Harley. So, what does it say about the fifth victim?" Mike said.

"Marie St. Dubois, fifty-five, worked in a flower shop, no family, lived alone. Nothing remarkable about her either. Except that she volunteered at the zoo in the—get this—snake house and, yep ..." Dan consulted the photo once again. "Here she is." For a moment the two were silent. "If I had to venture a guess, I'd say that these are the only cult members that moved to St. Louis and that if we tracked the rest of them down—"

"They'd all be dead too, but the cases are in so many various jurisdictions that no one's put it together yet." Mike said.

"It's a safe bet. We need to track down the boy."

"The one with the dark hair? We don't even know if he truly existed."

"He did. I'm sure of it. I just can't prove it. Doesn't your mom work at the orphanage outside of town?" Dan looked up.

"St. Agnes, yeah. What makes you think he was an orphan?"

"Call it a hunch. I don't think he was necessarily an orphan, but... abandoned."

CHAPTER 46

2:07 p.m.

Sadie woke from her nap disoriented. For a minute she thought she was still dreaming: she was in her parents' bedroom on their bed, their wedding picture in her hand. Dried tears itched her cheeks; then she remembered coming home. She hadn't meant to fall asleep; looking at the clock, she realized that she'd been out for hours. It was the best sleep she remembered having in a long time.

Getting off the bed, she took a moment to straighten the pillows and kiss the picture before placing it back on the nightstand. She'd been at the house longer than anticipated, and her stomach was beginning to rumble, but she still hadn't searched her father's study.

Downstairs, she went straight to the study. It was a beautifully appointed room; the walls above the dark wood wainscoting were papered in a tartan plaid, floor-to-ceiling mahogany bookcases lined three walls, and a huge two-person desk, the top of which was inlaid with leather, took up a large portion of the space.

Sadie's father had always had a flair for the dramatic, which is one of the reasons he was a superb courtroom attorney; he loved the pomp and flourish of a trial. However, his taste for drama didn't end there. In his study, he'd had a secret room built in behind one of the bookcases, and this was where he kept his files.

By pulling on a book entitled *Hidden Treasures,* a mechanism was triggered that opened the door in a whoosh. Sadie had loved playing in here as a little girl; the secret room fueling many spy fantasies when she was younger. Now, pulling on the book, she felt like she was a young girl again, opening the door to the unknown. The room, as well as the whole house, smelled a little musty, but it didn't detract from the wonderful, mysterious little room. Along one wall were more mahogany file drawers; along the opposite wall was nothing but shelves and cubbyholes for storage. And along the back wall was another door—this one led to the wine cellar that held her father's extensive collection of wines, many of which were inherited from his father, who had been a true connoisseur. Standing in "the room of mysteries," the name she'd dubbed it years ago, she again wondered why it had been so long since she'd come home, and she realized that she could never sell this amazing house.

She didn't know the woman's last name. All she had was Jane, so she decided she'd start there. Pulling open the drawer marked *J,* she thumbed through the files to the place where the file should have been. Nothing. Next she looked under *S* for Sister; nothing again. Finally, she even tried *C* for church or cult, then *S* again for snakes. Slamming the drawer, frustrated, she couldn't think of anywhere else to look.

"I know you had files on this, Dad. Where did you hide them?" she said, as she walked back out of the hidden room into the study and sat in his chair. Staring into the multitude of colors in the beautiful Tiffany lamp on the desk, she thought for a moment. This lamp had always been one of her favorite things; as a child she would sit for hours starting at it, fantasizing that the pieces of colored glass were really expensive gems that held the keys to mysterious wonders and wealth beyond imagination. Was it possible that he'd gotten rid of the files? After all, he'd dropped the case. Staring into the lamp's gemlike glass designs, she had almost convinced herself that the files didn't exist and was about to switch off the light when something caught her eye. A shape, in the glass, something that shouldn't be there. Vaguely outlined underneath one of the dragonfly's bodies was a key. Well-concealed, it was difficult to see. With her right hand she reached under the shade, and extracted the anomaly. A three-inch-long skeleton key. Key in hand, she settled back into the plush leather chair, turning the key over in her hand. while mentally comparing it with all of the doors in the house. There was only one she could think of that was a logical fit: it was deep in the bowels of the wine cellar. It was the key to a room she'd never actually been in. Her father's reason for keeping it locked was that it was unsafe and dirty in there, although he'd never specified an exact danger. A few times as a teenager, when curiosity and boredom had gotten the best of her, she'd tried to pick the lock; but she'd never succeeded in gaining access. Eventually, boys became the focus of her attention and the room had remained untouched and forgotten, until today.

But the house was hers now and, by default, so was whatever he was hiding. Sadie stood and pocketed the key.

Before heading to the wine cellar, she went out to her car and grabbed her emergency flashlight, testing it to make sure it still worked. As she walked back to the house, a sudden gust of cold air sprang up; a myriad of dead leaves swirling around her in a macabre dance. She shivered and picked up the pace until she was safely inside, slamming the door against the elements outside. A storm was brewing; of that she was sure.

The door to the wine cellar opened easily with a slight hiss as cold stale air wafted out. She felt inside along the wall for the light switch; soft yellow lights flickered on in the many sconces that lined the walls, giving the subterranean room a rather gothic ambiance. Her father's flare for the dramatic once again gave Sadie a half smile. Crossing the threshold into the cellar and descending the stairs, she felt a sense of anticipation rising in her. What was hidden behind that locked door? Would it turn out to be nothing but decades-old cans of paint and chemicals that her father hadn't wanted her getting into and possibly swallowing as a child? Tools and other things that could have lopped off a finger, if used improperly? Or was it something else?

Walking through the labyrinth of racks holding countless bottles of wine, Sadie noted the thick coating of dust and webs that had accumulated among the bottles. Along the way, a few of the bulbs flickered in their sockets, threatening to burn out, and she hoped that they lasted until she was gone before going out completely. Even though she had a flashlight, she preferred not to have to use it.

The door was simple but sturdy. A tarnished brass knob and lock were all the decoration that adorned it. A large, intricate spider web covered the top right-hand corner of the door, its inhabitant not home at the moment. "Sorry, spider," Sadie said knocking the web away with her hand and then wiping it on her jeans. She took the key out of her pocket. Holding her breath slightly, she inserted the key into the lock; it was a perfect fit. Inside the room was pitch black. She couldn't see past the threshold, the dim light from the cellar barely penetrating the gloom inside. Not knowing whether there was another switch inside, she felt her hand along the walls on both sides of the door, trying not to think about the multitudes of creepy crawlers that would love to inhabit a room like that. After the third try, she found a switch and flipped it up and down. Nothing.

"Of course." Sadie sighed and switched on the flashlight and shone the light around the room, its beam bouncing off of crates and candles. A small table sat against the far wall, and above it hung a golden cross.

"What the...?" That was the last thing she'd expected. Stunned, Sadie walked deeper into the room, using her flashlight to closely examine everything. The room was smallish, longer than it was wide. She assumed it must have been a fruit cellar at one time, before it had been turned into...an...*altar*. Lining the wall to her right were various crates and boxes; she made a mental note to pull them out into the light later to have a good look inside. But for now, she was drawn to the front of the room. The table, a small handcrafted one of unstained wood, held several white candles, an incense burner with the remains of incense still in it, a silver bowl, and a match book. It looked innocent enough.

Above the small altar hung an inordinately large cross of gold, which (although dulled by years of dust) still cast a dim gleam in the reflected beam of her meager light. Something appeared to be draped across the top of it. At first she thought it was probably just a cobweb, but as she looked longer, she realized that it was far too dense to be constructed of the gossamer strands secreted by a spider. She climbed up on the altar. As she straightened up, standing eye level with the cross, she carefully shone her light from the bottom up until it illuminated the object of curiosity . . . a snake's skin.

She reached out a tentative hand, half convinced that she was imagining it, and half hoping that once she touched the papery-looking skin, it would indeed dissolve into nothing but a cleverly designed web. When she touched it, it did crumble, but it was definitely something shed, not woven. Her mind seemed to shut down then and, stumbling off the table, she knocked off a picture that she hadn't noticed before. Stooping, still dazed, she picked it up and wiped the years of accumulated dust from the glass surface. The picture showed her father naked from the waist up, a rattlesnake in each hand and a look she had never seen before—one of unrivaled power—etched onto his face. Numb with disbelief, Sadie dropped the picture, only vaguely aware of the sound of the glass breaking as it hit the floor. She wanted to believe that none of this made any sense, but it did, and suddenly after all this time, the unexplained became explained, and the puzzle pieces finally started falling into place. Her rational mind, along with the little girl in her, wanted to disbelieve what she had seen, what was all around her, but the woman in her understood and felt resentment.

"He was a disciple of that nut job?" Sadie said loudly, suddenly wishing for a corkscrew. Right now, she felt like drinking everything in the wine cellar. Walking aimlessly back through the racks of wine bottles, she ceased to notice the spiders that scurried out of her path and the webs that clung to her clothes and hair. Her brain was on overload, and she needed to move, but she also needed to find out what else was in that room.

"What in the hell were you thinking, Dad?!" she yelled at the room. Bits and pieces of memories, of fights between her and her father, arguments, admonishments, and guilt flashed through her head, making her dizzy. Finally she stopped and, breathing deeply, tilted her head up toward the ceiling. "Well, Dad, you can't hide your secrets anymore." Walking back into the secret room with purpose in her stride, she began pulling its contents out into the light of the wine cellar one by one, examining each item as she went.

The first two boxes were heavy oak and topped with a thick wire mesh and a hinge at one end that acted as a lid or door. Inside each box was the body of a mature rattlesnake, now long deceased and desiccated. The fangs gleamed wickedly in the lamplight. The other two boxes were of heavy cardboard, the type used to pack and carry produce, and they were stamped "St. James Orchard." She lifted the lid off of the first box. Files, papers, and notebooks, were all crammed together. A spider scurried across the back of her hand as she rummaged through the sheaves of paper, startling her. Knocking the spider off of her hand, she quickly smashed it with one of the notebooks. Studying the spider, she noticed the distinct fiddle shape on its back, the tale-tell marking of a brown recluse, a poisonous spider whose bite left a wound that didn't heal. Suppressing a shudder, she gingerly carried the boxes upstairs, hoping that the spider lived up to his name and was indeed a recluse.

CHAPTER 47

3:35 p.m.

"I've got you!" Evie said triumphantly to the empty lab. "Come on, Adam, how long can it take to go to the bathroom?" she called out, making careful notes of her findings. She was impatient for Adam to return so she could share her news with him: the long hours spent studying the evidence had finally paid off, and she was sure they had a solid lead.

In St. Louis the guy had been meticulously clean; no fingerprints or fibers had been found, even at the place he'd been staying. He'd painstakingly scoured the residence before leaving, as if saying to the cops, "Okay, I'm done here now. You can come in, but you won't find anything." For some reason, though, the guy had gotten sloppy in Crystal Springs, and she'd not only collected hair and clothing fibers but managed to lift several perfect fingerprints from Birdie's apartment that didn't belong there. Of course, the only reason they'd found those is because he hadn't finished there. Bad luck for him, great luck for her.

She likened collecting and analyzing evidence to a game she played as a child, "Which one of these things doesn't belong with the others?" She had been very good at the game. She was still very good at the game.

Now all that remained to do was wait for the print to finish running through the comparison process with the National Finger-print Database, which would take a while. But she knew this was it, the piece of evidence that would lead to an arrest.

Hearing a noise in the hall, she turned around excitedly looking for her partner. "Adam, get your butt in here," she yelled. Silence was her only response.

"Hey, are you okay?" She was starting to worry; he'd been gone for a long time.

Evie walked across the lab, her shoes squeaking a little as she crossed the linoleum floor. Stepping out into the deserted hallway that connected the lab from front to back, she looked up and down the utilitarian walkway. The building appeared to be empty, except for her. Turning to her left, she walked the twenty feet to the men's room door and knocked lightly. "Adam, you okay?" When she got no response, she began to wonder if she'd only imagined hearing him. She started to move away from the door when she heard "Evie, go! Run!" from the other side of the door.

The hair on the back of her neck stood up when she heard his voice. It was weak but there was no mistaking what she'd heard.

"Adam?" She pushed on the door. "What's going on? Stop messing around." Her voice betrayed her uncertainty now, as she slowly eased the door open, "Oh my God! Adam!"

Evie rushed to Adam's side. He was on the floor wedged between the sink and the toilet, his six-foot-two frame making it a very tight fit for the small room. He'd been shot once in the neck. Evie realized that the gunman must have used a silencer, which is why she hadn't heard the gunshot. But she had heard something—or someone—in the hall outside the lab moments ago.

Adam was still alive, but barely.

"Hang in there, buddy, I'm not gonna let anything happen to you, I promise." Shrugging out of her lab coat, she covered him with it. Then, taking off her thin sweater, she tied it around his neck the best she could in an attempt to stanch the bleeding.

"Evie…no time…" Adam tried to warn her, but she cut him off.

"I'll get help. I won't be gone long." Evie only hoped she wasn't lying to her friend; she knew damn well that there was a good chance the killer was still in the building.

Evie grasped the door handle, her hand sweating, and pulled it open an inch. She peered up and down the hall; it was empty. All she had to do was get back into the lab, and she could lock herself in, call for help, and wait for the cavalry to arrive. The trip across the hall took an instant, but felt like a lifetime. She shivered and wondered whether it was a result of her growing fear or the fact that she now wore only a thin cotton T-shirt. She was certain it was the former and not the latter that was making goose bumps grow on her tender flesh. Pressing her face against the small glass window in the door of her lab, she surveyed the room. It appeared empty, but, there were many blind spots from this vantage point. Opening the door a crack at first and then wider, she was relieved to see that the room did indeed appear unoccupied. Hurrying in, she was halfway through the room when she saw him. The sight of him caused her to stop dead in her tracks. She had to stifle a scream that welled in her throat with a fierce urgency.

He was in her office, which was separated from the rest of the lab by only a partition of glass. He must have been in the file room, which is why she hadn't seen him before. If he turned around right now he would see her and she would be dead. Dropping to her knees behind the counter, which stood more than waist high, she quickly weighed her options. He was no doubt collecting any and all evidence on himself and destroying it. The reports and all of her findings were in her office; there was no way she would be able to get to them.

From her hiding place behind the counter, all was quiet. The only noises in the building were those of the police scanner she kept on at all times when she was in the building and the pounding of her heart. Her heart, she would swear, was the louder of the two.

She needed a phone, and she needed to get out of the building. Her cell and her gun were in her office with her purse and the killer, but Adam's cell, she knew, was always in the right-front pocket of his pants. She mentally kicked herself for not thinking about it earlier. Rising to her feet but staying low and keeping the high lab counter between them at all times, she crept stealthily across the lab, pausing only at the end of the counter. The door to the hall was only five feet away now, but it was five feet of open space with nothing to hide behind. Suddenly that small space seemed like an ocean. Mustering her courage and saying a prayer, she slowly edged her face around the side of the counter; his back was still turned to her. It was now or never. As fast as she could, Evie crab-walked to the door and managed to reach the hallway without incident, breathing a sigh of relief when the door shut silently behind her. She crossed the hall quickly and was relieved to see that Adam was still alive, though barely. "Hold on, buddy, you're gonna be fine," she said with more conviction than she felt. Fishing in his pocket, she retrieved his phone and quickly flipped it open—no signal. She would have to move. She snuck back out the door; she hadn't been in the bathroom for more than thirty seconds, and the hall was still clear. Being closer to the back door than the front, she hurried along the hall, fighting the urge to run. Running would make too much noise, and the last thing she wanted to do was let the killer know where she was.

Nagging doubts played at the corners of her mind; it had been almost too easy so far. Why hadn't he come after her as soon as he'd shot Adam? Her back had been turned and with the scanner on in her office, she wouldn't have heard much anyway. He could have easily snuck up on her. Maybe he thought she wasn't a threat or hadn't realized she was there, she reasoned with herself. Reaching the back door without incidence, she grasped the knob, turned and pushed; the door wouldn't budge. Pushing hard again, she tried to force it, but to no avail. It was stuck, blocking her escape. Somehow he'd jimmied the door.

She faltered for only a moment then turned and ran as fast as she could for the front of the building, only to discover that the front doors were barred as well, locked and chained, trapping her inside with him.

He was playing a sick game of cat and mouse, and she was the prey. She knew she had only seconds before he would emerge from the lab, seconds until she was dead … or worse. Risking everything she broke her silence, flipped open Adam's cell, and called Mike, realizing that the killer might hear her and come for her now. She prayed Mike was close enough to help her.

CHAPTER 48

3:49 p.m.

Dan was getting frustrated; although the trip to St. Agnes had not been a complete waste of time, he still had no real leads on who the black-haired boy was. Mike's mom had been there in the eighties and did remember a boy fitting the description coming to stay with them for a while. He was non-talkative, skittish, and overly sensitive. He also got kicked out for torturing and killing the house cat. But then he didn't really get kicked out—he ran away and as far as she knew, the authorities never found him.

But that was as far as the help went. He was a ward of the state. He had refused to give them a name. He said his name was Boy. The search for his parents came to a dead end. He was as much a mystery then as he was now. The only clear thing was that Dan knew in his gut that this was in fact the same boy from Sadie's visions—and the killer.

They were no closer to catching the killer than before they had started. "I hope Evie calls soon and with some good news." Just then Mike's cell phone rang, shattering the silence.

"Speak of the devil." Mike flipped his phone open and answered. "Hey, Adam-?"

"Mike, help me!" The urgency in Evie's whispered voice made the hairs on Mike's body stand on end.

"What is it?" Mike motioned to Dan.

"He's here. He's in the lab. Mike, he shot Adam, and he's jimmied the locks on the doors. I can't get out." The panic in her voice manifested itself into a cold rock in the pit of Mike's stomach.

"Stay with me," Mike said, putting the call on speaker phone so Dan could hear. "Where is he now?" At these words, Dan's eyes widened and he jammed the accelerator to the floor.

"He's in the lab, in my office," Evie whispered.

"Where are you?" Mike said over the sound of the engine racing.

"In the atrium. He's done something to the doors so I can't get out. Mike, he's going to kill me."

"No, he's not."

"911?" Dan asked.

"Did you call 911?" Mike relayed the question, as Dan sped down the highway swerving between motorists slow to get out of his path.

"No, the scanner's on in the lab. He'd hear the call." Mike could hear the unmistakable sound of tears choking her words.

"Okay, good thinking. Can you get to the tunnel?" Mike was thinking of the old underground passage between the lab and the main portion of the defunct pharmaceutical company's main office building.

"I think so." She swallowed hard, trying to sound calmer than Mike knew she was.

"Go now! We're almost there. We'll meet you. *Go!*" Even though they were close, the last few miles that separated them seemed vast. "Faster!" Mike commanded Dan.

The lab, a single-story building, set off by itself at the end of a one-way street, had at one time been the lab facility for a pharmaceutical company that had called Crystal Springs its home for a few years until heavy competition had driven it into bankruptcy. The company had erected an underground tunnel for employees to use in case of dangerous storms and also as a means to provide a higher level of secrecy for their projects. Although Dan had been in St. Louis when the company had closed, Mike was in college and had been in the tunnel many times for parties. It was in this tunnel years ago that Mike had first met Evie and where he hoped to find her now, very much alive. With regret, Mike ended the phone call with Evie as Dan dialed the chief's private number. Not wanting to alert the intruder to Evie's position, he also avoided calling 911, sure that the chief would move heaven and hell to get backup to them.

Pulling up to the main building, not the lab, Dan threw the car into park, and both he and Mike exploded from the vehicle at a dead run across the concrete portico that led to the building's main entrance. Pulling his gun as he ran, Mike fired at the locking mechanism, literally blowing the doors open.

Without words, the partners slipped into the building with Mike at the lead, on their way to the tunnel and whatever lay beyond.

CHAPTER 49

3:53 p.m.

Tucking the phone into the pocket of her jeans, Evie took a deep breath, wiped the tears from her eyes, and started down the hall, which although somewhat short, now seemed impossibly long.

She couldn't believe she hadn't thought of the tunnel herself. If she could get there, she might have a chance. The only problem was that the door to the basement and the tunnel was back at the opposite end of the hall, and to get there she would again have to pass the lab and him, and she wondered if her luck would hold out for a third and final voyage down the hall.

Tears of terror streaming down her cheeks, she crept back out into the hall on shaky legs; blessedly, it was still empty. Going as quickly as she could and still as quietly as possible, she was just about to pass the lab when the door flew open in front of her and a man with a sickening, malevolent grin on his face stepped out into the hall, a gun leveled at her chest, her files—with all of his information—tucked under his arm.

Pumped up by adrenaline and fearing that she was already dead, Evie surprised both herself and the killer by speeding up instead of slowing down. As the adrenaline coursed through her veins as never before, she had only one thought: *Live!* A second before impact, she dove to the floor, sliding between his legs, her arms outstretched and her hands clasped firmly in front of her. Using years of aggressive volleyball games as training, she hit him in the crotch harder than she had ever set a volleyball. Letting out a howl of surprise and pain, he fell to the ground just as she cleared his legs with her own. Sheets of paper from the files flew everywhere, and she thought she heard the gun fall as well; however, she didn't stop to find out. Self-preservation fueling her, she was up on her feet and running in an instant, not bothering to turn around, knowing that she had only given herself a few precious moments, and even those might not be enough.

Evie spun around the corner, just as something stung her shoulder, not unlike that of an angry hornet, and realized that he'd shot at her even though she hadn't heard it, the bullet grazing her shoulder. She felt her undershirt become sticky with blood. Yanking open the door to the basement, she pulled it shut behind her, and thumbed the lock into place, even though she knew it wouldn't keep him at bay for long, but if she was lucky, it would be long enough for her to get safely through the tunnel and into the vast warren of empty buildings on the other side.

The tunnel was pitch black, and Evie briefly considered switching on the light but opted against it. Instead she grabbed the emergency flashlight at the top of the stairs and ran.

Running as fast as she could, she tried not to think about how her shoulder stung and throbbed where the bullet had grazed her. She tried not to think about the blood she was losing. She tried not to think about the fact that she'd just been shot.

Remnants of parties past littered the ground, and graffiti on the walls around her flickered by in the bobbing beam of her flashlight. The tunnel was long, the length of a football field from end to end, and she was about halfway through when she heard the door open with a crash. Stifling a scream, she turned off the flashlight, plunging herself into a Stygian darkness.

"Fee fi fo fum," the voice of the killer reverberated through the darkened tunnel, echoing off the walls and sending chills down her spine.

"I smell the blood of a pesky lab rat." He switched on the light at the top of the stairs, flooding the tunnel with fluorescent light. Never before had Evie hated light so much. The killer let loose a barrage of bullets, many of them nowhere near to hitting her, instead ricocheting off of the concrete walls and imploding the lights above. He wasn't taking time to aim. He was lost to anger, and it showed in his marksmanship.

Adrenaline exploding in her bloodstream, she ran faster than she ever thought possible, reaching the stairs at the other end in record time. She was up the stairs and just about to yank open the door to escape when a second bullet sliced into her back and sent her reeling backwards down the cold concrete stairs and into oblivion.

CHAPTER 50

4:02 p.m.

From the opposite side of the building, the guys, with Mike in the lead, were running down the hall from the main foyer when they heard a door slam in the bowels of the building so hard it reverberated throughout the building, followed by a scream.

"Evie!" Mike disappeared around the corner and into a stairwell.

The stairwell echoed the sounds of their heavy footfall on the concrete steps as they raced toward the basement. At the bottom of the stairs Mike stopped. A thin film of perspiration coated his creased brow as he eased open the door that led into the basement hallway. Looking in both directions, Mike said, "Clear," and slipped out with Dan close behind. "That's the door to the tunnel," Mike said, indicating a gray metal fire door off to the side about twenty feet down the hall. Once both men were positioned on either side of the door, Mike was about to open it when it started to open on its own. It stopped and they heard several soft thuds like a sack of potatoes falling down a staircase. Pulling the door open, Mike had a brief glimpse of Evie lying bloody at the bottom of the stairs.

Bullets from the killer's gun had shot out many of the lights and left others sparking in the otherwise Dantean darkness. Through the flickering dark, Dan could hear heavy footsteps approaching; they were walking, not running.

Mike flew down the stairs to Evie's side, flagrantly ignoring the imminent danger approaching stealthily from the darkened tunnel beyond.

Knowing that Mike was acting on impulse ruled by emotion, Dan took over. "Police, stop, or I'll shoot," he said as he leveled his gun at the approaching menace. The footsteps stopped, and for a long uneasy moment, nothing moved or made any sound. The killer was standing just outside the last area of illumination.

Just as Dan was beginning to wonder if the guy was going to give himself up, a bullet whizzed past him, impacting forcefully with the door jam, inches from his shoulder.

"Get down!" Dan cried, returning fire over Mike's head. Both men returned fire into the darkness, neither one knowing whether or not they'd hit their target. When the gunfire stopped, Dan heard the sound of a door swinging open at the other end of the tunnel. Racing down the stairs to join Mike, he saw blood bubbling from a wound in his partner's leg. "Get him!" Mike yelled, tearing off his jacket and shirt to make a tourniquet.

Grabbing Evie's flashlight, Dan sprinted down the length of the tunnel expelling his spent clip, and exchanging it for a fresh one. At the far end, taking the concrete steps two at a time, he hesitated at the closed, gray, metal, fire door.

Above him all was quiet. Dan eased the door open, and was about to slip through when an explosion rocked the building. A blast of overheated air surged through the gap created by the open door, knocking Dan down the stairs backwards.

Almost instantly black smoke began curling through the opening, tainting the already stale air and making it barely breathable. Back on his feet almost as soon as he landed, Dan sprinted back up the stairs and kicked the door closed, the air at the top of the stairs already thick and hot.

"Can you walk?" Dan yelled as he ran, reaching the couple and skidding to a halt. Looking down, he saw that if Mike's leg had been even one inch to the left, the bullet would have hit Evie's temple. "Can you walk?" he said again, panting.

"Do I have a choice?" Mike grabbed Dan's outstretched hand and hoisted himself up. "Take care of Evie. Don't let her die, just... don't let her die."

"I've got her."

"Hurry, the building's coming down!" Mike said, pointing to a large section of concrete ceiling just as it gave way and crashed into the cement floor with a resounding thud.

"Go!" Dan prodded Mike ahead of him, as he picked up the unconscious Evie. Hoisting her into a fireman's carry, he mounted the stairs after Mike, who was leaving a bloody trail in his wake.

In the stairwell Dan held on to Evie with one hand while he stabilized Mike with the other, gently urging him up the stairs. Although the air outside the tunnel was cleaner and he doubted the fire would be able to reach them on this side, he wouldn't be comfortable until they were all safely outside.

As they reached the first turn in stairs, another explosion rocked the lab, causing the stairs to swing and sway under the trio like a wooden suspension bridge. As the stairs bucked beneath them, Mike lost his footing and fell hard on his hands and knees. He looked back over his shoulder at Dan. "Get her out of here." Mike commanded, his face hard with determination and pain.

"We will," Dan said, shifting Evie to his left shoulder and hoisting his partner back up with one arm under his armpit. With Mike helping as much as he could, the three of them made it to the top of the stairs.

The doorway at the top of the stairs proved to be a problem. To get through the door, Dan would have to either let go of Mike or Evie, which was something he really didn't want to do. He was in the process of trying to fit through sideways without banging Evie's limp head when he felt a pair of strong arms lift part of her weight from him. Startled and with no hand free to go for his gun, Dan started to protest. "Hey..."

"Dan, it's okay, give her to me. You get Mike." It was Paul Bennett, a fellow officer, his partner Jen Mackey right beside him. With Dan relinquishing his hold on Evie, Paul took her easily and headed for the door and the waiting ambulance, while Jen sidled in next to Mike and helped support his weight until they were out of the building.

"You have no idea how glad I am to see you," Dan said to Jen as they hurried awkwardly along the hallway. Mike was growing weaker with every step from loss of blood.

"Why didn't you answer us?" Jen asked, shifting her weight under Mike to get a more secure hold.

"Didn't hear you. How long have you been here?"

"Not long, showed up right before the first explosion. We were all the way across town when the chief called, got here as fast as we could." Even though it seemed like hours had passed since heading into the basement, he realized that in reality less than ten minutes had passed. *Time crawls when you aren't having fun,* he thought.

CHAPTER 51

4:11 p.m.

Across town, Sadie had just finished hauling the heavy boxes of files upstairs and loaded them into her Jeep when she heard a succession of loud thuds in the distance and looked up, scanning the horizon. "What the ...?" She saw a black cloud of smoke rise above the tree line, billowing across the skyline to the east. Sirens in the distance pierced the air. Somewhere close by, a terrible fire was raging, and instinctively she knew that it was not a coincidence. Fighting the impulse to call Dan, she locked the car door and headed back to the orchard. Badly shaken by the recent discovery in her father's private room, she felt in serious need of company and help. For the first time in a very long time, she admitted to herself that she not only wanted to talk to people, she needed to. Since her parents' death, she'd prided herself on being a strong and independent woman who didn't need anyone. Not letting anyone get close made it much easier to keep her wounds from reopening. As she drove, she silently hoped that Anna, Rocco, and Dan would not judge her too harshly for whatever her father may have done.

Feeling herself near tears, she found herself looking forward to another go at the punching bag in Dan's loft.

CHAPTER 52

4:23 p.m.

Inside the ambulance, paramedics worked furiously on Evie while Mike watched from the sidelines, feeling helpless. His own leg, bandaged and sore, would no doubt heal in time, but it wasn't his leg he was worried about. Even though he was only separated from her by a few feet as they rocketed down the highway, Mike felt as if an ocean engulfed the space between them. He longed to hold her, to comfort her, but instead he looked on as the woman he loved clung tenuously to life. As the paramedics worked on Evie, Mike pulled a jeweler's box from deep within his jacket and opened it. Inside was a perfect solitaire diamond in the shape of a teardrop that he'd been holding onto for months, waiting for the "right time," but never quite finding it. Now with the woman he loved fighting for her life in front of him, he hoped he hadn't waited too long.

The trip to the hospital seemed to take forever, even though they weren't more than twenty minutes away. Once inside, Evie was rushed into emergency surgery while Mike was wheeled in another direction. The last image he had of her was the stretcher being wheeled into the operating room, the doors swinging shut behind her, effectively separating them; he'd never been more scared in his life.

CHAPTER 53

4:30 p.m.

Standing in the parking lot, filling a red-faced Chief Baxter in on the events leading up to the explosion, Dan found he couldn't take his eyes off of the burning building. Fire men and women from Crystal Springs fought the flames with a rare form of courage that Dan found inspiring. In the distance he heard the sirens and knew that the team from Johnsonville would soon arrive to help.

The entire building was engulfed in flames, and he wondered what the psychopath had used as an accelerant.

"This had to have been part of his plan all along," Dan said.

"Why the whole cat-and-mouse game? Why not just blow up the building at night when no one was around and he could come and go without a chance of being caught? Seems like he took an awfully big risk," Chief Baxter said as he shrugged out of his warm jacket, the fire making the day feel more like the height of August rather then early November.

"I think this is what he considers fun." Turning to look at the chief, Dan could see the flames of the inferno reflected off the other

man's glasses. "Chief," he said, "I think you're right about the connection to the snake handlers and Sister Jane."

"Well, you're the only one."

"Did this Sister Jane have a son?"

"If she did, she kept him a secret. Why?"

Without mentioning where he'd gotten the information on the
black-haired boy, he told the chief what they had found out about
him.

"It's weak at best. There is nothing truly connecting him to the
group."

Except for Sadie's visions, but even then Dan had no idea how
she was connected to the boy or the group. "It's the only lead we've
got right now too." Just then Jen Mackey ran up an excited flush on
her cheeks.

"We've found a blood trail leading into the woods," she said
breathlessly. "Looks like you wounded him."

"Show me," Dan said. The day was starting to look up.

The trail of blood through the trees was easy to follow as autumn
had done a thorough job of thinning the foliage on the trees
and shrubs. Bright crimson droplets glistened on leaves of gold,
orange, and brown, marking a clear path for the searchers to follow.
The path, although obvious, was treacherous due to the numerous
exposed roots and limestone rocks that protruded from the earth,
obscuring their way and making the going slow. The path stopped
abruptly at an old service road; though rarely used now, it once
served as a main thoroughfare for Wilson's Mill. The gristmill,
prosperous in the 1920s, had closed completely in the early '40s,
and despite numerous attempts to sell the land or reopen the mill,
the site sat vacant. Ghost stories circulated town every October,
and despite the law's best efforts, it was impossible to keep the area
clear of thrill-seeking, hormonally charged teenagers. Now the mill
looked less ominous and more like a perfect hideout.

Wilson's Road ran east to west. To the west was the river, to the east the highway; freshly made tire tracks imprinted in the soft earth led to the east.

"I want road blocks set up at every major intersection," Chief Baxter started issuing orders. "No one comes in or leaves Crystal Springs without going through a checkpoint. Issue a bulletin to all hospitals and clinics within a hundred-mile radius. We don't know how badly he's injured, but there's a good chance he'll need medical treatment. *Go!*"

"Wait, get the dogs," Dan said, staring to the west toward the remains of the ancient mill. "He's not leaving town, and he won't go to a hospital," Dan said without looking away from the mill in the distance.

"You think he's holing up at Wilson's Mill." Chief Baxter took off his glasses and rubbed his eyes with the back of his fist.

"Too obvious," Dan said, after a slight hesitation, "but he wants us to think he is. He's smart, very smart and I don't think we can or should overlook the possibility that the tread marks are anything except an elaborate fake."

"So you think all of this is just a wild goose chase?" Chief Baxter was annoyed.

"Yeah—maybe. Let's secure the road blocks and check the hospitals, but it won't hurt to let the dogs tell us for sure which way he really went."

"Get the dogs," Chief Baxter issued the order. When the junior officers had dispersed to carry out his orders, he turned to Dan and said, "You know something, don't you?"

"I know he's not going to stop. He's like a hurt, angry hornet, and he's going to keep stinging until we stop him," Dan said.

"If he's hurt badly enough, he might go to a hospital."

"No, he won't; he can't and he knows it. Besides, if he went far enough away to be safe, he wouldn't be able to witness his destruction, and he needs that—he feeds off it. No, he's here somewhere," Dan said, turning 360 degrees.

He swallowed a shot of whiskey while he savored the victory that had been his today. Smiling, he picked up a plastic bag filled with pigs' blood that he'd used to bait them, leading them to tire tracks that, although had been made with his car, had been made yesterday and led off into the country, in the opposite direction of where he now sat. Whichever direction they turned, no matter how smart they thought they were they would never find him, thus leaving him free to finish what he'd started. Taking another shot of whiskey, he lay down. He would sleep this afternoon, for tonight the real games were about to begin.

CHAPTER 54

4:52 p.m.

The news of the explosions and the fire was all over the radio, and roadblocks were being erected at almost every intersection. Sadie drove faster than normal, impatient to get back to the orchard to see if Anna and Rocco had heard from Dan. The sky overhead turning a leaden gray didn't help to lessen the growing feeling of dread as it heralded the approach of an impending storm. A heavy wind buffeted the Jeep as she drove, and she had to strain her arms to keep the tall vehicle from crossing over the centerline and into oncoming traffic. It wasn't until she turned off the main road and onto the long tree-lined drive that led up to the orchard that she was able to relax a little, finally breathing a sigh of relief as the large farmhouse came into view.

Pulling around back and parking as close to the kitchen door as possible, Sadie almost made it inside before the sky opened, unleashing a torrent of fat, heavy raindrops all around her. Making a dash for the door, she felt the rain slice icily through her hair and fall cold on her scalp.

"Anna, I'm home," she called out as she shrugged out of her wet coat and hung it on a hook in the recessed alcove between the back-door and the kitchen. Instantly, she realized what she'd said and it gave her a slight pause; she'd called the place *home*, and indeed it felt like it.

"In here," Anna called from the next room.

Shaking the rain out of her hair, Sadie stepped into the kitchen to find Anna up to her elbows in flour, sugar, and spices in the kitchen with George curled in front of the fire. One batch of cookies was already cooling on a rack, and Anna was heartily beating something in another bowl with heavy slaps of a large wooden spoon.

"Sadie, thank God you're home," Anna said, setting down the bowl. "One less person I have to worry about." She hugged Sadie tightly. Sadie returned the hug, thankful for the comfort it provided.

"I heard the explosions from my folks' house, but I had no idea what had happened until I turned on the radio. I can't believe it. It's crazy out there; all of the streets are blocked. I saw Rocco manning one of the roadblocks at Main and Fifth."

"Yes, he left as soon as Dan called, all too excited to play hero." Anna resumed beating the cookie dough.

"Dan—is he okay?" Sadie asked nervously.

"Yes, thank God, he's fine. But Mike and Evie are both in the hospital." Anna shook her head. "He said he tried to call you, but the call never went through."

"Huh." Sadie dug her cell out of her purse. "The battery's dead."

"That's what he thought. Anyway, he didn't want you to worry. He said he'd call when he could, but he didn't think he would be back tonight, and he wants us all to stay put."

A clap of thunder, accentuated by a bolt of lightning, shook the floor-length plate glass picture window that encompassed the space on both sides of the fireplace. The kitchen, in contrast to the day outside, was cheerful and warm and smelled of cinnamon, nutmeg, and clove. A fire danced merrily in the brick fireplace.

"The cookies look wonderful." Sadie eyed them hungrily.

"Help yourself; there will be plenty more where that came from. The pumpkin cookies just came out of the oven and might be a bit hot still; if you wait fifteen you can have chocolate chip with Macadamia nut."

"These are delicious," she said around a mouthful of pumpkin cookie.

"It's a good thing we all have high metabolisms around here," Anna said. "I bake when I'm upset or nervous, and right now I'm both." She paced as she whipped the contents of the bowl. "Dan said the entire lab was completely destroyed, and if they hadn't gotten out in time, they would have, well could have …" Anna stopped talking and continued beating the contents of the bowl in silence. Finally, her fury spent for the time being, she set the bowl down and added copious amounts of chocolate chips and Macadamia nuts.

"Would you like some help? Sadie asked. "I've spent the last hour …" She let the words trail off, the rest of the sentence lodged awkwardly in her throat.

"You found …" Anna prompted, cocking her head, "… something?"

"In the last few hours, I've rediscovered and lost my family all over again." Sitting down heavily at the wooden kitchen table, she stared out the window beyond Anna, the driving rain obscuring the orchard from her view; the weather seemed to reflect her feelings perfectly.

"It was difficult to go home again?" Anna prodded gently. She scooped generous-sized lumps of raw cookie dough onto a shiny silver baking sheet.

"Yes and no. I thought it would be, but when I finally mustered the courage to step across the threshold and walk in, it was … good … and I realized how much I miss not having a family. But then …"

Anna wiped her hands on a cotton dishtowel and pulled up a chair opposite Sadie while she waited for her to continue; the cookies could wait.

"My dad was … a snake handler … a disciple of Sister Jane." She spoke so quietly it barely came out above a whisper. A tear took her by surprise, followed by another, and another and soon she was unabashedly crying in front of Anna. The tears felt good and cleansing, and soon she felt better. Drying her eyes with the back of her hand, she noticed that Anna had set a box of tissues in front of her and a glass of water. Taking a moment to compose herself, she wiped her nose and took a drink. Then, taking a deep breath, she related her afternoon and her discovery to Anna.

"I brought the boxes of files back with me; I was hoping that you and Rocco might help me go through them. Maybe we can find something that will help Dan and the police."

"Are you sure you want us to? It's quite personal, and we would certainly understand if you—"

"No." Sadie cut her off softly but firmly. "There have been far too many secrets in my life already, and I have a strong feeling that if we are going to stop these killings, we need to know what's in those files. My father's days of hiding are done, and I will not pay for his wrongdoings and neither will anyone else I love."

"Rocco and I would be happy to help you then," Anna said.

"What would we be happy to do?" Rocco said, emerging through the back door and shaking off the chill and the wet, wintry weather.

"Helping me solve a riddle," Sadie said, standing. "But I really need to take a shower first. Anna, would you mind filling him in? I don't feel up to repeating it again right now."

"Of course, dear. Take your time. I'll fix something to eat, and Rocco will get the boxes out of the car."

"Thank you." Sadie hugged both of them and headed upstairs. Rocco just looked at his wife, his eyebrows raised. "What the devil is going on?"

As Anna recounted the events of Sadie's day, George hopped up onto Rocco's lap and kneaded for a few minutes before settling down into a loud, lazy purr as Rocco stroked his furry back. Anna's recounting of Sadie's day left Rocco chilled to the core despite the warm, pleasant atmosphere that surrounded him.

"I'll be damned. I never would have guessed."

"She's terribly upset."

"I'm not surprised. I'll get the files." Rocco picked up the cat as he stood and set him back down on the chair before putting his raincoat back on. "That poor girl, to find out after all this time ..."

She's going to need a lot of support," Anna said as George climbed into her lap. "I have a feeling that this is just the tip of the iceberg, and when she finds out what's in those files she's ..."

"She'll be fine," Rocco said, hugging his wife from behind. "We'll make sure she is."

"Have I told you how much I love you lately?" Anna stood and wrapped her arms around her husband, tilting her head to look up at him. George, now completely fed up with people, decided to bathe on an empty chair by the fire.

"No more than I love you." Rocco kissed her lightly on the forehead and then the lips. Outside another clap of thunder shook the windows. The couple stood silently for a moment in each other's embrace, until the gentle, yet insistent pinging of the timer on the stove sent Rocco to retrieve the files while Anna took a tray of hot cookies out of the oven and replaced it with another.

W hen Sadie reappeared from her shower, she saw that Anna and Rocco had emptied the files from the boxes onto the large dining room table and sorted the notebooks, files, and loose papers as best they could. By the time they were finished, the entire surface was filled. Taking a small stack at a time, they adjourned to the kitchen to puzzle over the contents.

"I'll start with this." Sadie picked up a leather-bound diary, securely tied with a strap of leather. The diary was identical to the one Dan had that belonged to the killer, only she had no way of knowing that. "Did either of you ... did you know about my dad?" Sadie found she couldn't make eye contact with either Anna or Rocco.

"No. I'm sorry; your dad was very..." Anna began but found she didn't know how to finish.

"Secretive. My father was a loner who preferred reptiles to his own daughter."

"I'm sure he loved you fiercely," Anna said.

"I used to think so. I used to think I knew him but I don't. I never did. I am so mad at him."

"He also did do a lot of good for this town," Rocco added quietly but firmly. "Whatever he may or may not have done, he helped a lot of good people too."

"Thank you for that and I hope someday I can see him again in that light. But I ... I'm just ..." She faltered on her words then sighed heavily. "I don't want you to judge me for my fathers' mistakes." Looking from Rocco to Anna, she said, "I had ..."

" ... nothing to do with any of it. And don't worry, no matter what we find in here, you'll have our support."

"And Dan's," Rocco added.

"Yes, and Dan's," Anna said.

Anna supplied them each with a notepad and a pen for taking notes. As the afternoon grew short and the storm continued to rage outside, the trio pored over the files from the strange altar room. A large plate of cheese, crackers, sausage, and apples sat in the middle of the table, and they nibbled as they read. A warm fire crackled in the brick fireplace, while a pot of chili simmered on the stove. Dan called briefly to say that he was unhurt and would be home as soon as he could, but not to expect him before late, if he was able to make it at all.

CHAPTER 55

8:00 p.m.

The night had finally come! By dawn everyone would know who he was and why he was here, but it wouldn't matter because soon after, they would all be dead. "May you rest in eternal discord," he said to the empty chapel as he finished the preparations for the night. Satisfied that everything was in perfect readiness, he left. After the sound of his footsteps faded away into the night, the only other sound in the small, dark room was a rattling of tails.

CHAPTER 56

8:45 p.m.

"According to this, Sister Jane was born on January seventh, nineteen fifty-four, to Samuel and Jenna Alcott in Mounts Par, Kentucky, Appalachian area. According to her birth certificate, her real name is Janice Marie Alcott," Rocco read from the notes he'd taken. "Her parents were both snake handlers in a church that went by the name *The True Path*. It doesn't look like much of a church though. There's an old photo of it here." He passed the picture around.

"It looks more like a gas station," Anna said, adjusting her glasses. "I can see where the pumps once stood."

"Must not have had a big following," Sadie said, as she studied the picture.

"Hmm, what are you?" Anna unfolded a small square of parchment that was stuck between the pages of the old Bible she was studying.

"What have you got there?" Rocco added another log to the fire.

"It looks like a crude family tree. According to this, Jane ... Janice ... you know ... had two children, one born in nineteen seventy-six, and the other born a few years later in seventy-eight. I guess one of them died at birth or something because there is only one name listed here: Marcus."

"The boy," Sadie said, shaking her head. "It has to be the boy."

"What are you talking about?" Anna set down the family tree and studied Sadie.

"There was boy, with black hair and blue eyes that haunted my dreams when I was a girl. He was always surrounded by snakes, terrified, crying. I wanted to help him but I couldn't. My father told me he was a figment of my imagination and that I needed to stop thinking about him. But I couldn't. I used to have terrifying visions of him being tormented by large, writhing snakes." Suddenly Sadie stopped talking and closed her mouth. She realized that both Anna and Rocco were staring at her, and she realized that they had no idea what she was talking about. For a long time no one said anything. "I'm sorry," Sadie said, finally. "I—"

"You talked about him in your dreams the other night. But I didn't realize it meant anything," Anna said, nodding. "When did you meet him?"

"I never did. I never knew he was real. I still don't."

"I think we all know he's real," Rocco said, with finality. "And you must have met him; you just don't remember it."

"I guess that's possible." Sadie couldn't believe they were so accepting of her—of what she said.

"You said the family tree showed that she had two children. Who's the other?" Rocco picked up the parchment and studied it. The name was scratched out. "According to this, Marcus was born on November third—that's today—nineteen seventy-six, and the other child, the one with no name, was born on November third as well, just two years later in nineteen seventy-eight."

"Two children born on the same day two years apart. What are the odds?" Anna shook her head at the coincidence.

"Here's another coincidence that's more than a little alarming," Sadie said. "November third, today, is my birthday too," Sadie said as she reached for the thin parchment, holding it up to the light and examining it closely. "This can't be right. It's impossible," she said firmly. "That woman was clearly insane."

"Happy birthday," Anna and Rocco said simultaneously.

"Why didn't you tell us? We could have celebrated," Anna added.

"Birthdays aren't that important to me. Besides with everything that's going on … it just wouldn't feel right to celebrate." Sadie smiled briefly before returning to the parchment. "Something was written here once. But I can't make it out. It looks like it might begin with an E … I can't tell for sure."

"Do you really think it's that important?" Anna said. "The other one probably died or was stillborn, and she erased the name."

"It's creepy that we all share the same birthday." Sadie shuddered. "And why erase the name? Why not just add a date of death, even if it's the same day as the birthday?"

"I don't know, maybe it was too painful," Anna said.

"Okay, let's move on. What else do we know about her?" Rocco picked up his pad and rifled through his notes.

"Not much; the details of her life are pretty sketchy. She was born and raised a preacher's daughter. She ran away from home at fifteen. It doesn't say why she ran away, but it looks like it coincides with a couple of mysterious deaths in her parents' church," Anna said, shaking her head.

"Death does seem to follow her," Rocco said.

"It does. Only this sounds like a terrible way to go. One of the original deaths was from strychnine poisoning." Anna read from a yellowed 1970 news article from the *Kentuckian*.

"Strychnine?" Rocco raised his eyebrows

"According to this, the quote-unquote true believers not only played with venomous snakes but drank poison as well, as testament that they were really God's chosen people. It also corresponds to the quote from Mark 16:18 that she has underlined in her Bible." Anna passed the book around so that the others could read it as well.

"It sounds like the apple didn't fall far from the tree," Sadie said.

"So after things got too hot in Mounts Par, she decided to make

Crystal Springs her new home and started her very own snake cult right here."

"What a wacko," Rocco said, shuffling his stack of papers and files into a neat pile before standing up and stretching.

"Motion seconded," Anna took off her glasses and rubbed her eyes. When Sadie didn't say anything, husband and wife exchanged glances with each other across the table. Sadie sat still, a confused look on her face, the journal she'd been studying closed in front of her, and in her hand she held a single sheet of paper.

"What did you find?" Anna asked, breaking the girl's trance.

"This is…this says…well, it's wrong, of course. To your knowledge, did Doc Conway ever have an assistant that he fired for incompetence?" Anna and Rocco exchanged puzzled looks.

"What are you talking about?" Anna asked.

"This." Sadie handed the paper to Anna, who took it with one hand while adjusting her glasses with the other. It was a birth certificate. Reading the document, Anna quickly saw the reason for Sadie's confusion. Saying nothing, she handed the paper to Rocco. It was a birth certificate dated November 3, 1978. The name on the certificate read Sadie Elizabeth Mozart, born at 8:05 p.m. and died at 8:08 p.m.

"Well, I'll be damned; says here that you're dead."

"Funny, I feel pretty lively for a dead girl."

"It looks authentic enough," Rocco said, running his toughened fingertips over the embossed seal in the lower left corner of the document. "Notarized and everything."

"May I?" Anna held out her hand. After studying the document again for another moment, she mused "It was signed by your father and Doc Conway."

"I know that isn't my birth certificate…wait a minute. I'll be right back."

"Where are you going?" Anna asked.

"Last month, before all this mess, I got my birth certificate out of my safety deposit box to get a passport made." Sadie bounded up the stairs. "It's still in my purse," she called back. In the guest room, her purse was sitting on her bed where she'd left it. In a hurry, she unceremoniously dumped the contents onto the bed, extracting the small, white folded document from the pile just as the lights went out.

Sadie froze, the sudden darkness smothering her; she felt trapped, and then just as quickly the lights flickered and came back on. Relieved, Sadie turned to leave and found something else startling—not only were the house lights on now, but lights throughout the orchard had suddenly come to life. Sufficiently spooked, Sadie hurried back downstairs, anxious to rejoin the others.

"What happened?" Sadie asked, handing the document to Anna.

"The storm must have knocked down a few power lines," Rocco said. "I wouldn't be surprised if the whole town is down." Rocco noticed how ashen Sadie looked suddenly and realized how much the brief blackout had really scared her.

"But, the lights are on—everywhere." Sadie was confused.

"When the storm knocked out the power, the generators kicked on. I ran them to the house as well as the orchard; the St. James are never without power," Rocco said a little proudly.

"I, for one, am thrilled not to be stranded in a blackout," Sadie said, realizing that her sense of light-born safety was in reality nothing more than a gossamer veil, that if *he* wanted her she was powerless to stop him, but for now it would have to do.

"Me too," Rocco agreed. "Now let's see what this says," Rocco said, looking over his wife's shoulder. Anna and Rocco both read the birth certificate together. It was identical in every way except there was no time of death.

"According to this one you were actually born a little earlier but on the same day," Rocco said, comparing both documents side by side.

"Is it possible your mother was carrying twins?" Anna asked.

"And only one of you survived," Rocco added, seeing where his wife was going.

"And they gave me my dead sister's name?" Sadie looked horror-struck.

"You're right. That's unthinkable. I'm sorry." Anna looked truly aghast at what she'd proposed.

"No, I'm sorry, I shouldn't have snapped." Sadie sank down into the chair at the table and looked up at the couple, shaking her head in bewilderment. "Just hours ago I woke from a nap on my father's bed. It was the happiest I remember feeling in a long time. And then not an hour later I discover that he was a member of a cult with a serious snake fetish, run by a woman who thought she was some sort of a pharaoh. And now this! I feel like I'm losing my mind."

"There is someone who could clear this up," Rocco said.

"Yes, there is," Sadie said, gathering both birth certificates and standing. "If Dan calls, tell him I'm paying a visit to the good doctor."

"Why don't you just call," Anna said, worry reflected in her voice. "Dan asked us all to stay put."

"I know he did, and I also know that he had good reason to, but I'm tired of lies and half truths, and it is too easy to lie over the phone. I need to confront him, this," she said, waving the papers, "in person and it can't, I can't, wait until morning. I'm sorry, but I have to go now." Sadie crossed the kitchen and lifted her coat off the hook by the door.

"Sadie…" Anna started to protest but stopped when she felt Rocco's hand on her shoulder.

"Do you want me to go with you?" Rocco offered.

"I would love you both to go with me, but I have to do this alone." She could see they were about to protest. "After my dad was killed by the drunk driver, Doc Conway stepped in and filled that void in my life. We've spent every holiday together that I can remember; he was the only 'family' I had at my college graduation, and now I find out that my entire life, my father and Doc kept a secret from me. This is obviously something I was never meant to see," she said, shaking the piece of paper in her hand. "I think it will be easier if I confront him alone, I don't want him to feel like we are strong-arming him; I just want the truth." And with that Sadie headed outside to her Jeep, pulling her keys from her jacket pocket as she went, and headed for whatever answers lay beyond in the cold, wet November night.

"Godspeed," Anna said as she heard the Jeep's engine roar to life outside. She had a terrible feeling that they had just made a mistake letting her go alone.

"We couldn't have stopped her if we'd wanted to," Rocco said, stirring the chili on the stove.

"I know." Anna frowned.

"You would have done exactly the same thing," he said, holding a spoonful of chili out for her to sample.

"I know. Mmm…perfect as always," she said, savoring the spicy warmth of the soup on her tongue.

"You want me to call Dan and tell him?"

"I do," Anna said, sitting back down at the table and pulling over the black leather journal that Sadie had been reading all evening. She was determined to get to the bottom of this mystery. The stack of papers she'd been reading before were nothing but pure claptrap. It consisted of several passages from the Bible, either completely rewritten or interpreted insanely. It seemed like nothing more than the ramblings of a fiction writer, and it was hard to take seriously. So far she hadn't found anything that would help stop the killings.

"Dan's going to get over to Doc's as soon as he can. He's at the hospital checking on Mike and Evie." Rocco rubbed Anna's shoulders while he talked, his big hands gently kneading her tired muscles.

"Thank God they're all right," Anna said, shutting her eyes and letting her head fall forward slightly as she enjoyed the impromptu massage.

A s husband and wife worked together in the warm kitchen, the storm continued to rage outside. Jagged bolts of lightning split the sky around her in an angry pattern and lit the black sky like daylight. Thunder roared and shook the heavens as Sadie fought to keep the Jeep on the road in the high winds. The unusual storm made her question the wisdom of her decision, but she had already gone too far to turn around. Just then a bolt of lightning struck a tree up ahead, splitting it in two with a wrenching crash. Before Sadie had time to react to the strike, half of the tree crashed to the ground in front of the Jeep. With reactions owing more to adrenaline and instinct than actual driving skill, she swerved onto the shoulder, coming within inches of a line of giant oaks, and then back onto the road. Bringing the Jeep to a jarring stop with a squeal of tires, Sadie whipped around in her seat and stared open-mouthed at what very easily could have been her death. "I wonder if that's a sign," she said, hoping that it was not a harbinger of things to come. "God, I hope not." Even though the rest of the drive was uneventful, Sadie nevertheless breathed a sigh of relief as she turned off the main road onto the quiet drive that led to the doctor's house.

CHAPTER 57

9:38 p.m.

The sky overhead was an inky black, the stars obscured by the heavy rain clouds, leaving the landscape outside Dr. John Conway's bay window bleak and desolate. Somewhere in the back of his mind he heard lightning strike a tree close by, but his thoughts were a million miles away. He had only experienced one other such night in his life, where the sky—the world, in fact—seemed void of light, of hope. Staring out into the night, a glass of Crown Royal grasped tightly in his hand, he let his mind travel backward in time to that first black, starless night years ago when he was just a boy of ten.

Where so many of his other childhood memories had faded with time, that night in January stood out, refusing to be pushed aside, forgotten. It had been a hard winter, and that night was bitterly cold. Winds howled like banshees through the trees that even then were giant. Sleeping fitfully, he had just dozed off when he woke again suddenly, a terrible feeling buried deep in his gut. He knew something was wrong.

John wished that Sam, the family dog and his best friend, had come to bed with him. But the large German shepherd was nowhere to be seen. Sam usually came upstairs and settled on the floor by his bed after the rest of the family went to sleep. His door shut to the hall, he realized that Sam couldn't have come in; his stupid brother must have shut his door. "Jerk," John said uneasily in the darkness. He hated the dark, and his older brother, Ben, knew it and loved to tease him about it. His dad tried to help him a few weeks ago, on his birthday, by telling him that he was a young man now and that meant that the monsters would be scared of *him* now, that he had no reason to be scared of them anymore because the monsters would never bother him again. He hadn't bought it; he'd been ten for practically two weeks, and he was just as scared of the dark as ever.

Lying in the dark, he realized that he was not just feeling scared but that he really had to pee and there was no way he would be able to hold it. Although the prospect of opening the door to the hall and facing whatever was out there made his heart pound and his palms sweat, the alternative was far worse. Slipping out of the relative safety of his bed, he padded barefoot across the cold hardwood floor to the door, which suddenly looked ominous and malevolent. The old house creaked and groaned around him—this was what his dad called "settling"—John wasn't sure he bought that either. He was positive that just on the other side of his sturdy door lurked something nasty, with bulging eyes and wickedly long, pointed teeth salivating at the prospect of ten-year-old boy for dinner.

But he really had to pee. Dancing from foot to foot, he screwed up the courage, placed a shaking hand on the glass doorknob, and turned it. But before opening the door all the way, he stopped to listen. With the exception of the wind outside, all was silent. In his head he envisioned himself flinging the door open and stepping bravely into the hall, thereby showing the monsters that he was unafraid. Instead he opened it only a crack and peeked outside, ready to slam it shut in an instant. All was quiet and with much trepidation, he stepped out into the hall, his heart thudding, sure an attack was imminent. But the hallway was quiet and monster-free.

The old farmhouse was quiet and still smelled faintly of the roast they'd had for dinner that night. Quickly he made his way to the bathroom he shared with his parents and older brother.

After relieving himself, he felt decidedly better and concluded that his aching bladder had been the cause of the bad feeling—not the boogeyman. Feeling triumphant for having conquered his fears, he decided to make himself a celebratory late-night snack, the way his dad and brother sometimes did in the middle of the night. It was a man thing, and he was definitely a man now.

Walking ever so carefully on tiptoe, he crept down the hall, past his parents' room to the staircase. All thoughts of monsters forgotten, he pretended he was an intrepid explorer in a distant, exotic land, much like the hero in the book he was reading. The hero in the book would never be scared by stupid monsters, and now neither would he. Knowing that the third step down creaked loudly, he held onto the heavy oak banister as he warily extended the toe of his right foot until it touched the next step down, skipping the telltale creaking board altogether. It seemed to take forever to get past that step, and when he did, he noticed that he'd broken a sweat. After that the rest was smooth sailing, and soon he was in the kitchen with his head buried up to his shoulders inside the refrigerator.

Pulling out several thick slices of leftover roast, bread, mayonnaise, and cheese, he was about to put his snack together when the same bad feeling that had awakened him came back—only stronger. And now he *knew* something was definitely wrong. It was then that he realized he still hadn't seen Sam... Sam, who always slept either at the foot of his bed or outside his door... Sam, his faithful friend who would—should—be here at his side begging for food, but was nowhere to be seen. And then from outside, past the darkened porch, he heard Sam barking in such a way that turned his veins into rivers of ice. Dropping his gathered bounty onto the floor, he sprung to the back door, unlocked it, and flung it wide with such force that it bounced off the wall and back onto him. Not caring if he woke the whole house, not caring about anything except his best friend, he started across the deep screened-in porch. He was about halfway through when he heard a sound he would never forget. It was a sound that to this day sent shivers down his spine. It was the baying of hungry wolves.

His heart stopped and then started again at about six times the normal speed. Straining his eyes against the black night beyond, he searched in vain for Sam. He couldn't see the dog or the wolves; he could only hear them. Sam sounded terrified and the wolves sounded hungry.

Adrenaline coursed through him, washing away all traces of fear. John screamed, "*Get away from my dog!*" He was about to lunge out the door into the night when he saw his dad's shotgun leaning against the wall, the one he kept there for emergencies, the one John was still forbidden to touch without his father present. Grabbing the gun, John raced out into the night. Somewhere in the back of his mind, he was aware of the door slamming hard and reverberating in its frame—boy, his mom would be pissed—as he bounded across frozen ground hard beneath his bare feet.

Running hard, he saw his breath turn into vapors against the icy night air. Then he saw them by the barn and skidded to a stop. They were black silhouettes against a dark backdrop in the night void of light. His dog was backed against the side of the barn, surrounded on three sides by malicious, hungry predators. Sam growled and stood his ground, but John could see that he was favoring his front paw. He was hurt. Blind with fear and anger, John raced toward the pack of wolves, the shotgun raised, screaming like a warrior plunging into battle. He was vaguely aware of shouts coming from behind him. His father and brother were yelling for him to stop, but he couldn't. His legs were on autopilot.

Instead of scattering, as he had hoped, the pack turned and looked at him—hungrily and simultaneously, as if they were all separate parts of the same malevolent entity. Sam was barking louder now. Just then one of the wolves, the largest one, broke away from the pack and leapt at John. He shot wildly, missing the beast by miles. In that split second he saw his entire life flash before his eyes, all ten years of it. The wolf hit him with the impact of a speeding locomotive, and he went down with the shotgun still clenched in his hands, his arms and the gun held tightly in front of him, the only thing keeping the monster's jaws from ripping his throat out. He could feel the hot, sour breath of the beast on his skin and knew that he was done for. Then suddenly, he was free, the wolf knocked aside, Sam holding its neck.

Sam and the wolf tumbled over and over in a fury of fur until finally the wolf lay dead, thick blood spilling from its mangled throat. Although Sam bled from many wounds, he held his ground in front of John, the protector until the end, as the rest of the pack moved in for the kill. As if in slow motion, John saw the second wolf lunge, this time at Sam. And he saw himself raise the shotgun, take aim, the way his father had taught him, and fire. The roar of the gun reverberated through the night as the wolf exploded backwards upon impact.

The next thing he knew, he was being lifted off the ground and carried away while several more shots rang out into the starless night. His mother carried him into the house while his father and brother took care of the remaining menace. Sam had survived, but from that day on he walked with a profound limp and preferred to stay inside whenever possible.

Tonight, fifty or so years later, John had that same feeling deep inside: he knew a dangerous predator lurked outside. The insistent pounding on the door sliced through the silence of the big old house, the same one he'd grown up in, his family and Sam long gone now. He was now alone with the wolves. Setting his drink down, he picked up his Colt 45 revolver and a flashlight and headed for the door.

CHAPTER 58

10:07 p.m.

"Sadie?" He looked worn and tired.

"Am I?" Sadie withdrew the birth certificate from her pocket and held it out to him. "Because according to this, I'm dead."

Doc Conway neither spoke nor made a move to take the proffered paper, but it seemed he aged another ten years in the span of seconds.

"Doc, come on, I need to understand this."

Still, he remained silent, staring past her into the storm, lost in some other place. Frustrated, Sadie thrust the paper into his hand. "Go on, look at it. It says I died." But when he didn't respond again, Sadie gave up. "I can't believe you're shutting me out." And with that she turned to go.

"Sadie, wait." Outside the rain began falling harder as more thunder and lightning rattled the skies. "Come inside." Doc Conway backed up, making room for her to squeeze past him into the house. It was only then that she noticed the gun in his hand and paused.

"Just keeping my hands busy," he said, and with that he reached around her, pulling the door closed against the dark storm raging outside and locked it. Without another word, he turned and led the way back down the hall.

CHAPTER 59

10:13 p.m.

Doc Conway led the way to his study, a large formal—yet comfortable—room in the back of the house. A room she knew well. Every holiday she could remember, before and after her own father's death, had been spent here.

Sadie gravitated toward *her* spot: one of two high-backed leather chairs.

"Can I get you a drink?" The question was stiff and formal.

"No. I don't want a drink. I want an answer."

Nodding, Doc turned away from Sadie and busied himself at the bar, refreshing his own cocktail. For a time the only sounds in the room were the clinking of ice cubes and the crackling of the fire.

"That night … was … still seems … unreal. We thought we were doing the right thing. You have to believe that." He looked up from the fire now, his deep green eyes locking with hers.

"Go on," Sadie said, her voice shaking a little as she realized, not for the first time, that the doctor's eyes were so like her own.

In words almost too hushed for Sadie to hear, he said, "Both Marilyn and her baby died on my table that night."

The words seared Sadie's brain, the news hitting home like a freight train. As much as she wanted to deny it, she couldn't. In a way she realized she'd always known or at least suspected something, an affair maybe, but not this.

"I..." She found she had no words, her brain jumbled and fogged. "Who am I?" And for the first time in her life, Sadie saw Doctor John Conway tremble. "It's a simple question. If I am not me—Sadie Elizabeth Mozart..." Sadie bit back a wave of revulsion as the bile in her stomach churned restlessly. "...who am I?"

"Marilyn had a very difficult pregnancy. She bled frequently and—"

"Why do you keep calling her Marilyn? She's my mother."

"No she's not."

Stunned into silence, Sadie went to the bar and poured herself a healthy shot of bourbon. Doc didn't continue until she'd sat back down; his naturally penetrating gaze became glassy, and he turned to face the fire. Sadie was sure, though, that he wasn't seeing the licking flames on the logs but some long-ago event that changed his life and hers forever.

"It was a miracle that the baby survived for that long with the amount of venom in her bloodstream." He stopped for a moment, gathering strength for what was coming next—for the truth. "Your father was devastated. He blamed himself."

"Why? What did he do?" The words seemed to scratch Sadie's throat on the way out.

"Marilyn, a devote Catholic, was appalled by Sister Jane and what she represented. And for his part, your father did everything to keep that part of his life separate, but he got sucked in just like the rest of us. There was nothing she couldn't make us do, make us want to do."

"I don't want to know this. Just tell me what it has to do with me," Sadie spat, disgusted.

"The wine cellar was your father's special place. He loved his wines and often spent hours in there when he needed time to think, and Marilyn always respected his space. But that night was different. She'd started having false contractions and was worried. She needed him to bring her to me. At that time I wasn't the county coroner, but the town physician. Instead of knocking, she just walked in and …" He stopped talking for a moment and sipped his drink; he seemed to shrink smaller in his chair as he prepared to continue.

"Don't stop now." Her compassion was long gone.

"Her timing was terrible. Stephen had taken to handling even when he wasn't in church. And that night he'd been restless and gone downstairs to pray. When she walked in, he was in a state of rapture."

"Rapture." The word sent shivers up Sadie's spine. *Rapture… Andre.*

"The height of worship, when one becomes one with the Lord through the snake. It's …"

"I get it—just go on," she said, even though she didn't get it at all. Sadie's head spun with the insanity of what she was hearing. This was something bad TV movies were made of, not real life, and certainly not *her* life. But at the same time she couldn't help admitting on some level that it all made sense—that her entire life, her night terrors, somehow it was all connected together.

"She screamed when she saw him on his knees with the serpents raised high above his head. Before he could stop it, both snakes leapt out of his arms and struck her in the abdomen, injecting her with a lethal amount of poison."

"Why didn't he have anti-venom?"

"Because he didn't think he'd ever need it. If he was bitten, it was the Lord's will as to whether he lived or died. He wasn't the only one that felt that way, we all did. Only I did have anti-venom; being the town doctor, I had to keep it on hand in case …"

Sadie didn't hear what he said next. The word *we* thundered in her head.

"What do you mean, *we?*"

"Sister Jane had a large following."

"She was a blight on the town."

"True, but we didn't see it then—couldn't. She was ..."

"You know what, I don't want to know. Just tell me who I am."

"Very well." In his mind he could see everything just as it was. "Marilyn wasn't the only woman who gave birth that night, nor the only one bitten. Another woman had been bitten as well, in almost the exact same spots, only her body was much more adept at handling the poison since it was something that she had become addicted to over the years."

"How is that even possible?"

"It is, and it happens more than you know. It was raining and cold outside, much like it is tonight," he said, staring out the window into the blackness beyond. "I had just finished delivering a beautiful baby girl—you." He turned to smile at Sadie, but she looked away, sickened by the sight of him. Seeing that she wasn't going to respond to him, Doc released a tired sigh and continued, "When Stephen burst through the front doors with Marilyn in his arms, he was babbling like a madman. No matter what you may know about him now, please believe that he loved her very much."

"Sure he did; he loved her so much, he killed her." Sadie felt sick to her stomach.

"Marilyn was already in labor when they arrived, and the baby came fast, very fast, but it was too late ..." He trailed off, staring into the fire for a moment before resuming. "Stephen was despondent. He raged at me to make it better, to fix it, he was out of his head, until ..."

"Until what?" Sadie prompted. Although she wanted to run from this house of horrors, she was rooted to the chair.

"We hadn't heard her come in, but suddenly there she was, standing in the doorway. She wore a thin cotton gown, a light shawl wrapped around her shoulders, her baby in her arms. Then she did something truly remarkable ... she placed her daughter in your father's arms."

"No!"

"'You take her. You lost yours because of me; let me repay you. She'll keep us bonded forever. Her name is Elizabeth.'" Just then

Doc broke off and walked slowly across the room and retrieved a wooden box from a high shelf. From within it withdrew a neatly folded piece of paper, which he handed silently to Sadie before sitting back down.

It was another birth certificate, dated the same as the others: November 3, 1978. The child was listed as Elizabeth Marie Conway, daughter of Jane Alcott and John Edward Conway.

"I was a pawn."

Doc Conway said nothing as he turned his gaze first to the fire and then out into the night.

"She used me to keep both of you her henchmen. What else did you *do* for her? Did you kill?"

"No! Never! I'm a doctor. The very thought is abhorrent."

"But you did—you covered up for her—twenty years ago, during the *suicides*. They weren't accidental at all, were they?" It was Doc's silence now that spoke loudest. Large wet tears filled the corners of his eyes and coursed down his ruddy face. "You know who's responsible for the killings, don't you? That's why you have a gun."

"She was so beautiful and graceful, filled with so much raw power and charisma; there was nothing either one of us could deny her."

"That's not what I asked."

"Yes, the first two were suicides but not the third. She killed Dr. Black, hit him over the head with a rock until he lost consciousness and then set the snakes on him."

"She couldn't have carried him to the river. She was too small. Who dumped the body?"

"I don't know, truly."

"But you falsified the death certificate."

"Yes." The word was barely audible over the storm. "I love you."

"And I despise you." Grabbing her jacket, she ran through the house to the front door.

Doc ran after her. He had to get her back; he had to explain, to try and make things right between them again, although deep down inside he knew that would never be possible. When he reached the front door, Sadie was already to the Jeep. Then Doc saw him in the shadows and knew him for the wolf that he was.

"Sadie! Look out!" It was too late; he had her. As Sadie went limp in the killer's arms, Doc began to raise his gun, only to realize that he didn't have it. It was on the table next to his drink in the study. Helpless against the predator in the storm, he watched the young boy he knew so long ago look up at him and grin.

Doc's heart froze as he looked into the face of pure malevolence. Slamming the door and locking it, he raced for the gun and the phone. With the gun in hand, he headed deep into the black farmhouse, suddenly glad for the lack of power: no one knew the house better then him, and he wasn't about to give the intruder any advantages. Fishing his cell out of his pocket, he dialed 911.

At the kitchen table, Anna and Rocco stared at the photograph in front of them. "How could Doc Conway have been one of them? He's never missed church a day in his life," Anna said, still disbelieving.

"To keep up pretenses," Rocco offered.

"First her father and now Doc."

"If this guy is going after members of the cult, then Doc is probably not too far down on the list." Panicked, Anna fumbled the keys of the phone twice before managing to get Dan's number dialed correctly. For the first time she wished she had taken time to learn how to use the speed-dial function.

As Anna dialed Dan, Rocco picked up the leather journal again and flipped through the pages. His heart ached for the young girl who had already become like family in such a short time. "I can't imagine what Sadie's going through." He started to stand when something in the book caught his eye: it was a poem.

CHAPTER 60

11:15 p.m.

"Aren't you supposed to be in your room?" Dan found Mike pacing clumsily on his crutches, outside the hospital's ICU. The surgery was over, but the doctors still wouldn't let Mike in to see Evie.

"The power went out in the middle of her surgery." Mike's voice hit an unnaturally high tone.

"Only for a few seconds; the hospital's generator is working fine. Hell, the only place in town better lit than this place is Mom and Dad's."

"Evie is—"

"Going to be just fine. I talked to the nurse; the bullet didn't impact her spine. She's gonna pull through, and she'll be able to run circles around you again in no time." Dan put an encouraging hand on Mike's shoulder.

"I love her so much," Mike said softly, his eyes trained on something in his hand and not on Dan.

"She loves you too." Dan followed his partner's gaze and saw that Mike was holding the engagement ring he'd purchased months ago. "Give it to her when she wakes up. She'll say yes." Just then Dan's cell phone rang. It was Anna.

"Hi, honey." Dan could hear the worry in his mom's voice. "Sadie isn't back from Doc's yet."

"I'm sure she's fine, probably just waiting out the storm." Dan hadn't been too worried about Sadie going over to Doc's. At least he knew where she was.

"Doc was one of them—a snake handler. I'm sure he'd never hurt Sadie but…"

"I'm on my way," Dan said. He was about to hang up when Anna said, "There's something else, Dan. We think we found directions hidden in a poem." Motioning to Mike, Dan put the phone on speaker so they both could hear it.

"To the north the sparkling serpent winds
Coils round of perfect symmetry give refuge to the true believer
In her belly we rejoice
In her venom we find strength
In her acceptance we find savior."

"Good work, thanks. I'll have Sadie home soon." He made one other urgent call, to Chief Baxter, who went silent as he listened but promised that Jen would be there with satellite maps and other necessary files ASAP. When he turned back to Mike, Dan was surprised by his partner's sudden transformation—the worrying boyfriend gone, a man bent on justice in his place.

"Are you sure you feel up to it?"

"Sitting on my ass while my friends are getting killed? Hell, no!"

"Good to have you back. The doctors aren't going to like it."

"Screw the doctors. If there is anything there to find, I'll find it." Mike had definitely turned a corner, and Dan could see his eyes light with focus and determination.

CHAPTER 61

12:00 p.m.

Dan knew something was wrong as he wound his way up the gravel drive to Doc's house. As he emerged from the cover of trees into the circle drive in front of the large house he saw Sadie's Jeep; then he saw her on the ground beside it. Dan also noticed the open front door; the lock blown to pieces. Throwing the car into park, he raced to her side. She was alive, just unconscious, soaking wet in a puddle. Her skin looked ashen in the ambient glow cast through the cold rain by his headlights. Dan had just lifted Sadie out of the puddle when he heard a shot ring out into the night, reverberating in the stillness left after the storm.

Not wanting to leave her, but not having any other choice, he raced up the walkway and into the blackened house, "Police! Drop your weapon and come out with your hands up!"

Just then Dan heard what sounded like an explosion of glass coming from the room at the opposite end of the hall and off to the left—the doctor's study. Moving cautiously down the hall, he now heard only the sound of his shoes on the hardwood floor. Turning the corner into the room, he saw that the plate-glass window had been shattered outward, with a hole large enough for a man to clamber through. The doctor was on his back convulsing, a pool of blood spread beneath him; it looked black in the orange light cast by the dying fire. He was still breathing, but barely. Just then a foot came out of the shadows kicking him in the side of head and sending him reeling. His gun flew out of his hand. He had assumed the killer had fled through the window. Instead he had used it as a trap to bait Dan into letting down his guard a fraction, and a fraction was all it had taken. He was on the floor now crawling after his own gun, and he had almost wrapped his hand around it when a heavy boot connected with his head, the force of the kick flipping him over onto his back. Then he heard and felt two bullets hit his chest, point-blank range, and everything went black.

CHAPTER 62

12:17a.m.

Dan regained consciousness to the sound of sirens; he had no idea how long he'd been out. His chest hurt like hell where the bullets had struck him, and he felt a knot growing on the side of his head where he'd been kicked. The IIIA vest he'd been wearing had saved his life. The bullet, a .44 fired at such close range, would have torn a hole through him otherwise. He was lucky that it had just been a handgun, because anything larger would have penetrated the vest, and at that close range, probably not stopped until it reached the floor.

Outside, he heard the screech of tires, as his backup arrived— too late, he feared. He moved stiffly over to where Doc Conway lay, barely breathing and still convulsing. "Hold on, Doc. Help is on the way."

"Police! Drop your weapon and come out with your hands raised!" Dan recognized the voice of Jen Mackey from the front entry.

"It's clear," Dan yelled back. "Doc's been shot. I need an ambu- lance, now!" It hurt him to yell; his chest had been severely bruised from the bullets, but at least he was alive. Thankfully the killer had aimed at his heart and not his head.

It didn't take long for the paramedics to stabilize the doctor and move him into the waiting ambulance.

With nothing more he could do for Doc, Dan looked around the room for any clues that might help him piece together the rest of the puzzle. A glint of firelight, reflected off of a small piece of broken glass, caught Dan's eye and he almost dismissed it as a shard from the window. But the window was broken from the inside, meaning that the majority of the shards would be on the lawn outside, and this fragment was on the other side of the room, too far away to be from the window. On closer inspection he saw that it was actually a broken vile of brown glass. Frowning he nudged it with the tip of his pen, turning it over so that he could read the label. Strychnine. *So the killer hadn't been just satisfied to shoot the doctor, but poison him as well.* Careful not to touch it, as Strychnine can be absorbed by the skin and be just as damaging as if ingested, he examine it closely. It had blood on it. *Had the killer cut himself?*

"What have you got there?" Jen said coming up behind him.

"Poison."

"This is good." Jen said.

"Good?"

"At least we know what we're up against now. Maybe there's a chance to save the Doc."

Dan didn't comment, only nodded before turning away to continue his search. He left Jen with the task of calling the hospital and securing the evidence. Right now he had only one person he cared about saving. Sadie.

That's when he saw the two birth certificates. It didn't take him long to appreciate their significance. *God, Sadie must be devastated.* But then he saw something else, a piece of white paper poking out from a wooden box high on the doctor's study shelf. Doc was a neat man, which made the bit of paper stand out against the room's ordered ambiance. Extracting the paper, Dan saw that it was a copy of the same poem that his dad had found.

Dan fished his cell phone out of his pocket and dialed Mike; he paced impatiently while he waited for the call to be answered. Finally, after what felt like an eternity, but in reality was only three rings, Mike came on the line. "I was just gonna call you; I found it," Mike said before Dan even had a chance to say hello.

"Where?"

"It's under the Great Sink." Mike sounded positive. The Great Sink was the largest and most unstable sinkhole in the area. It was completely off limits to everyone but researchers and other trained professionals, which meant that every year adventurous souls too stupid or headstrong to heed the warnings got lost down there.

"How do I get there?" Dan asked, starting his car.

"You can't go in there, Dan. It's dangerous, and you have no idea what you're doing down in the caves."

"We don't have any other options. Mike, he has her. He has Sadie down there. I'm going in. Just tell me what to do, and I'll do it."

"Wait, Dan, think about it. If you get hurt or lost, you'll be …"

"No, I know the risks and I'm going to find her." Mike knew this was the final word on the subject.

"Okay, but at least go prepared."

"What do you suggest?"

"Go to the ranger station at the Springs, the main one. I'll call ahead so they know you're coming. Everything you'll need is in the locker I keep there. In my equipment you'll find a set of high-pow-ered walkie-talkies. I'll have one of them brought to me; you keep the other one on you and on at all times," Mike continued giving his senior partner directions as Dan sped for the Springs.

CHAPTER 63

1:23 a.m.

The light of what seemed like a hundred candles burned her eyes as Sadie slowly regained consciousness; she quickly squeezed them shut again. Groggy and disoriented, her head was pounding, and she had a vile taste in her mouth. She remembered running from Doc's place—from her father—and then nothing but total and complete blackness. The clammy fabric of her wet clothes clung to her uncomfortably. She was cold and her arms and legs tingled as if they'd fallen asleep, but when she tried to sit up, she couldn't.

Panicked, she struggled against the rough ropes that bound her hands and feet. The more she strained against the bonds, the tighter they became, abrading her tender flesh. Fastened around her neck was another rope that traveled the length of her body, connecting her hands and feet as well and thus ensuring that she was helpless, for with every move, the rope around her neck grew tighter.

"The more you move, the tighter the knots will become, eventually cutting off all circulation and, if I tied them correctly and I'm sure I did, the oxygen to your brain." His voice, neither hateful nor harsh, but matter-of-fact came from somewhere in the dark void behind the ring of light cast by the candles.

Sadie said nothing as her heart froze in her chest. She stopped struggling, and silence ensued. For what seemed an eternity, only the telltale sounds of his footfall in the darkness and her own quick breathing filled the vile space. Straining her eyes in the direction of the disembodied voice, Sadie could not see him.

Sadie lay on her side in a large earthen pit surrounded on all sides by rough-hewn rocks that extended about three feet from the floor of the pit. She could see only a portion of the room from her vantage point on the floor of the pit. But what she did see caused an uncanny feeling of déjà vu to wash over her, and she didn't need to see beyond the candlelight to know where she was. It was a place she'd seen a thousand times in her dreams. It was the place where the boy fought the snakes and lost—every time.

Set back from the pit were what looked like bleachers, row upon row of wooden benches, each higher than the one below it. The pit apparently formed the focal point of the coliseum-style seating. The candles had been set up on the front two rows of bleachers, and Sadie felt like the injured lion waiting for the gladiator to finish the job. Although she couldn't see one, she knew there was an altar somewhere, probably very similar to the one she'd seen in her childhood home just hours before, what already seemed like a lifetime ago.

"I know this place," she finally broke the silence, unable to endure the metronome rhythm of his footsteps.

"I know it better," he said with a smirk.

"What do you want with me?" Her throat felt hot and dry; it hurt to talk.

"I want to finish the job I started so many years ago. I want to be free of this curse that plagues me. I want to sail the Caribbean and drink margaritas on the beach like Jimmy Buffett. I want to play and cavort, to smile and be happy. I want a normal life. But that's impossible. She saw to that. They all did." As he spoke, his footsteps became progressively harder and faster. He seemed to be walking in one continuous circle around her. Then he stopped and the silence was deafening.

"What curse?"

"You! You stupid cow. You're the bane of my existence, the thorn in my proverbial paw. I hate you." The matter-of-fact tone was gone, and what replaced it chilled Sadie to the core. It was the sound of total madness.

"How could I have hurt you? I don't know you!" The words flew out in a desperate flood of fear and frustration.

"Don't you? Don't you really? Sis." And there it was. Neither one spoke again for the time being, and for several minutes she heard nothing, even his relentless pacing had quieted. Then slowly she was able to discern a second noise, a gentle lapping of water. Confused, Sadie tried to calm herself by concentrating on her surroundings. If she knew where she was, she had a better chance of— what—escaping? *Not likely.*

Above her, indeed all around her, stars sparkled in the darkness, and she thought for a moment that the storm had passed and they were outside, until she realized that his footsteps echoed; she couldn't be outside. And suddenly she knew she was underground. She was in a cave. The stars above and around her were crystals. She was inside the belly of the Springs.

Slowly he began pacing again, a predatory cat stalking its prey in the darkness.

"How do you like the place?" His tone was now conversational, as if they were discussing nothing more important than window treatments.

"Not exactly my style." Sadie surprised herself with her response. Slowly the fear was subsiding and being replaced by a strong desire to survive.

"No, if I remember correctly, you're more into that whole shabby chic look—more shabby than chic."

"What have I ever done to you?"

"You were born."

"Sorry, I didn't really have any control over that."

"No, that's true, and it's not your fault that they chose to keep you separate from the church. Maybe, if they had delivered the same tortures onto you, I wouldn't have to kill you now—maybe, but they didn't. No, you got to live out your fairy tale princess life safely away in the big white house with the columns and the dad that bought you everything you could ever want or need. I got nothing, and if I complained, I got beaten."

"You're my brother."

"So? I'm supposed to have some deep fraternal bond to you whereby I would never hurt you and always feel a deep-seated need to protect you?"

Sadie found her words swallowed by a deep penetrating fear.

"While we're on the subject of family, though, aren't you curious about who *my* father is?"

"Doc?" Sadie had to struggle to make her voice audible.

"Try again."

"I don't know."

"Jane loved her male disciples. And they loved her."

"You don't even know who he is."

Then there was silence as she heard him make his way out of the bleachers, moving toward her at a constant pace.

"It's ironic actually," his voice came softly from the shadows, conversational almost. "The man you grew up knowing as daddy, the man who taught you how to ride a bike, kissed your knee when you fell off and skinned it, and bought you a double scoop of choco-late peanut butter and vanilla caramel nut ice cream in a waffle cone when you got back in the saddle and didn't quit till you were a 'real pro'—that man was really my father." Venom dripped from his words, and his voice got louder as he spoke until he practically screamed the word *father,* and then he was silent again, the word ominously echoing off the cavern walls.

"You're insane," Sadie said defiantly, but inside she was more shaken now then she had been. Every single thing he'd just described was exactly what happened the weekend she learned to ride a bike. A shiny red Schwinn her father had surprised her with one day after getting straight A's on all of her spelling tests for a month. He had it, right down to the flavors of the ice cream. Sadie racked her brain to come up with a reasonable explanation as to how this stranger would know such intimate details of her life.

"Fine, don't believe me. But do you believe your own eyes?" Suddenly there he was, looming above. It was like looking at a photograph. He was the spitting image of the man she had known as *Daddy*. He had the same build, that of an athlete, and he was attractive. His black hair fell in the same loose colic, but what really penetrated her stubborn mind were his crystalline blue eyes. It was true.

"So what? I got a bike, so you want to kill me?" Anger now boiled where just moments ago fear had lived.

"Yes."

"Oh good, and for a second, I thought you were insane."

"That's your stunning retort? Your witty response? You cheated in school, didn't you? And here I thought you were the smart one." Spittle flew from the corners of his mouth as he yanked hard on the ropes that bound her, forcing her into an awkward sitting position before disappearing back into the shadows again. "You are exactly two years younger than I am. As if your existence wasn't bad enough, you had to steal my birthday too?"

"That's crazy."

"And again you amaze me with your wit. Yes, Jane was crazy as a loon, but she was smart too, amazingly so. She hated children, which is one of the reasons she had no trouble giving you away without ever shedding a tear. In fact, she often told me that she truly believed that it was God's first sign to her that she was chosen to give you up, since he saw it fit to have his mighty serpents destroy the life that came from that other woman's womb."

"Her mighty serpents bit her in the belly that night too."

"True, which is one reason I have no remorse in killing you. God never wanted you to be born."

Before Sadie could formulate a retort, he began again on another tirade.

"It was all about power, which was the only thing she truly

loved. Mom was smart, giving you away. She was convinced that her act of selflessness would bind the two men to her forever in the secret that they shared. And for a time it did."

"Until you went crazy and started killing people?"

"No, I had nothing to do with those murders—that was all mom. By that time she had so much power all she had to do was look at a disciple the wrong way and they offed themselves."

"If she had so much power, why did she get arrested? How did she become the town pariah?"

"Her flock turned on her. You're bright enough to get that, right?" His tone was mocking now as he continued. "When the death toll started piling up, her followers started leaving her; one-by-one they began filtering back to the church in town. Dad stayed true almost until the end, until I tried to kill you."

The blood in Sadie's veins ran like ice as she tried to process this flood of information. "What?"

"You don't know? Is it possible that you've blocked it? That's just...delicious." Again he paced outside the light, and again silence ensued. It was obvious he was deciding something. Finally, he said, "I think I won't tell you just now how you almost died."

"You tried to drown me in the river with the snakes."

"So you do remember."

Although Sadie knew it was true, she still couldn't remember exactly what had happened that day.

"But I failed. They found us too soon and stopped me. After that she left town and abandoned me here. For a while they sent me away to an orphanage, but it didn't work out." She detected a distinct smirk in his voice. She didn't need to know what he'd done.

"Why Andre? Birdie? All the others? Why not just come after me if you hate me so much?"

"Haven't you figured it out yet?"

"Because you're a psycho with venom for blood."

"Venom for blood, hmmm, I never thought of that; that's good. But, no, that's not it. I'm here for revenge. While you lived your perfect little life, full of parties and friends, I was forced to sit in a pit with rattlesnakes." With that he jumped down from the riser on which he was standing and kicked something hollow with his booted foot, causing what sounded like dozens of warning rattles to emanate from within. Sadie didn't need to see it to know what it was.

In the middle of the startling revelation, she had a clear image of him as a boy in the pit. "I didn't put you in this pit."

"And if you would have—could have—stopped it, you would have." His voice was slick with sarcasm.

"I would have tried."

"It's funny, I actually believe you. I never would have tried to help you."

"Why did she…why did they do it?"

"Why put me in a pit filled with snakes?" When Sadie didn't respond, he continued. "I was the savior—the son of the goddess. If a disciple sinned, they would come down from the pews," he said, standing as he waved an arm around the room in a large flourish. "Mom would invite them to stand with her here in the inner circle, and they would kneel before her as they unburdened themselves of their sins. Then she would prance around yelling and shaking her fists, dancing and chanting for their souls, all the while kicking the boxes that held the snakes, agitating the vipers within, and then at the very height of her frenzy, she would…" He danced around crazily, stomping and kicking the many wooden cages that surrounded her prison. He looked like the devil's favorite marionette as he twirled and danced in the jittery light cast by the candles. After minutes of his wild dance, he stopped, suddenly leaning over the edge of the pit, his face inches from her own, his sweat running in rivulets off of his face and onto her own, "…and then she let the snakes loose." Standing again, he moved over to sit on the wooden bleacher, his voice heavy with exertion. "If they bit me, the person was guilty in God's eyes; if they didn't, the person was either innocent or had already been forgiven."

"How did that punish *them?*" She had to keep him going; she had to keep his attention diverted as long as she could. She had to keep him from opening the cages and letting the snakes out.

"That was the best part. It depended how many bites I received. Each bite was worth money; the more severe the bite, the more it was worth. She would come up with a figure, usually in the hundreds of dollars, that would absolve them of their sins."

"That's crazy," Sadie said.

"Obviously. The distinction between insanity and genius is a fine line, and Jane was both. She managed to walk that line, at least outwardly, with aplomb. But inside, she had the blackest soul I've ever known. So the snakes bit me, and the good people of the congregation paid her to save their insignificant souls from fiery damnation. They hocked their family jewels, signed over the deeds to their family estates, and much more, all to regain favor in the church's eyes. It might come as a shock to you, but over half the town ended up signing their property over to her. And now that she's dead, it's all mine."

"If you had been bitten that many times, you would have died."

"You forget that your father, the good town doctor, was one of her staunchest supporters." He let the words sink in for a moment before continuing. "Sometimes she would milk the vipers before the show, so when they bit me—and she always made sure they did—there was little or no venom. She did this when she was feeling generous." He laughed a cruel laugh. "Over the years, I grew resistant to the poison. It can't hurt me. But you, on the other hand..." He let his words trail off.

The next thing she knew, he was standing above her again, looking down at her in the pit. The way he looked at her, with his head cocked to one side, made her feel like a giant bug on display. "Now if you'll excuse me, I have to go. And if you think your hero cop boyfriend will be coming to your rescue, think again. I shot him." With that, he opened the first cage and shook it until the snake fell onto the earth in the pit just feet from Sadie. After that, he moved methodically around the circle opening cage after cage until all of the snakes were in the pit surrounding her. Then he disappeared into the night.

CHAPTER 64

2:15 a.m.

The drive out to the ranger station took almost an hour, even with Dan speeding along the country roads in excess of ninety miles an hour, an incredibly reckless speed on these roads. It was all he could do not to go faster.

The ground beneath the Springs was honeycombed with a warren of ancient, underground caverns and tunnels, some of which had given way long ago and developed into massive sinkholes. The Sinks covered a vast portion of the countryside, with over a hundred different sinkholes, in varying sizes. The area was remarkably beautiful and had been featured in a recent National Geographic special as one of the nation's most awe-inspiring places. But as many beautiful things, it was deadly as well. As the rose is not left unprotected by her thorns, the Springs and the Sinks within were not left without a deadly yin to the area's awesome yang. Not only was the area home to several species of poisonous snakes, but the ground itself was unstable, and the caverns beneath, miles upon miles of tunnels and hollows, had served as the final resting place for many a man, bird, and beast over the centuries. Once you found your way in, it was nearly impossible to find your way out again. Several amateur spelunkers had become lost and trapped there over the years. Dan felt sick with the thought that the woman he loved was now being held prisoner by a beast more fearsome than the Minotaur in that underground labyrinth.

Finally, through the trees the ranger station appeared like a beacon, light emanating from every window and the open front door. Skidding to a stop, Dan threw the Jeep into park and flew out of the vehicle and up the walkway. The scene inside made him stop in his tracks: he was flabbergasted. Inside, the small station was crammed full of people, men and women, all decked out with expensive, high-tech gear. There had to be thirty or more people crammed into the little space. In every space that wasn't filled with a person, kerosene lamps burned brightly.

A burly-looking mountain of a man was the first one to greet him. "We're all yours, Dan," he said as he pumped Dan's hand with one hand while slapping him amiably, yet seriously, on the back with the other. "You know my wife, Lana," he added, putting his arm around a petite woman, the same one who had rounded up the snake from his apartment earlier.

"Ben, Lana, what's going on?" Dan asked, shaking his head, happily amazed to see the amount of support that Mike had been able to pull together in such a short amount of time.

"Good to see you again, Dan, don't worry. If Sadie is down there, we'll find her." Lana took his hand in her own. Her hand was warm, and her shake, firm and reassuring.

"This is Keith Mitchell, and over here is Paul Nebbit, one hell of a tracker," Ben introduced a couple more guys who eagerly pumped Dan's hand, saying that they would help with anything he needed and not to worry. Some of the people Dan knew through work, most of them rangers with the Parks Department. The rest were friends of Mike's and Evie's—fellow spelunkers and caving enthusiasts—people who made the Springs, and the Sinks in par-ticular, much more than an idle hobby, people who knew the terrain backwards and forwards. They were Dan's best hope of finding Sadie alive.

"We're here to help, Dan. Just tell us what you want us to do," Ben said.

"Time's wasting. Let's get you suited up," a familiar voice said, behind Dan. Turning around, he was stunned yet again. "What the hell are you doing here?" Mike hobbled to a stop beside him, grinning like the Cheshire cat, a pair of crutches wedged under his arms. "You didn't think I was going to let you have all the fun, now did you? I'm mission control." Mike handed Dan a radio. "I want you to stay in contact with me at all times and do as you're told."

"How did you do this?"

"Rescue round robin. It's not the first time someone's gotten lost in the caves. We're all prepared twenty-four-seven to initiate a rescue response, and everyone here is highly trained and qualified—except you," Mike said pointedly. "Hell, I wouldn't let you go in there if I thought I could stop you. Fact is, you don't know the terrain, and you have no idea how to use the equipment. You are what we would call a liability. But you are strong and a fast learner and I absolutely know you will do everything Ben here tells you to do." Mike's eyes seemed to bore through Dan. Dan knew he was right.

"I wouldn't exactly call myself a liability," Dan said.

"There are several ways to get into the cavern." Mike moved awkwardly over to a sturdy wooden table in the middle of the room that had several maps laid out on it. "This is Bertha," Mike said, using the Great Sink's nickname and pointing to a map that showed the locations of the sinkholes, indicating the largest one with the index finger of his right hand. Dan's eyes flew over the map; he didn't say anything for several moments as he surveyed the lay of the land. There was something about the way the different sinkholes were aligned that made him pause. For a time all sounds seemed to fade into nothing; all he could hear in his head was the poem and all he could see was the map. The sinks spiraled in on themselves, coiling round and round on each other growing larger and larger until…

To the north the sparkling serpent winds
Coil round of perfect symmetry give refuge to the true believer
In her belly we rejoice
In her venom we find strength
In her acceptance we find savior.

"They spiral." Dan looked up at Mike, who nodded.

"In her belly, we rejoice," Mike repeated. "The church is directly under Bertha. We know exactly where it is too."

"I thought that area was off-limits," Dan said.

"Exactly."

"So you've been down there more than once?"

"Naturally," Mike said.

"Are you positive this is the right place?" Dan felt the cold fingers of futility crawl through his hair and over his scalp.

"It has to be the place," Lana confirmed.

"It's perfectly hidden too; unless you knew what you were looking for, you wouldn't find it. You could literally walk right past it and never know any different. We sort of stumbled upon it," Ben said.

"But we had no idea what it was or had been used for." Lana briefly described the pit in the center and the wooden bleachers set around it.

"It's the perfect place," Mike said.

"To hold secret meetings," Dan finished.

"Completely protected from prying eyes," Mike continued. It all made sense.

"So who is this guy?" Ben asked, breaking the rhythm of the partners.

"Best we could piece together, he's the son of Sister Jane, and if we're not mistaken, and the church was in the caves, he grew up there," Mike said.

"And knows them better than any living person on the face of this earth," Dan said, uncomfortable with the idea of taking civilians into the lair of a demented killer.

"Maybe back then," Ben said, "but there have been numerous cave-ins since those days. The tunnels he used to follow may no longer be passable."

"True," Mike said, "but if what we are surmising is accurate, then he feels proprietary over everything down there. According to him, those are *his* caves, *his* tunnels—and we're about to enter *his* turf." Everyone in the room was silent as the weight of Mike's words sank in.

"Look," Dan said, turning in a circle as he spoke, looking everyone in the eye as he addressed the room. "You can't know how much I appreciate you being here, but this guy is seriously dangerous, and I can't ask any of you to risk your lives. It would be suicide…"

"It would be suicide without us," Lana spoke first.

"You're stuck with us, pal," Ben said.

"Whether you like it or not," someone from the back chimed in.

"This may have been his world twenty years ago," Mike said, "but it's ours now." Looking from face to face, Dan saw nothing but dogged determination, and he knew that not one of these people would back down.

"Well, I guess I better stop wasting time trying to discourage you," he said, giving in. "How do we get there?"

"There are a couple of ways in; one is big enough to drive a car in. It's the main entrance and close to where we want to be."

"What the hell are we doing here then?" Dan seethed with frustration.

"Hold on, it's not gonna be that easy. If he is down there right now as we suspect and he is holding Sadie alive, then he will surely kill her the second he hears us. If we go in that way, there is no way he won't hear us coming. It would be…"

"Suicide," someone said.

"It would be murder," Dan acquiesced, seeing the truth in his partner's words. If Sadie was still alive, they needed the advantage of stealth. "Okay, so what now?"

"There are three other entrances to the caves, but only one that's a direct shot. You'll go with Ben, Lana, Keith, and Paul,"

Mike said. "You're team number one. Do everything they tell you, and hopefully, you will find Sadie and have her back here by breakfast. I'm going to have the other teams stake out the additional entrances, but they won't enter unless they're needed for rescue or in case of a cave-in."

"I don't know, Mike, this guy is dangerous and armed. I don't think it's a good idea to take civilians down there. If he's down there, then he's been down there for a while, and he knows his way around."

"All of us are armed and dangerous too," Ben said, and from the look in his eye Dan believed him and was, at that moment, glad to have him on his side.

"Look, there's no time to argue, we have to get moving, now. Besides, there's no way to stop these guys. They're more stubborn than I am," Mike said.

"You're the boss," Dan said, giving in.

"Good, now let's get moving."

CHAPTER 65

2:51 a.m.

In the short time since leaving the ranger station, they'd covered an impressive amount of ground, Dan easily keeping up the others. Although he'd lived in the city for a long time, a country boy never forgets his roots, and he felt less and less like an alien the farther they moved into the dense thicket of trees.

After a time of moving steadily over the rugged terrain, Ben stopped and held up a hand, signaling the others to stop as well. "We're here," he informed Mike, speaking in a hushed whisper into his radio.

"See anything along the way?" Mike came back surprisingly clear.

"Nope. Just a nice midnight hike in the woods," Ben sounded so amiable that Dan wondered, not for the first time, if these good Samaritans had any idea what they could potentially be up against.

"Teams two and three have already checked in. Their entrances all look clear, no signs of recent activity."

"Roger that," Ben said. "Over and out."

"Godspeed," Mike said and then the radio went quiet.

"Have you ever gone caving?" Lana asked Dan, as she dropped to her knees.

"No, I … um … how are we supposed to get inside? I don't see an entrance." Dan scanned the rocky outcroppings surrounding him on three sides, but he saw nothing but solid rock.

"Not up there," Lana said, bringing Dan's focus back to the ground. "Down here." She stretched out on her belly and then disappeared feet first into what looked like an oversized rabbit-hole in the rock, pulling her pack with her. A moment later came two flashes from her light, signaling that she was okay and it was clear for the next person to follow her down.

They'd made a decision not to talk unless it was absolutely necessary once they were in the caves. Just in case they were not alone, they would need as much stealth as they could muster.

"We're going in there?" Dan mouthed to Ben, who just slapped him on the back as they watched Keith and Paul disappear into the earth, each of them giving the "okay" signal with their flashlights as soon as they were clear of the tunnel. Giving Dan the thumbs-up, Ben dropped fluidly to his stomach and slipped into the opening, sort of like a snake in reverse. Dan was stunned; the hole hadn't looked big enough for Lana to fit through, much less her burly husband, but as Dan watched in disbelief, the large man disappeared, leaving Dan alone in the night. He suddenly felt very conspicuous. Then came the two flashes: it was his turn. Taking a deep breath, he lay face-down on the cold limestone, and feeling a bit like Alice going down the rabbit hole, he wondered how soon he would run into the Mad Hatter.

Dan slid backwards on his belly for several feet until suddenly he realized there was nothing supporting the lower half of his body; yet he kept sliding. Trying to use his arms and hands as much as he could in the confined space to slow his descent, he was nevertheless about to fall, when he felt several pairs of hands on his legs urging him lower. Finally giving up to gravity, he allowed himself to drop freely to the floor of the cave. Looking up, he saw himself surrounded by the reassuring faces of the rest of team one. They all nodded and gave him the thumbs-up sign; he in turn flashed his light twice.

They were in a smallish cavern, barely big enough to hold all five of them; it was twice as tall as it was wide. As soon as Ben ascertained that Dan was indeed all right, he nodded and once again dropping to his belly, squirmed snakelike into another tunnel that angled down farther into the earth. This time Lana indicated that Dan should go next, and saying a silent prayer, Dan followed suit, this time crawling headfirst. The going was slow and painful; every time Dan moved, he felt the bruises on his chest sting with pain. Gritting his teeth, he pressed on.

CHAPTER 66

3:21 a.m.

Sadie lay frozen in fear, her eyes squeezed shut, her breath frozen in her chest. The weight of the snakes felt like a thousand pounds on her chest, arms, and legs. Silent tears of terror slid down her cheeks and pooled in the dry earth below her as she waited for them to start biting. Minutes that felt like hours passed, and nothing happened.

Afraid to move, afraid to breathe, afraid to die, she lay there holding her breath until her chest burned for lack of oxygen and her head started swimming. Slowly she let the air out of her lungs, her eyes still squeezed tightly shut. One of the vipers, already agitated, rattled its tail close to her head. Remaining as still as humanly possible, she inhaled shallowly, afraid to move even that much. The rattling by her head stopped as another one started, this time the sound came from her feet. *I'm going to die.*

Her muscles tensed and quivered as she lay still, waiting for the inevitable.

Yet still nothing happened.

Foolish as it was, she thought that if she kept her eyes closed, maybe the snakes wouldn't bite her; if she didn't acknowledge them, maybe they would leave her alone too. And suddenly, out of the depths of her memory, she realized that that had been exactly what her brother had thought so many times in the past, and she cried.

Sadie wasn't sure how many rattlesnakes lay on and around her. She had passed out after Marc dumped the first snake onto her; she had a feeling that that was the only reason she was still alive. She knew from the rattling earlier that there was one coiled very close to her right ear, not touching her but within striking distance. She hoped it would move farther away, although she feared that it, as well as the others might be drawn to her body heat. One snake lay heavily across her throat, pinning her head in place. She had no idea how long the snake was or where its head was and imagined that if she opened her eyes she might see it looming over her face, forked tongue flicking, fangs bared, ready to strike. Using every bit of willpower she had, she forced herself to remain calm and instead continued her inventory: there was at least one on her torso, and a few wrapped around her legs, which were starting to tingle and become numb. As she lay there, she felt the smooth underbelly of one whose body was as thick as her wrist slither across her face; inexplicably, it left her unscathed. As time passed and the rattling quieted, she began to feel a faint shimmer of hope until she remembered that Dan was dead.

Time stood still, and Sadie had no way of knowing how long she'd been there.

She thought of Edgar Allen Poe's famous story "The Pit and the Pendulum," and although there wasn't an actual razor-sharp pendulum swinging ever closer, threatening to saw her in half, she nevertheless identified with the hero of that story. Even if she could somehow manage to free herself from the pit and the snakes, she had no idea what fate awaited her outside the confines of this awful cavern. It could be better, but it could also be worse—much, much worse.

CHAPTER 67

3:35 a.m.

Dan could only hear the movements of the others, the light on his miner's hat illuminating just the area immediately in front of him. He couldn't even see Ben's boots. The progress was slow and seemed to take forever. Frustrated, Dan pressed himself harder until he was forced to stop and wait for Ben to clear the tunnel first.

There was no way that the killer could have brought Sadie in this way. Ben and Mike had opted for this route because, although it was the most difficult approach, it was the most direct way to the belly of Bertha. It was also impossible for anyone to sneak up on them, and most important, this entrance wasn't on any of the maps: Evie and Mike had discovered it just over a year ago, and they were certain that no one else but their group was aware of it.

Gradually, the tunnel began to grow larger, until there was enough room to crawl; then suddenly it opened out into a room large enough for all of them to stand. When all five of them were out of the tunnel, Lana took the lead, acting as scout. It had been predetermined that she would lead the party once inside the main portion, since she and Ben knew the area the best, and because she was the smallest, most agile, and quickest. She was also better with a firearm than most men. Although Dan had wanted to protest, he knew he was being old-fashioned and that it was smarter to let her go first.

Lana's small feet made almost no sound as she hurried ahead of the group, giving the "all-clear" signal at intervals with her flashlight. She moved quickly through the subterranean landscape, making their progress faster than Dan would have thought possible. Lana was often finished scouting and waiting on them to catch up at the designated checkpoints. And so the group moved forward, sometimes single-file, sometimes climbing, sometimes slinking on their bellies, sometimes crawling on their hands and knees, and sometimes walking like spiders on barely visible ledges around pools of brackish water.

After a few dozen twists and turns, Dan completely lost his sense of time. Despite the horrifying purpose of their journey, he was surprised around almost every turn by dimly lit glimpses of nature's incredible wonders. He had no idea that the belly of the earth could be so beautiful. In the larger caverns, stalactites and stalagmites grew from the floors and the ceilings, their immense size dwarfing the scouting party. Some of them had grown together over the years, forming columns so large that three men couldn't wrap their arms around them if lined up side by side. Crystals in every shade of the rainbow danced in the lights of their miner's hats and flashlights. An underground river wound its way through the caverns, sometimes forming shallow pools, sometimes rushing and other times just barely trickling. But as beautiful as Dan found it, he prayed that it wasn't the last sight that Sadie ever saw. With each minute that dragged on, with each step they took, a feeling of dread took a greater hold on his heart.

CHAPTER 68

4:03 a.m.

Alone in the room, deep in the pit, Sadie thought she heard muffled footsteps. Holding her breath, she strained to hear anything against the silence. It was no use; she couldn't hear anything, although she could have sworn she'd heard *something*. For a second she was convinced that he'd come back to finish her off. But he didn't have to come back; she would die of dehydration in a couple of days, if the snakes didn't kill her first. She had a very real sense that this pit would be her grave.

Sadie had no idea how long she'd been in the pit; she'd begun drifting in and out of reality. The complete and utter silence of the large cavern, with the exception of the sounds of the water, was almost deafening. The snakes had long since stopped issuing warnings; it was almost as if they'd accepted her. In and out she drifted, snatches of visions from her youth surging to the forefront of her memory for the first time in decades. Memories she had worked so hard to suppress, to hide from. Things that she had known to be true then but had come to mistrust over the years. How her father must have been mortified to hear her describing her "dream" about the chapel in the ground with the snakes and the boy in the pit. Through her mind's eye she had witnessed every torment that sick women had visited on her son ... Sadie's brother ... her father's son. But he wasn't really her father. She had even downplayed the number of times she's woken bruised, bitten or bloodied—her psychic wounds. In adulthood she'd convinced herself it was a rare occurrence, when in reality it had been all too frequent. If every wound she received her brother bore she was lucky—for she hadn't had to feel the pain. Again her heart went out to the little boy who'd been destroyed in this very room.

Then with a sudden clarity that broke through her daze, she remembered in vivid clarity the first time her brother had tried to kill her. As she did, she cried out against the night, causing the vipers to become restless once again.

She had been here once before, many years ago. That day he had been lingering just beyond the trees that bordered her father's backyard, and she had known him instantly. She'd called out to him, but he ran and he was fast. By the time she'd reached the spot where he'd been standing, he was already gone and for a moment she thought she'd lost him. She wondered if he'd really been there at all. Was she hallucinating? But then she caught sight of him again, and the chase was on.

Every time she fell behind, he would stop and wait; then when she was within sight of him again, he would take off, leading her farther and farther away from town, deeper and deeper into the Springs. And then suddenly, he stopped and waited, grinning, beckoning her to him.

He stood just outside the entrance to a cave large enough to drive a convoy into. Finally, she reached him, out of breath but excited. Then taking her hand, he led her into the cave without a word. She tried asking him questions, but he only shook his head—always grinning—and eventually she followed quietly. She felt a deep connection with him. It wasn't until they actually reached the inner sanctum that he turned vicious, knocking her unconscious with a large rock.

Sadie didn't regain consciousness until she hit the water. Shocked and confused, she struggled to the surface but he held her under, his hand entwined in her long hair, exerting constant pressure. He was strong—so much stronger then she was—and even though she fought, she was no match for him. And then she saw them, the snakes. The last thing she remembered was the needle-like piercing of her flesh as they attacked her en masse.

The next thing Sadie knew, she was at home in bed. She had no memory of getting there. Everything hurt and a multitude of bandages covered her arms and legs. One sat ominously on her neck, and blood still seeped from a deep gash on her forehead, staining the bandage red. Curious, she eased away the gauze covering, revealing twin puncture marks reminiscent of a vampire.

That was when she first heard the woman and her father arguing. She had followed their angry voices to her father's study. And now, twenty years later, she finally remembered what the woman had said: *I don't know why you're worried. They can't hurt her. She's just like me—immune to the venom—not like the boy. I should have chosen her for my disciple, not that weakling.*

As quickly as the memory had come over her, it evaporated again, and she became aware once more of her surroundings—glad for the knowledge but saddened by it all the same. She couldn't help finding irony in the fact that her most acclaimed pieces of blown glass all incorporated snakes. So the boy—her brother—who so desperately wanted her dead so many years ago, was about to finish the job, or so he thought. If she truly was immune to the venom, then she had nothing to fear from the snakes, but there were so many other variables. Dan was dead, and the Springs were immense. It could feasibly take rescuers days to find her, and that's if they even knew to look in the Springs. What if they were looking in town or worse ... *no, she wouldn't let herself go there!* They would find her. They had to!

What happened next surprised her. Sadie found a deep well of tears never before acknowledge, and she cried. She cried as much for the boy who had been damaged beyond repair in this pit so many years ago as she cried for herself. He never had a chance. She wondered what each of them would have grown up to be if their roles had been reversed. Would he be an aspiring artist and she a broken, deranged killer?

The floodgates now open to the past, she let all of the remembered visions free, reliving each one as if she were her brother—as she had lived it then with him. If only she could make him understand that what they did to him they had done to her as well.

She could see images of people, their faces expectant and—what was it—*hopeful*—as the snakes were put to the little boy. She could see her "fathers" now, one on each side of Jane, holding the snakes aloft, on their faces the look of raw power mixed with ecstasy. And Sister Jane between them, her hands intertwined with theirs, the same look on her face as well—all the while inflicting pain and degradation on a scared little boy. Finally, the horror was too much and she cried out, her wails echoing throughout the forsaken chamber. It was then that the biting frenzy began, but Sadie didn't feel anything as the snakes sank their fangs deep into the same spots where they had bitten her so long ago.

CHAPTER 69

4:23 a.m.

"Sadie!" Adrenaline, like liquid fire, shot through Dan's veins. *She was alive! But for how long?*

Her scream echoed through the corridors of the labyrinth. She was close, and she was in trouble. Pushing past Ben and Lana, Dan ran, frantic to find her, but all the tunnels were blocked.

"We're close now." Lana tried to calm him with a gentle hand on his elbow. "She's alive; we'll get her out."

"How? This is a dead end! She's on the other side of that wall, I know it, but there's no way through!" Dan felt like he was about to explode. Just as Sadie's scream rang out, the group had emerged into a large cavern with a pool of water at one end, fed by a magnificent underground waterfall.

"The water is going under the wall," Keith said, motioning to it with his light.

"So?"

"So," Ben said, "follow Lana." And as if by magic, Dan watched Lana disappear behind the wall of water. Only now she held a nine millimeter in front of her.

"You're next." Ben also had his gun pulled and at the ready.

Dan followed Lana behind the cascade of water. The tunnel was narrow, and the sound of falling water drowned out every other noise. Dan couldn't see an outlet; the passage looked like a dead end. Then suddenly Lana disappeared behind a giant slab of limestone into what Dan had originally thought was nothing more than a fissure in the rock. In the almost complete dark he felt Lana's hand tugging on his wrist, pulling him after her into the rock.

This passage was narrower than the first; after they'd gone about five feet, it turned sharply to the right, and then back to the left, like a Z. Suddenly Dan could see light—bright light—coming from an opening just ahead, and he could hear rattling. Easing himself in front of Lana, Dan was the first to emerge into the cavern, gun drawn. The room, large and open. It took him only moments to determine that the killer was not there but Sadie was.

"Sadie!" Dan ran to the edge of the pit, skidding to a stop on his knees just inches from the edge. At the sound of his voice, all the snakes turned and looked at Dan in unison—as if they were of one mind. There wasn't an area of exposed skin that didn't display angry bite marks. They were on her face, neck, and hands. "She's been bitten!" Dan could only assume that they were also on her arms and legs as well, the clothing being no match for the rattlers' razor sharp fangs.

"We've got you." Lana shrugged off her pack and immediately handed the anti-venom kit to Ben to prepare. "Hang on, Sadie. Everything will be okay."

The snakes, upset by the bevy of sudden activity, began sounding ominous warnings. Huge pools of fresh tears pooled in Sadie's large green eyes and spilled over her beautiful face. "You're alive," she said to Dan, smiling.

"So are you." Dan couldn't believe how strong she was. The look on her face was not one of terror or agony but of wisdom marked by deep sadness.

"No sudden movements, anyone," Lana said, surveying the situation. "Sadie, I'm going to get you out of there, okay? But you have to stay very still." Reaching once again inside her pack, Lana extracted a long pole that, when opened up and snapped into place, looked like the one she had with her at Dan's apartment earlier that day.

"Okay, guys, I need those crates over here now." Within seconds she had expertly looped one of the snakes, depositing it into the crate as soon as Keith set it down.

Sadie didn't move while Lana worked. She kept her eyes locked on Dan's. He was amazed by the intense look of calm strength looking back at him. It seemed she was comforting him, not the other way around.

"I have to stop him," Sadie said.

"I'll stop him, but first we need to take care of you," Dan promised. "I'm not going to let you die."

"I won't. I'm fine." Again her words came out smooth and cool, and he realized that somehow during this ordeal a warrior had been born.

It killed him that she had been forced to suffer at the hands of that maniac. He hated the sight of her hog-tied like an animal. The rough rope used to bind her had cut into her tender flesh, leaving lacerations around her throat and wrists; thick winter socks protected her ankles, and her sweatshirt had kept the rope from cutting into her stomach.

As soon as Lana had extracted the last snake, Dan jumped into the pit and gently cut the ropes that bound Sadie's hands, feet, abdomen, and neck. As he freed her from the ropes, the rest of the room seemed to fall away. All he could think about, all he could see was the woman he loved. He didn't even realize that tears were streaming down his cheeks until Sadie kissed them away. Throwing her arms around him, she burrowed her head into him and held on tightly as he lifted her out of the pit to Ben. "Ben's got anti-venom, and there's a team of paramedics close by. You're going to be fine."

"I don't need it."

"You've been bitten dozens of times. You need the anti-venom," Dan insisted. Then he said to Lana, "Does rattlesnake venom cause hallucinations?"

Before anyone could answer Dan, Sadie spoke up louder yet still calm. "I'm not hallucinating. I can't explain it. I can't even feel them. Dan, seriously, I'm fine." Sadie could see that Dan was about to object when she cut him off, "I've learned a lot down here. I'm immune to their venom. They can't hurt me."

"I'll be the judge of that," said Keith, a trained emergency rescue paramedic, who guided Sadie to the first row of bleachers and gently nudged her into a sitting position. Sadie allowed the examination without complaint.

"How long ago were you bitten?" Keith asked.

"Just before you found me."

"The venom can take anywhere from fifteen minutes to an hour to take effect. As happy as I am that you are not suffering at this point, I am going to have to insist that you allow me to administer the anti-venom."

Dan could see that Sadie was about to object. "Please, Sadie, I believe you, but do it for me anyway."

Sadie merely nodded her assent and allowed Keith to do what he felt he needed to. As he did, she sought out and found Dan's hand and grasped it tightly. "How did you find me?"

"It was the poem."

"Poem?"

"Come on, let's get out of here. I'll explain it to you on the way," Dan said.

"No argument there," Sadie said. And as soon as Keith was finished, they were on their way.

It took considerably less time to get out of the caves than it had to get in. This time they took the direct route through the large cavern—the one Sadie had come in through so many years ago.

As soon as they were out of the caves, Dan radioed Mike. "Mike, you there?"

"Dan, where are you? Did you find her? Is she alive?"

"Hi, Mike," Sadie said into the radio over Dan's shoulder.

Static. "Dan..." *Static.* "...possible situation..." *Static.* "...orchard..." *Static.* "Hurry."

"Trouble." Sadie's eyes mirrored Dan's thoughts.

"Pick up the pace," Dan said to the group.

CHAPTER 70

5:06 a.m.

Once inside the ranger station, Chief Baxter and Mike rushed forward, steering Dan away from Sadie, speaking softly and urgently. Sadie didn't need to hear the hushed conversation to know what was going on. Anna and Rocco were in trouble, and every member of the police force was in the ranger station with her. Guilt burned in her gut like a fiery worm. She would not let them suffer and die at the hands of her brother.

But why? Why kill them? And then she knew. He couldn't, he wouldn't, let anyone live who had given her what he had never had—a loving home. Even though it had just been a few days, it had been enough. He would kill them. Of that, she was certain.

"The ambulance is waiting to take you to Memorial General," Lana said, as a pair of uniformed medics began leading her back outside, away from Dan.

Sadie's first instinct was to pull away. She didn't have time for this. She needed to talk to Dan; she needed to get to the orchard and stop her brother. Pulling away, Sadie ignored them and headed for Dan, who was simultaneously heading back to her. "Sadie, I have to go," he said. "I'll come to the hospital as soon as I can."

"It's your folks, isn't it? He's gone after them," Sadie said, and judging by the look on his face, that was exactly what they'd been talking about.

"We can't raise them on the phone, land line or cell," Dan said, the worry creasing his handsome face. "It could be the storm, though; it knocked down a lot of lines."

"No, Dan, it's Marc. And he has a huge head start on us."

"Sadie, go with the paramedics, please. I'll be there as soon as I can." Dan's eyes pleaded with her.

"You need me, Dan. I know him; I know him better than he knows himself. You have to trust me."

"I do trust you, Sadie, but I'll be damned If I'm going to lose anyone I love to that monster. Please let me do my job." Sadie was so stunned she didn't even realize she was being led to the waiting ambulance until they were halfway there.

CHAPTER 71

5:18 a.m.

Anna paced the kitchen while Rocco laid more logs on the fire, and for the first time in her life, she found it impossible to draw comfort from the familiar surroundings of her home.

"Stop pacing, you're going to wear a path right through the floorboards," Rocco said, easing himself up from his kneeling position on the hard floor, his joints not quite as flexible as they used to be.

"He shot Dan," Anna cried, suddenly craving a cigarette for the first time in over twenty years.

"Dan had on his vest." Rocco poured a shot of bourbon into a glass and handed it to her.

"How can you be so calm?" she snapped, taking the glass from him and sipping on it. The amber-colored liquid warmed her tongue and the insides of her cheeks.

"I'm anything but calm, precious," he said, putting his arms around her. "But I know my son."

"So do I," Anna said into his chest. "It's just that I thought we'd put all of this behind us when he moved home."

"So did he, so did he." Rocco gently soothed her. In truth, he was just as upset as his wife, but he refused to give in to his emotions, not just yet anyway. When this was over and Dan was safe, Rocco would have quite a go at the punching bag hanging in the barn loft. "Mike said he'd call when he knew something."

"I am so mad at him." Anna slapped the table with the flat of her hand, something that was so uncharacteristic for her, it made Rocco jump.

"He had to go, Anna. You know he did."

"I know that, you big galoot, but he didn't even tell us himself. Mike told us our son had been shot." Anna drank the rest of the whiskey in one quick yet graceful swallow. "My son, my only son, has been shot not once but twice in the chest by a lunatic. Sadie is missing, presumably dead, and Mike runs off to play the hero—on crutches. My God, if this were a novel, I'd tell the author to stop drinking while writing," Anna fumed.

"You're just plain mad at the world, is that it, then?" Rocco surmised.

"Damn straight, and you should be too." Then Anna softened a little. "I just don't want to do this again. I still remember the last time we got a call like that. I swear, it aged me ten years. I thought that when Dan moved home from the city, we wouldn't have to go through this again." Anna stopped talking and rested her head on Rocco's shoulder. He didn't say anything; he didn't need to. He knew exactly how she felt, and he was feeling it too. The night she was referring to was just weeks before Dan quit the force in St. Louis and moved home to Crystal Springs. Even though Dan hadn't actually been injured that time, it was too close for comfort. Anna shook silently as she cried on Rocco's sturdy shoulder.

CHAPTER 72

5:22 a.m.

"A team's on their way to the orchard. Don't worry; we'll get this bastard." Chief Baxter squeezed Dan's shoulder encouragingly, but Dan could see the worry etched all over his bosses face.

"No, wait." Dan shook his head stubbornly. "I have to go in by myself."

"Are you crazy or just insane? Did you fall and hit your head in the cave?" Mike practically shouted at him. "That's a suicide mission, and I have no intention of breaking in a new partner, partner."

"I hear you, Mike. Believe me, I wish you were at my side, but you can't be. I have to do this alone."

"Mike's right. It *is* suicide," Chief Baxter chimed in, laying down the law without actually coming out and saying it.

"Look," Dan said, calmly looking from man to man, holding each of their gazes steady with his own. "This guy is seriously unhinged and unpredictable."

"My point," Mike said, clearly frustrated.

"And no one knows the orchard better than I do," Dan continued. "If we go busting in there like hell's bells, Mom and Dad are dead for sure. Hell, there is no way of knowing that they aren't dead already," Dan had to work to keep his voice level and calm, when inside he was screaming.

"Dan, you've been through a lot tonight. Let us handle it." Chief Baxter tried to reason with Dan, but in his heart he knew he would be doing the exact same thing.

"Look, Chief, Mike ..." Dan took a deep breath. "It isn't that I don't appreciate everything you are saying, and I'm sure I would be saying the same thing if the situations were reversed, but if you go in there with me or instead of me, you will get my family killed. Not only do I know the lay of the land, but he thinks I'm dead." He took a breath, bolstered a bit by the fact that neither man interrupted him or tried to talk over him; they were waiting for him to finish. "Just give me a head start—a few minutes to go in and survey the situation. You can have me wired from here to Sunday, place cruisers from every jurisdiction at the bottom of the hill, but for God's sake, promise me that you won't move until you have my word." The other men were silent for a few ticks of the clock, and suddenly everything in the small room seemed preternaturally quiet. "I hope you know what you're doing, son." Chief Baxter finally nodded granting a begrudging assent.

"So do I, Chief. So do I."

CHAPTER 73

5:30 a.m.

Dan hated wearing wires, and he found it hard to stand still; the ticking of the clock seemed louder than normal. It seemed to be saying, *Time's running out; hurry, or your family will be no more.* He felt safe in the knowledge that at least Sadie was finally out of harm's way. At least she would live through the night—even if he didn't.

Finally, the wire was in place, and Dan flew into his shirt and out the door to his Jeep, fumbling with the buttons as he listened to the chief's last warnings and instructions. Slamming the door to the Jeep, Dan waved briefly at Mike and the chief before jamming the car into reverse and gunning it out of the parking space.

Dan was about a half mile away when Mike's voice broke from the car's radio. "Dan, we have a situation. Sadie is missing … Repeat … Sadie is missing."

"What the hell!?" Dan slammed on the brakes and spun the wheel hard enough to make the tires squeal as he did a fast 180 in the middle of the highway.

"The medic said he went to get her a soda and when he got back, she was gone."

"Damn it!" He had been so sure that Marc had left and Sadie was safe.

"I'm not missing, Dan. I'm fine," Sadie's voice emerged from the back seat.

"Sadie?!" Dan came to a hard stop in the middle of the deserted highway. "What are you doing here?"

"I'm coming with you," Sadie said as she climbed into the passenger seat.

"The hell you are," Dan replied, heading back toward the ranger station.

"Turn around, Dan, please. We have to hurry; he's there already. He has them, and he's going to kill them unless I—unless we can stop him." Her tone was soft yet firm.

"Sadie, I know you mean well, and I love you more for it, but I can't let you. It's too dangerous."

"Fine, just go to the orchard, and I'll stay in the car. But we don't have time to waste. Now *go!*"

"Promise me you'll stay in the car."

"I promise."

"Dan, stay put. I'm sending a cruiser to pick her up," Chief Baxter's voice crackled out of the radio. Dan had momentarily forgotten about the wire.

"No can do, Chief." And with that Dan did another 180 and headed down the highway toward the orchard with the pedal all the way to the floor.

"How do you know they're still alive?" Dan asked Sadie as he ignored his boss's repeated attempts to get him to pull over. He kept driving, turning the volume on the radio down so that he couldn't hear the chief.

"I just know," Sadie said quietly. "I feel it. I also know he's been bitten. I saw it happen right before I passed out. He's got venom running through his veins right now; and unlike me, he's not immune, although he thinks he is."

Dan drove fast, almost recklessly. "Then the venom could stop him."

"No, he's not immune, but it won't kill him. It just hurts him, and it will only make him even more dangerous. Every bite he sustained as a boy contributed to the monster he is today. It's eaten away at him, changed him. He's no longer like you and I. He's not like anyone. But he is my brother, and what happened to him could have as easily have happened to me."

Dan listened as she filled him in on everything—what she had found at her parents' house, what had been in the files, everything that Doc Conway had told her about her birth and her real parents. Then she told him what she had learned while being held captive by her brother.

"And you think you can reach him?"

"Probably not. I have a feeling that he's beyond help. But I can stop him. I know I can."

"Sadie, you promised me."

"I know."

C hief Baxter and Mike rode in silence, listening to Sadie's story. They were only a few miles behind Dan, a bevy of cruisers in their wake. The chief was no longer fuming at his renegade officer. He was more concerned than angry, and he wondered if, put in the same situation, he wouldn't have done the exact same thing.

CHAPTER 74

5:38 a.m.

Outside he sat watching the couple as they consoled each other at the kitchen table. It had taken him much longer than anticipated to reach the orchard because of roadblocks. He'd been forced to take many off-the-beaten-path roads to reach his destination. But no matter, he was here now. Walking around to the back door, he let himself inside. It took several seconds for the couple to realize that they weren't alone.

"**W**hat the hell? Who are—." Rocco stopped, instantly recognizing the man in front of him. He was the spitting image of Stephen Mozart, and suddenly Rocco understood. "This entire thing is about a bad case of sibling rivalry? You've got to be kidding me."

"Sit down." Marc motioned toward the table with his gun, a wicked-looking nine millimeter with a silencer attached.

"Oh God," Anna said, recognition dawning on her face.

"Not quite, but my mother used to think she was," he spoke amiably, as if he were a close friend who had just stopped in to say hello. "And just in case you're curious, this *is* the same gun I shot your son with. Allow me to introduce myself," he said, flourishing the large semi-automatic handgun at Rocco as he'd started to stand.

"There's no need. We know who you are," Anna said as she stared directly into Marc's eyes.

"That certainly does make things easier."

"What do you want with us?" Rocco, though directly in Marc's line of fire, refused to be intimidated. He noticed too that Anna was putting up an equally stubborn front. Neither of them would be cowed; neither one would give him the fear he needed to feed on.

"To kill you. But I would rather not do it just yet. No, first I want a little bit of what she got."

"She?" Anna shook her head confused. "Your mother?"

"No, you imbecile. Why would I want anything that she had? The whore. I'm talking about my sister. I'm talking about Sadie. I want to be—I *deserve* to be treated just like family." Marc pulled out a chair at the table and plopped down just like he always sat there. Then in a very convivial tone he said, "I'm parched. What have you got to drink around here?" He smiled. Anna and Rocco just glared at him.

"I said," he repeated louder, a distinct tone of unbalanced aggression in his voice, "what have you got to drink? I've had a hectic night, and I am quite thirsty. Now do be a good hostess and see about your guest's needs, won't you, Anna?" He pointed the gun at Rocco as he addressed her.

"Of course, dear, what would like? Water, wine, beer, arsenic— what's *your* poison?" Anna smiled as sweetly as possible through her own seething rage.

"Hmmm … that's quite a selection … a beer, I think. Yes, a beer sounds great. Thank you." He beamed. "Now that's more like it, nice country hospitality. And Anna darling," he said as she began to stand, "don't try anything funny while you're up, and don't even think about leaving the room, because if you do, I'll put a nice little bullet right between your husband's eyes and then I'll come for you."

Scooting her chair back and standing up from the table was the hardest thing she'd ever had to do in her life, but Anna wasn't about to show fear to this fiend. And a fiend, much more than a man, is exactly what he resembled. His face and body were slicked with sweat, and he had a pronounced tic in his shoulders and face that frightened her. She grabbed the first bottle her hand came in contact with, and without looking, she shut the refrigerator door and crossed back to the table—to her husband and the killer.

"Enjoy," Anna said sarcastically as she set an icy St. Pauli Girl down in front of him, along with a bottle opener.

"Cute. Open it," he said. Sighing, Anna opened the bottle. She'd hoped that he'd put the gun down for just a second and that maybe, just maybe—but he'd seen right through it.

"Ah, now that really hits the spot after a hard day's killing." He drank deeply, finishing half of the bottle in one long swallow. "Now for the formal introductions, my name is Marcus Anthony Alcott. I know, I know, Marc Anthony—but what can you do? Mom was a total loon." He paused, waiting for a response from his captive audience. When none came he continued, a bit less jovial than before. "I am the man who just killed your son and Sadie." Marc stopped, suddenly overtaken by a spasm that contorted the muscles of his face into what Anna would later describe as the face of a demon—of the devil himself. After a moment he was fine. It happened so fast that neither Anna nor Rocco had time to react and make a move against him.

As soon as he had himself under control again, he continued, "And will be killing you very soon." *What was happening to him? The convulsion was new. The venom had never done that to him before. That bothered him almost as much as the fact that he hadn't received the welcome he'd imagined. They weren't cowering in fear and begging for their lives. They were being sarcastic; they were—looking down on him.* "Dan, the hero cop, always saves the day. I guess he's not really as good as all the hype."

"You bastard!" Anna exchanged glances with Rocco, squeezing his hand hard under the table. *That's better,* Marc thought, and he started to relax and enjoy himself again.

"That's right. Think of how lucky you are."

"Lucky?" Rocco bit the words out of anger.

"Certainly, how many people get to meet their only son's executioner?" Marc took a long pull from his beer and realized it was empty. "Another," he said, waving his empty bottle at Anna, his gun still trained on Rocco.

Anna stood from the table slowly, reluctant to let go of Rocco's hand for even a second, but she realized that this might be her chance to tip the scales. She needed a weapon … something … anything. Taking the long way around the kitchen to the fridge, she scanned the countertops; everything was too big. The things that were heavy enough to knock him out were too heavy for her to lift, much less throw. The knives were all in a drawer, and her aim— well, that was questionable at best.

"What's taking so long, sweetie?" Marc tapped the gun on the table for emphasis.

"I'm s-so … sorry," Anna stammered. "I've never been held hostage before."

"Oh, my bad. Of course, you're terrified." Now his voice came out almost soothingly, which, to Anna, was far more disturbing. "Just be a good girl and move a bit faster."

Anna quickened her pace; she had almost given up trying to find a weapon, when she saw it. There on the counter on a cutting board next to the refrigerator was Rocco's Swiss Army knife. He'd been using it to cut an apple earlier, just before the phone call from Mike. They'd both forgotten all about it. Hurrying now, she crossed the rest of the kitchen quickly. Pretending to trip just as she reached the large refrigerator and bumping hard into the counter, she quickly palmed the knife, sliding it into the front pocket of her jeans.

"Oh my, don't hurt yourself now. That's my job. Just take your time. I'm not going to kill you—yet." It was obvious that Marc felt he held all of the cards. He seemed to be thriving on their discomfort. "What a gracious hostess," Marc commented as she returned to the table with the beer. "Just set it on the table, and open it like before." Anna did as she was told, and Marc nodded for her to sit.

"Your son was a complete waste of space," Marc said, throwing the empty beer bottle into the fireplace. It was meant to be the exclamation point at the end of his sentence, but a spasm overtook his arm as he released the bottle, causing him to miss. The bottle struck the brick wall outside the pit. Shards of glass from the force of the hit exploded back into the kitchen. A piece of green glass hit Marc square in the face; he felt blood trickle down his cheek.

Wiping the blood away with his hand, he felt insecurity and anger begin to well up inside of him. He hated looking stupid. It was the strychnine. It had to be. The only effect the rattlesnake venom ever had on him was that of excessive thirst, and a little numbness, which was usually a welcomed thing. But the strychnine, that hadn't been intentional. Doc had bitten him on the hand when he'd been forcing the poison down the old man's throat, and the vile had shattered, spilling its contents into his open would. Yet he'd still managed to get most of it into the old man. Still he doubted that could hurt him seriously. He hoped.

"Would you like a band-aid?" Anna asked.

"No," he said, the casual smile now gone, replaced with a sick grimace. Anna could see the soul of a viper in the face of the man before her, and it scared her to her very core. Under the table she grasped Rocco's hand again, even tighter this time.

CHAPTER 75

6:45 a.m.

Dan eased the Jeep off the road and onto a hidden gravel road that was more like a path.

"Where are we?"

"Taking a shortcut; it'll take us right to the back door. No one really knows about this. It's how I used to sneak in and out in high school and not get busted. I don't want to risk coming up the front drive. I doubt he knows about this." And Sadie didn't doubt it was true. The road looked more like an accidental opening in the trees, and the way was rough going. Only a four-wheel drive vehicle would be able to make it up this path.

After a few minutes the lights from the orchard began to glow through the trees, and Dan switched the Jeeps lights off and pulled to a stop. "This is far enough. From here I'll go in on foot."

"Dan, let me come with you. I can help you."

"Not a chance. Here's the plan: I go get the bad guy and you stay put." There was a finality in his voice that didn't allow argument.

"What are you going to do?"

"Whatever I have to," Dan said, pulling her toward him, his

hands on either side of her face, and kissing her full on the lips before he moved to get out of the Jeep. "The cavalry is just a few miles behind us, and they can hear everything. As soon as I give the word, they'll swarm the place like a plague of locusts. Trust me, he's not going anywhere. Now sit tight and I promise I'll see you soon." In moments Dan had disappeared from sight into the thick copse of trees.

Sadie watched Dan disappear into the woods. Turning around, she scanned the road behind her. It was dark and empty, but she knew that soon she would have lots of company, and then she would never be able to get away. "You need my help, Dan, whether you know it or not." She had a plan, and it was a good one. Without her, Dan and his parents would be dead, of that she was certain. She hadn't bothered trying to convince him, though. It wouldn't have mattered—both of their minds were already made up.

A cold mist had begun to rise, and Dan moved like a ghost through the copse of trees, every one familiar to him, his every step easy. This was his territory, and no one knew it better. The mist was good; it would help obscure his movements, mask his sounds. It was almost as if Mother Nature was on his side. His plan was simple: first he had to determine where, exactly, everyone was and if they were still alive. Then he would do whatever it took to save them and apprehend Marc. Although Dan was not a killer by nature, he knew that if pushed he would defend his family in any way that he could.

CHAPTER 76

6:48 a.m.

Sadie ran through the woods, heading straight for the barn. The ground fog was growing heavier, and she had to pay attention to her footing so she didn't trip over an exposed root. It would have been faster to go by way of the road, but she couldn't risk having her footsteps on the gravel drive heard or having Dan see her and come after her instead of going after his parents and Marc. She prayed that she got to them in time—before Marc killed them all.

Although the orchard was bright, it was hard to see. The lights turned the dense fog an opaque white, making it difficult to see through. Finally the barn came into view; if everything went according to plan, in less than one minute the tide would turn against Marc and in their favor, or so she hoped.

Inside the barn, Sadie quickly spotted the flashlight she'd seen earlier hanging just to the right of the door. She jerked it off the hook and tested the batteries; they worked. Hurrying through the building, she quickly located the series of generators that ran power throughout the orchard. With a quick prayer, Sadie pulled the levers attached to the big purring machines, and section-by-section the orchard went dark. There was one last thing she had to do before leaving the barn, and without wasting precious time she flew upstairs into the loft and yanked open Dan's closet door.

D
an could see the kitchen now; pulling a pair of binoculars out of his coat pocket, he trained them on the house. What he saw made his blood boil. Inside Marc sat in his chair, the very one Dan had sat in from the time he was old enough to sit at the table. His legs were propped up, a beer in his hands, and he was talking. Dan couldn't read lips, but he could tell from the look on his face that he was angry and getting angrier—more unstable—by the second.

His parents were alive. He had to let them know he was there; he had to give them hope. Cupping his hands around his mouth, he let out a cry, which to the untrained ear sounded exactly like the call of an owl. Rocco had taught him the call years ago, when he was very young and had gotten himself turned around and lost in the orchard among the endless rows of trees. When Rocco had finally found him, he was crying and miserable, not only for getting lost like a big dummy, but for crying like a big loser. Rocco had asked Dan how he'd gotten lost in the first place when he was always supposed to stay on the path, and Dan had explained that he'd been following an owl as she hunted and eventually followed her to her kill. As he'd watched, she'd swooped out of the sky as fast as lightning, grabbed a snake in her beak, and flown off again to have her dinner. By the time Dan had finished watching, he'd gotten himself turned around, lost, and scared. That night Rocco taught him to hoot like an owl, and told him that it would be their secret call. No one else would know about it, and if Dan ever needed him, all he had to do was hoot.

Now a lifetime later, Dan hooted not for rescue but to let his loved ones know that help was on its way. The irony that the owl is one of the snake's natural enemies was not lost on him either.

CHAPTER 77

6:59 a.m.

"Well, it's been fun, but I really think I've overstayed my welcome." Marc's twitching was becoming so pronounced that he could barely hold the gun with one hand any longer. He needed both hands just to keep it steady, yet this barely comforted the couple. Even though he was decidedly unstable he was anything but weak. In fact, he seemed to swell larger with every moment. The veins on his face and neck stood out like taut cords of flesh.

"The only thing I haven't decided yet is which one of you to kill first." He moved the gun from Anna to Rocco and back as he spoke. Just then, an eerie hooting call emanated from outside. It was close. Anna thought she saw something flicker behind her husband's eyes for just a moment.

"What was that?" Marc's eyes were wild.

"Just an old hoot owl," Rocco said. Anna could have sworn just then that her husband seemed almost happy.

"Owl, huh?" Marc said and jumped as the call of the night bird came again, louder this time, closer. "I never did like owls." His words slurred as his face contorted, but his eyes never lost their focus.

"Owls eat snakes," Rocco said. Now Anna was sure she saw the hint of a superior smile playing around the corner of his mouth, but for the life of her, she couldn't understand why he was so happy to hear an owl.

"Yeah, well, I shoot owls," Marc sneered at the older man, his attention torn between the couple and the big plate glass window next to the fireplace. The sound seemed to come from right outside.

"Well, no matter," Marc said. "If it's one owl, or a hundred, it won't save you." He turned his attention away from the window and once again focused on the couple. Just then a third set of eerie calls emanated from outside, louder and closer than before, and all of a sudden the lights went out, plunging them into total darkness.

CHAPTER 78

6:59 a.m.

"Sadie," Dan said as soon as the lights went out. "You little rebel."
And in that instant he loved her more than he ever would have
thought possible. He'd been sitting out here for what seemed like
hours, but in reality had just been a few minutes, watching the horrifying scene transpiring in his family's home. His parents were
strong, stronger than he ever would have given them credit for, but
they were also afraid and he hoped neither of them would try anything before he got there.

Marc, on the other hand, was falling apart. His hair was wet
with sweat that dripped from his forehead and trickled down his
back, making his shirt stick to him. He kept twitching, and it
looked to Dan as if he were having some sort of fit. The venom
was affecting him but not enough to make him any less of a threat;
in fact, it made Dan considerably more nervous, which is why he
hadn't rushed the door as soon as he'd gotten there. He hadn't quite
figured out exactly what his next move would be when the orchard
went dark.

"What the…" Marc's voice was high and tinny. Then, as if out of nowhere, a voice sounded behind them.

"Lower your weapon slowly, and put your hands above your head," Dan said, as he moved into the room. On his head he wore a miner's helmet from the cave; in his hand he held his gun. Both light and gun were trained on Marc.

"You're dead!" Marc howled with rage and exploded backwards from the table, grabbing a fistful of Anna's hair he pulled her with him, his own gun pressed against her temple.

"Let her go," Dan said through clenched teeth.

"Drop your gun, and get that light out of my eyes," Marc demanded, pulling hard on Anna's hair making her wince under the strain. His voice wavered with insecurity, "I will kill her."

"Let her go," Dan repeated. He was not about to give up any ground. "It's over. The place is surrounded. Give yourself up."

"Bullshit. Every cop in the tri-county area is an hour away trying to save your girlfriend."

"Wrong. They're at the bottom of the drive waiting for my signal to roll in and take you out. You've got one chance to walk away from this alive, and that is only if you give up now."

"It's already too late for her. I made sure of it," Marc went on as if he hadn't heard Dan. "I put the snakes to her. She's dead."

"You've got to the count of three to put down your weapon and surrender," Dan said, "One…"

"Even if you're telling the truth, you won't let them move in, not as long as I hold your precious mother's life in my hands. If you move, she dies. If they come in here, she dies. So it's really your call, Danny boy—how do you want this to go down? Do I shoot your mother and splatter her brains on the pretty white cabinets?"

Time stood still for Dan. He felt like a cat waiting to pounce. All he needed was an opening, for Marc to drop his guard just a little. Even though he was an excellent marksman, he couldn't risk firing with his mother so close, and Marc knew it.

Seconds ticked by slowly; then something caught Dan's eye. It was Anna. She was moving. Dan watched as she carefully reached into the pocket of her jeans. She had something.

"What are you doing?" Marc jerked up on Anna, making her wince once more in pain.

"Nothing. What could I do?" Anna held her hands up in the meager light. Her eyes showed frustration and disappointment.

"Keep them where I can see them." Marc sounded less confident than he wanted to; it was evident on his face. His twitching was even more pronounced now. He was becoming more unstable by the second.

Neither man showed any sign of backing down. Then suddenly Marc, his eyes wide with disbelief, stared at something past Dan, outside. Turning slightly, Dan saw Sadie standing just outside the full-length picture window; she seemed to be illuminated from behind. She wasn't wearing the jeans and sweatshirt she'd had on earlier. Now she was wearing a dress—a dress that looked strikingly similar to the one Sister Jane had on in the photo. The ankle-length white dress clung to her curves and made her look sultry. In her eyes she wore a look of complete power.

Sadie stood with her arms behind her back. A luminescent mist swirled around her, obscuring her legs and feet; she seemed to be floating above the ground—an apparition. Her eyes were trained only on Marc as she slowly began to raise her arms out to the sides and above her head. In each hand she held a snake. And Dan realized that she had become her mother.

The apparition at the window shook Marc to the core. It was his mother ... it was his sister ... it was *her.* He shook his head but she was still there—a phantom surrounded by an unearthly glow, snakes raised above her head. *She had come for him!* And then she was gone. Screaming, he ran across the kitchen, dragging Anna with him to the window where the specter had appeared, but there was nothing there. Outside the mist continued to swirl and dance among the trees, but it was devoid of ghosts. Then the mist cleared once again, and there she stood—dead, yet impossibly alive.

Marc's brain was no longer functioning on a higher level. He had become as base an animal as a human being could become. There was no fear now, only the need to survive, the need to hunt, and the need to kill. Without a second's hesitation, he threw Anna to the floor and leapt through the plate glass window.

Marc hit the window with the force of a speeding locomotive, causing the glass to shatter into millions of silvery, sharp fragments that rained down all around Sadie. She could feel them like little blades biting into her hands and face. Tripping backwards, she managed to stay on her feet and out of his grasp as he landed hard on his hands and knees, but she wasn't fast enough and he managed to snag one of her ankles in his fist. It took all of her strength not to panic; kicking for her very life, she heard a satisfying thud as her foot connected with his head and he was off of her. Sadie lurched to her feet and ran, disappearing into the trees.

In the background she heard gunfire and sirens, but she didn't stop or turn around. She couldn't. Sadie knew that only one of them could walk out of this orchard alive.

Dan followed Marc through the rain of glass, landing hard on his side. As soon as he saw that Sadie was away, he gave the command and began firing, hitting Marc square in the shoulder. But the bullet did nothing to slow him. Marc was like a junkie jacked up on PCP; he couldn't feel anything, and nothing short of a miracle was going to bring him down. Dan needed backup, and now. "Get the teams moving. They're headed into the west grove, toward the river." Dan knew they couldn't let Marc get that far. If they did, Marc could easily escape back into the Springs, back into his own world until the next time he decided to come out to hunt and kill.

CHAPTER 79

7:08 a.m.

The trees looked eerie in the fog. The full moon, obscured behind a black cloud, cast the orchard into an almost impenetrable darkness. Sadie shivered as she ran through the miserable November frost with nothing on but a light cotton sundress. She had seen the dress the first time she'd been poking around in Dan's closet; at first, she'd felt a twinge of jealously until she realized that these were Anna's, since Dan was no longer living there she used the extra closet space. It had been perfect. The illusion had been easy to create; Dan also had a pair of plastic snakes, piled on one of his shelves, left over from childhood. Items long forgotten and dusty. It had been enough, and in the dark she knew it would unhinge him—that she could draw him away from the St. James.' Now she hoped desperately that he wouldn't catch her ... that she wouldn't die.

She could hear the heavy pounding of Marc's feet behind her; he was closing in. Then she heard a thud as he tripped in the dark and confusing grove.

"I hate *you*," Marc yelled from behind her, the last word disappearing into a guttural howl of rage that pierced the night and shook Sadie to the core. Picking up her pace, Sadie ran as fast as she could through the midnight forest of trees.

Marc didn't feel the pain from the bullet wound. Something completely primeval had taken over—something raw and powerful—and he ran with only one thought: to kill. On autopilot he pursued his prey relentlessly. Around him the world fell away, and all he knew was the hunt.

He could hear her just ahead of him, her feet crunching on the autumn leaves, but he couldn't see her. Then, for just a moment, the fog seemed to lessen, and he could see her shape moving amongst the trees. Encouraged, he started to move faster until the wind shifted again, and suddenly the haze was so thick he could no longer see at all. Moving like a blind man, he groped his way along, toward her.

CHAPTER 80

7:12 a.m.

The mist was so thick now that Sadie couldn't see her hand in front of her face. Within the span of a breath the entire world had been blotted out, including all sights and sounds. She knew Marc was here, but she had no idea how close or far he was. She also had no idea if she was moving away from him or directly toward him. In the white world of the cloud, she'd lost all sense of direction and relied solely on keeping her feet moving in the same direction.

Then, for just an instant, the mist thinned and she could see him; he was close, too close. He was standing still, listening for her, just as she was for him, only a hundred or so paces back, a distance he could cover in no time once he spotted her. Her heart stopped and for a moment she felt like a doe caught in headlights, but then the fog rolled in again, so blessedly thick it obscured everything.

She knew this wouldn't stop him. She had to move! On the ground they were at an equal disadvantage. As long as the fog remained this thick, they could wander, just a few feet from each other, and never know it. But as soon as it lifted, and it would, he wouldn't hesitate; he would kill her, unless she somehow had the upper hand. And then it hit her, to have the upper hand she needed to go up. Reaching above her head, she felt along until she found a limb low enough to grasp and strong enough to hold her, and as quietly as she could, she scrambled up into the apple tree's branches.

Sitting in the lower limbs of the big tree, Sadie tried to pierce the mist with her eyes and her ears, but it was no good. Muffled sounds of snapping twigs seemed to come from all around; she couldn't pinpoint an exact location. At least, she reasoned, if she couldn't see him, he couldn't see her either.

It wasn't long before she felt, as much as heard, him approaching. Then slowly, a dark shape emerged through the thick vapor; he was directly beneath her. So close she could smell his acrid sweat.

Sadie held her breath, scared that even the slightest noise would betray her. He seemed to pause for an unnecessarily long time directly beneath her. Then suddenly she could see him more clearly. The fog was beginning to lift. If he looked up, she was dead. Her leg was within his grasp; all he had to do was reach up and he would have her. Under her dress, strapped to her leg, she felt the weight of the hunting knife she had also borrowed from Dan, and though she hated to use it, she knew that she might have no other choice. She hoped he would move on, but somehow she knew he wouldn't. She would have to fight him. Fight him to the death.

Then, almost as if he'd sensed her, he slowly began craning his head backward, looking up.

This was it.

Pulling the bowie knife from its sheath, she mustered all the strength she could and sprang out of the tree, a cat pouncing on its prey. Sadie hit him hard as she landed, the impact sending both of them sprawling.

"Argh," Marc growled, lunging at her and hitting her like a battering ram. Sadie's head swam with stars as it bounced off the hard earth, once and then again. Her ears rang and she tasted blood on her lip. She had bitten her tongue. Marc rolled and pinned her underneath him, tearing frantically at her hand, trying to wrench the weapon free. But his coordination was off. He couldn't quite seem to focus. Each time he grabbed for the knife, he was just a fraction of a second too late, and she was able to keep the weapon out of his reach. And for a brief moment Sadie felt hope, but then he pulled it together and managed to grab onto her wrist with a vice-like grip.

Desperate not to lose the only weapon she had, she bit down on his wrist. A hot torrent of blood cascaded down the back of her throat, making her gag, but she refused to let go and held on. Shrieking in pain and disbelief, Marc let up a little, and in that instant she jerked the knife free and jammed it into his side with all the strength she had, at the same time kicking and bucking. She was moving purely on instinct, her will to live fueling her fight.

D an more heard than saw what was going on up ahead. For a few minutes, when the fog thickened, time slowed to a crawl; he no longer heard the pounding of footsteps. Everyone had stopped, it seemed, and then he heard a scream.

"Sadie!" Dan ran toward the sound of her voice.

The sounds of the scuffle were louder now, though he still couldn't see them. Then the wind picked up again, and the fog began to dissipate. Through the thick tendrils of cloud he saw them locked in a death grip, rolling over and over each other on the cold November ground, each trying to get and maintain the dominant position. Dan ran toward them, trying to find a clean shot but unable to. Blood was everywhere—on the ground, on the two people struggling—and he had no idea who had been hurt or how badly.

M arc flipped Sadie on her back again, as his hands closed around her windpipe. Blood from his open wound fell on her face as she struggled. Even with his wounds and the blood loss, he was strong, stronger than she ever would have thought possible. Stars swam before her eyes; she couldn't break his grip. Then suddenly his hands were gone, and she could breathe again. Gulping air, she realized why he'd let her go—he was going for the knife. It was not enough to strangle her to death; he had to maim her. He had to make her suffer. She tried to roll away from him, but he was stronger than she was. Then he had her hands over her head, locked in one of his own hands, as he used the other to free the knife from his side.

"I hate you," Marc said, brandishing the knife slick with his own blood above her. Just then Sadie saw Dan. Seeing him gave her a renewed strength, and for the first time since the chase had begun, she knew she would live.

"I'm sorry," she said to Marc as she dug her fingers into the open wound on his wrist and twisted away from him.

Dan was about to jump in and pull Marc off Sadie, when she opened her eyes and looked at him. In the brief time that their eyes locked, they communicated perfectly. Dropping to one knee and taking aim, Dan watched as Sadie literally threw Marc off her. As soon as she was clear, Dan fired, hitting Marc in the chest, in almost the exact same spot he'd been hit earlier in the night.

CHAPTER 81

7:28a.m.

The sound of the gunfire reverberated through the orchard; suddenly there were people everywhere coming out of the trees from all directions.

"Sadie!" Dan scooped her up, cradling her against his chest. "Are you hurt?" Using his eyes and hands, he checked her all over for injuries, but she was uninjured.

"He's still breathing," she said.

"He can't hurt you anymore."

Sadie looked at him. "Are you mad at me?"

"I should be. I should be furious with you, but I'm not. I would have done the same thing." He used his shirt to wipe the blood off of her face. "Can you walk?"

"Yeah, I'm okay," Sadie said and let Dan lead her out of the trees. The sight that greeted them when they emerged onto the gravel drive was one that Sadie would remember forever: Rocco, Anna, Mike, and Chief Baxter all running or hobbling toward them as fast as they could. Everyone hugging, everyone safe, Sadie had finally found her family; it had only taken a lifetime.

EPILOGUE

The next day at the hospital

"We'd like you to be the best man," Evie said as she toyed with the ring on her finger. Mike sat by her bed, holding her hand. The hospital room, a single, was already filled with bouquets of flowers and baskets of fresh fruit and chocolates.

"Like you could stop me," Dan joked.

"Congratulations, you guys," Sadie said, beaming as she kissed both Mike and Evie on the cheek.

"I can't believe he finally worked up the courage to do it," Dan teased Mike good-naturedly, clapping him on the back.

"He didn't," Evie said, playfully ribbing Mike. "The ring was on my finger when I woke up."

"That's kind of assuming a lot there, champ." Dan pulled a chair over next to the bed and sat down, pulling Sadie onto his lap. Even though she was less than a foot away, it had seemed too great a distance after almost losing her twice in the same day.

"I asked her when she woke up." Mike smiled sheepishly.

"He did and I said…"

"She said what the hell took you so long, idiot?" Mike finished for her, looking like a man who had just won the lottery, despite the bullet wound in his thigh. Just then a nurse walked in and announced that visiting hours would be over in ten minutes.

"You guys better go. Nurse Hanna is serious about visiting hours," Mike said.

Sadie stood abruptly. "Will you guys excuse me for a minute?"

S adie stood in the doorway of Doc Conway's hospital room. Tubes and wires ran between him and various machines, all making their own individual beeping or whirring noises. Even though Sadie felt betrayed, a part of her mourned for the man in the bed; he was her only real family, her father. Years of memories flooded her mind and filled her with grief, and she wondered if she would ever be able to forgive him. A part of her wanted to walk away from the hospital and never look back, but something kept her feet glued to the ground.

"I thought I'd find you here," Dan said, coming up behind her and putting his arms around her.

"I thought it would be easy." She didn't move away from him, but she didn't turn to face him either.

"Saying good-bye?" Dan asked.

"Uh huh."

"Do you really want to?"

"Shouldn't I? He hurt so many people."

"He made some bad choices, but he didn't kill anyone. In a way he's a victim in this too."

"I don't hate him, but I don't think I can ever love him, or trust him again."

"Come on—let's go," Dan urged gently.

"Can we go back to your place, lock the doors, and not come out for a week?" Sadie finally relaxed and leaned against Dan.

"Afraid not."

"Why?"

"Mom and Dad would be terribly upset if the guest of honor

missed her own birthday party," Dan said, as he led her down the hall toward the exit sign.

"Birthday party?" Sadie laughed.

"Yeah, but don't let on that you know. It's supposed to be a surprise."